"A fun mystery novel . . . entertaining."
—**TheMysterySite.com**

DEAD CENTER

"Entertaining . . . witty . . . perfect."
—*Publishers Weekly* **(starred review)**

"Enjoyable . . . entertaining."
—*Portland Tribune*

"Rosenfelt is a very funny guy who's got the gift of glib."
—*Kingston Observer* **(MA)**

"Rosenfelt adroitly mixes drama with humor . . . Those who like the added complexity of character-driven mysteries will find much to enjoy in this award-winning series."
—*Booklist*

"Written with flair and humor . . . If there aren't any real-life lawyers as entertaining, as witty, and as willing to tilt at windmills as Andy Carpenter, Edgar®-finalist Rosenfelt's engaging hero, then there should be."
—*Publishers Weekly* **(starred review)**

"A terrific tale . . . Fans of the series will enjoy *Dead Center*."
—*Midwest Book Review*

"Witty . . . cleverly plotted . . . very enjoyable."
—*About Books*

SUDDEN DEATH

"The author handles the material deftly, mixing humor and whodunit but never letting the comedy overwhelm the mystery."
— *Booklist*

"Another touchdown!"
— *Publishers Weekly*

BURY THE LEAD

A *TODAY SHOW* BOOK CLUB PICK

"Absolute fun . . . Anyone who likes the Plum books will love this book."
— JANET EVANOVICH

"A clever plot and breezy style . . . absorbing."
— *Boston Globe*

"Exudes charm and offbeat humor, sophistication, and personable characters."
— *Dallas Morning News*

FIRST DEGREE

SELECTED AS ONE OF THE BEST MYSTERIES OF 2003 BY *PUBLISHERS WEEKLY*

"Entertaining . . . fast paced . . . sophisticated."
— MARILYN STASIO, *New York Times Book Review*

more . . .

PLAY DEAD

Also by David Rosenfelt

New Tricks

Dead Center

Bury the Lead

Sudden Death

First Degree

Open and Shut

PLAY DEAD

DAVID ROSENFELT

GRAND CENTRAL
PUBLISHING

NEW YORK   BOSTON

Copyright © 2007 by David Rosenfelt
Excerpt from *New Tricks* copyright © 2009 by David Rosenfelt
All rights reserved. Except as permitted under the U.S. Copyright Act of 1976, no part of this publication may be reproduced, distributed, or transmitted in any form or by any means, or stored in a database or retrieval system, without the prior written permission of the publisher.

Cover design by Claire Brown
Cover photograph by Evan Hurd/Workbook Stock

Grand Central Publishing
Hachette Book Group
237 Park Avenue
New York, NY 10017
Visit our Web site at www.HachetteBookGroup.com

Grand Central Publishing is a division of Hachette Book Group, Inc.
The Grand Central Publishing name and logo is a trademark of Hachette Book Group, Inc.

Printed in the United States of America

Originally published in hardcover by Hachette Book Group
First mass market edition: August 2009

10 9 8 7 6 5 4 3 2 1

For Mike, whom I could never beat
at anything . . .
And for Rick, whom no one would
ever want to beat at anything.

Acknowledgments

I'm not a big fan of acknowledgment pages; most of the time I refuse to even acknowledge them. I especially hate when authors drop names of famous people as a way to impress the readers, and then go on to tell heartwarming little anecdotes to show how tight the author is with those bigshots.

Not me; that's not what I'm about. I make my acknowledgments short and to the point, and I don't go scrounging around for impressive names. I let my literary achievements do my showing off for me. If someone has been helpful or inspirational, I thank them . . . if not, I don't. No one gets a free pass.

So, in no particular order, I would like to acknowledge . . .

Michael Jordan
Bill Clinton
Dwight and Mamie Eisenhower
Debbie Myers
Jonas Salk
Britney Spears
Clarence and Marlo Thomas
Bob Castillo
Babe Ruth
Wolf Blitzer
Wolfman Jack
Stacy Alesi
Gandhi
Jessica and Homer Simpson
Little Anthony and the Imperials
Derek Jeter
Susan Richman
Wayne and Fig Newton
Puff Daddy
My Daddy
My Mommy
Alex Trebek
Various Rosenfelts
Golda Meir
The Barbara sisters: Bush, Streisand and Walters
Nelson Mandela
Ozzie Nelson
Ozzy Osbourne
Les Pockell
Kevin Costner
Kevin Federline
Robin Rue
George Costanza

Joe Montana

The entire state of Montana

David Divine

Bruce Springsteen

Walter Cronkite

Norman Schwarzkopf

Tony Blair

Tony Gwynn

Tony Soprano

Kristin Weber

Bialystock and Bloom

Ralph and Alice Kramden

Bobby and Gladys Knight

Doug Burns

George Burns

Henry Kissinger

Trixie and Ed Norton

June Peralta

The Taylors: Lawrence and Elizabeth

Cal Ripken

Paris and Conrad Hilton

Tokyo Rose

Al and Nancy Sarnoff

The Bird Brothers: Larry, Charlie
  and Big

Warren G. Harding

Stephanie Allen

Celia Johnson

Magic Johnson

Andrew Johnson

Johnson & Johnson

Norman Trell

Gracie Allen

Ernest Hemingway

The Jacksons—Michael,
  Stonewall and Phil

Simon & Garfunkel

Scott and Heidi Ryder

Joe Frazier

Christopher Columbus

Christopher Cross

Sandy Weinberg

Sam and Whitney Houston

Anthony, Bernard and Johns Hopkins

Muhammad Ali

John and Carol Antonaccio

The Rogers: Kenny, Roy and Ginger

Rocky Balboa

Geraldo, Chita and Mariano Rivera

George Kentris

Abbott & Costello

Chief Justice John, Julia and Robin
  Roberts

Michael, Sonny and Don Corleone

I apologize if I left anyone out.

On a serious note, please e-mail me at dr27712@aol.com
with any feedback on the book. Many people have done
so in the past, and I very much appreciate it.

PLAY DEAD

• • • • •

"Andy, you're not going to believe this."

This is the type of sentence that, when said in a vacuum, doesn't reveal much. Whatever it is that I am not going to believe might be very positive or very negative, and there would be no way to know until I see it.

Unfortunately, this particular sentence is not said in a vacuum; it's said in the Passaic County Animal Shelter. Which means that "positive" is no longer one of the possibilities.

The person speaking the words is Fred Brandenberger, whose job as shelter manager is an impossibly difficult one. There are far more dogs that come through his doors than potential adopters, and he therefore must helplessly supervise the euthanasia of those that are not taken. I know it drives Fred crazy; he's been in the job for two years, and my guess is he's not going to last much longer.

It bothers me to come here, and I rarely do. I leave this job to my former legal client, Willie Miller, who is my partner in the Tara Foundation, a dog rescue operation. We rescue a lot of dogs, over a thousand a year, but there are many more worthy ones that we simply do not have room for. I hate making the life-or-death decisions on which ones we will take, and Willie has been shouldering that responsibility.

Unfortunately, Willie and his wife, Sondra, are in Atlantic City for a few days, and we've got some openings for new dogs, so here I am. I've been dreading it, and based on what Fred has just said to me, I fear that dread has been warranted.

Fred leads me back to the quarantine room, which houses dogs who are sick or are unavailable to be adopted for other reasons. The other reason is usually that the dog has bitten someone; in that case they are held for ten days to make sure they don't have rabies, and then put down. "Put down" is shelter talk for "killed."

Fred points to a cage in the back of the quarantine room, and I walk toward it, cringing as I do. What is there turns out to be far worse than expected; it's one of the most beautiful golden retrievers I've ever seen.

Golden retrievers do not belong in cages. Ever. No exceptions. The dog I'm looking at is maybe seven years old, with more dignity in his eyes than I could accumulate in seven hundred years. Those eyes are saying, "I don't belong in here," and truer eye words were never spoken.

I can feel myself getting angry at this obvious injustice. "What the hell is this about?" I ask as Fred walks over.

"He bit his owner. Eleven stitches," Fred says. "Not that I blame him."

"What do you mean?"

"Well, for one thing, the owner is an asshole. And for another, he might not even be the owner."

"Tell me everything you know," I say.

It turns out that Fred doesn't know that much. A man named Warren Shaheen, who had just come home from the hospital, called him to a house in Hawthorne. He said he had been bitten by his dog, Yogi, for no reason whatsoever. He wanted the dog taken to the shelter and put down.

As Fred and Yogi were leaving the house, a young boy who claimed to live next door approached. He said that Warren was always kicking the dog, and he was sure that the dog bit him in retaliation. Further, he claimed that Warren had found the dog wandering on the street less than three weeks ago and apparently made no effort to find the real owner.

"What are you going to do?" I asked.

Fred shrugged. "You know the drill. After ten days, we put him down. We're not allowed to adopt him out."

I ask Fred if he'll open the cage and let me take the dog out. He knows he shouldn't, but does so anyway.

I take Yogi into a small room where potential adopters go to get to know the dogs they might take. I sit in the chair, and Yogi comes over to me. He has cut marks on his face, clearly visible in this light. They look old, perhaps remnants from some long-ago abuse. It's likely that Yogi has not had the best life.

He puts his paw up on my knee, a signal from goldens that they want their chest scratched. I do so, and then he rests his head on my thigh as I pet it.

Fred comes over to the room, looks in and sees me petting Yogi in this position. "Pretty amazing, huh?"

"Fred, I'm aware of the regulations, but there's something you should know."

"What's that?"

"Nothing bad is going to happen to this dog."

• • • • •

I HAVE COME to the conclusion that the entire "work ethic" concept is a scam.

Hardworking people are to be admired, we're told, though no one mentions that the very act of working is contrary to the natural order of things. It falls to me, Andy Carpenter, philosopher extraordinaire, to set the record straight.

I believe that humans have an "enjoyment drive," which supersedes all others. Everything we do is in the pursuit of that enjoyment. We eat because it's more enjoyable to be full than hungry; we sleep because it's more enjoyable to be rested than tired; we have sex because . . . I assume you get the picture.

We work simply to make money, because money makes our lives more enjoyable in many ways. If you take money out of the equation, the work system falls apart. Without the desire for cash, who is going to say, "I think I'll spend ten hours a day for my entire life selling plumbing supplies"? Or waiting tables? Or repairing vacuum cleaners?

There are people, I will concede, who would pursue certain occupations independent of money. For example, artists, politicians, or perhaps entertainers might do what they do for the creative satisfaction or the power or the acclaim. But that's only because they *enjoy* creative satisfaction, power, and acclaim.

Which brings me to me. I am work-ethically challenged. Simply put, I'm a lawyer who has never been terribly fond of lawyering. Since I inherited twenty-two million dollars a few years ago, money has ceased to be a driving force, which means I don't exactly have a busy work life.

There are exceptions to my aversion to plying my craft, which fit neatly under my drive for enjoyment. I've handled a number of major, challenging cases in the past few years, most of which became big media events. The key for me is to treat them as sport, as a challenge to be relished, and that's what I did.

But those cases were as important to me personally as they were professionally, which elevated the stakes and made them that much more enjoyable and exciting. They ignited my competitive fire. If I were representing some stranger in a divorce or suing an insurance company over an auto accident, I'd rather stay home.

Right now I can feel my juices starting to flow as I head for the office. On the way there I call my associate, Kevin Randall, on his cell phone.

His "Hello" is spoken in a hushed whisper.

"What's the matter?" I ask.

"I'm at my urologist," he says.

Kevin is the biggest hypochondriac in the Western Hemisphere, and five out of every ten times I might call him he's at the doctor. "You have your own urologist?" I ask. "That's pretty impressive."

Kevin knows I am unable to resist making fun of his devotion to his perceived illnesses, but he is equally unable to resist talking about them. "You don't? Who do you see for urology issues?"

"I have no tolerance for urology issues," I say. "I piss on urology issues."

He doesn't like the way this conversation is going, which makes him sane. "Why are you calling me, Andy?"

"To ask if you could meet me in the office. When you're finished at the urologist."

"Why?" he asks. Since we haven't taken on a case in a few months, it's a reasonable question to pose.

"We've got client issues," I say.

"We have a client?" He's not successfully masking his incredulity.

"Yes."

"Who is it?"

"His name is Yogi," I say.

"Yogi? Is that a first name or a last name?" Kevin knows nothing about sports, so he is apparently not familiar with Yogi Berra. However, I would have thought he'd know Yogi Bear.

"Actually, it's his only name, and probably not his real one at that. Listen, Kevin, I'm pretty sure he can't pay our fee. Are you okay with that?"

"Of course." I gave Kevin half of a huge commission we made on a case a while back, so money is not a major issue for him, either. Additionally, he owns the Law-dromat, a thriving establishment at which he dispenses free legal advice to customers who bring in their clothes to be washed and dried. "What is he accused of?"

"Assault," I say.

"Where is he now?"

"On death row."

"Andy, I sense there's something unusual about this case."

"You got that right."

• • • • •

"WHAT ARE YOU doing here?"

This is the greeting I get from Edna, who for fifteen years has been my secretary but who now insists on being called my "administrative assistant." In neither role has Edna ever done any actual work, but as an administrative assistant she can do nothing with considerably more dignity.

Like all of us, Edna strives to satisfy her enjoyment drive, and she does so by doing crossword puzzles. She is the greatest crossword puzzler I have ever seen, and possibly the greatest who has ever lived. Just as art collectors seem to discover DaVincis or Picassos at flea markets or in somebody's garage every month, in three hundred years crossword puzzle devotees will be finding long-lost Ednas and selling them for fortunes.

She is polishing off today's *New York Times* puzzle

when I walk in, and her surprise at seeing me is justified. I haven't been here in at least a week.

"We've got a client," I say.

"How did that happen?"

Her tone is somewhere between baffled and annoyed. "I was in the right place at the right time. Come in with Kevin when he gets here."

I head back to my private office with a window over-looking the finest fruit stand on Van Houten Avenue in Paterson, New Jersey. If I ever blow my money, it's not going to be on office space.

I use the time to look through some law books and browse on the computer, finding out as much as I can about dog law in New Jersey. What I learn is not encouraging; if there's a dog lover in the state legislature, he or she has been in hiding.

I'm fifteen minutes into finding absolutely no protections for canines under the law, when Kevin and Edna walk in. As soon as they sit down, I start in.

"Our client is a dog named Yogi, who is currently at the shelter. He's scheduled to be put down the day after tomorrow."

"Why?" Kevin asks.

"He's alleged to have bitten his owner."

Kevin shakes his head. "No, I mean why is he our client?"

I shrug. "Apparently, no other lawyer would take his case, probably because he sheds. What do you know about dog law?"

"Nothing," Kevin says.

"Then you take the computer and I'll take the books."

"Do I have to do anything?" Edna asks, openly cringing at the prospect.

I nod. "You might want to get some biscuits. We'll need them when we meet with our client."

Edna goes out, and I explain the details of Yogi's situation to Kevin. We then spend the next hour and a half researching the law. Kevin is far better at this than I am, and my hope is that he'll come up with something.

He doesn't. "Yogi's got big problems," he says.

He explains that the animal control system's regulations prohibit them from letting anyone adopt a dog who has bitten someone. It is considered a matter of public safety, not reviewable under any statute. Under certain conditions the owner can take the dog back, but Yogi's owner doesn't want him. Nor would we want Yogi to go back to someone who was kicking him.

"Andy," Kevin says, "are we sure the dog isn't really dangerous?"

I nod. "I'm sure. I looked into his eyes."

"You always told me you never make eye contact," he says.

"I was talking about with people."

"Oh. Then, are we sure the dog actually bit the guy?"

I nod again. "Apparently so. The neighbor said the guy was kicking him, so . . ."

Kevin notices my pause. "So . . . ?" he prompts.

"So . . . it was self-defense." I'm starting to get excited by what is forming in my mind. "Yogi was a victim of domestic violence."

"Andy, come on . . ."

There's no stopping me now. "Come on, the dog was being abused. He couldn't call 911, so he defended himself. If he was the guy's wife, NOW would be throwing him a cocktail party."

Kevin is not getting it. "If the male dog was the guy's wife?"

"Don't focus on the sex part," I say. "We've got a classic abuse-excuse defense here." I'm referring to the traditional defense used by abused wives who finally and justifiably turn violently against their husbands.

Kevin thinks about it for a moment, then can't hold back a grin. "It could be fun."

"The hell with fun," I say. "We're going to win."

Now with a strategy to work with, we spend another couple of hours plotting how to execute it. This defense, when the client is a dog, is obviously not something the justice system or the legislature has contemplated, so there is little for us to sink our teeth into. We're heading into uncharted territory with few bullets in our legal guns.

Kevin heads down to the courthouse to file for injunctive relief on Yogi's behalf, which essentially amounts to a request for a stay of execution. The court does not have to see merit in our position to grant it; it need only recognize that not granting it would result in Yogi's death, which would in effect be ruling against our overall case before we've had a chance to present it. Pleading self-defense on behalf of a dead client is not a terribly productive use of anyone's time.

After his stop at the courthouse, Kevin is going to attempt to interview Warren Shaheen, the man with Yogi's teeth marks in his legs. Kevin will get his side of the story and try to persuade him to see the merit of our position. Shaheen may well not want to get taken through the torture I've got planned for him, and Kevin is going to suggest some alternatives that we've come up with.

The first hurdle we'll have to overcome is to get a judge to consider our request tomorrow, the scheduled last day of Yogi's life. I head home to think about that problem in the way that my mind functions most clearly. I take my own golden retriever, Tara, for a walk in Eastside Park.

Tara's official name has changed a few times over the years. Right now it is Tara, the Greatest Creature on This or Any Other Planet and if You Can't See That You're an Idiot, Carpenter. It's a little long, but apt.

I rescued Tara more than eight years ago from the same shelter that currently houses Yogi. Just looking at her now, enjoying the sights and smells as we walk through the park, easily reaffirms my commitment that I will never let another golden die in a shelter, not if it takes every dollar I have. Fortunately, it doesn't.

Tara and I pass a number of our "dog friends" as we walk. These are the same people, walking their dogs, that we meet almost every time we're in the park. I don't know any of the people's names, and we merely exchange pleasantries and minor canine chitchat, yet we have a common bond through our love of our dogs.

Each one of these people would be horrified to know of Yogi's plight, and I don't share it with them. At least not now. But I do come to the realization that my only hope lies in sharing it with all of them.

Yogi is about to become famous.

I call my friend Vince Sanders, editor of the local newspaper and the most disagreeable human being I have ever met. As a terrific journalist, he will take a heartwarming story and run with it, despite not having the slightest idea why it is heartwarming.

Vince's long-suffering assistant, Linda, answers the phone. "Hey, Linda, it's Andy. What kind of mood is he in?"

"Same as always," she says.

"Sorry to hear that," I say, and she tells him I'm on the phone.

"Yeah?" Vince says when he picks up. "Hello" and "good-bye" are not part of his verbal repertoire.

"I've got a big story for you," I say.

"Hold on while I try to come to terms with my excitement," is his deadpan answer.

I tell him to get a photographer and meet me at the animal shelter. He doesn't want to, but he trusts me a little from past stories, so he considers it. I close the deal by promising to buy the burgers and beer the next time we go to Charlie's, our favorite sports bar.

I drop Tara off at home and then go down to the shelter. Vince hasn't arrived yet, so I use the time to bring Fred up to date on the situation. I think he likes what he's hearing, because every few sentences he claps his hands and smacks me on the back.

When I'm finished, he says, "You think you can pull this off?"

I nod. "I'm most worried about the timing."

"What do you mean?"

"I've got to get the judge to move much more quickly than judges like to move. I don't want anything to happen to Yogi in the meantime."

"Don't worry about that," Fred says. "I've got a hunch I'm not going to be able to find my syringes."

He's telling me that he won't put Yogi down on schedule, at least not until he's heard from me. He's taking a risk, particularly since this will be a well-publicized case, and I appreciate it. As will Yogi when he hears about it.

Vince and his photographer arrive, and I explain the situation to them. When I'm finished, I take them back to the quarantine area. "This is him?" Vince asks. "This is the big story?"

"It's a human interest story, Vince. Which means that if you were an actual human, you'd have an interest in it."

Fortunately, Vince's photographer is a dog lover, and he eagerly gets to work. I make sure that all the pictures are taken through the bars of the cage; I want Yogi's miserable situation to be completely clear in each photograph.

When he's finished, he shows Vince the picture he thinks is best, and we both agree. It captures Yogi perfectly and dramatizes the injustice of his plight.

Tomorrow that picture will be everywhere, because Yogi is about to become America's dog.

• • • • •

SOMETIMES THINGS COME together perfectly.

It doesn't happen often; usually something can be counted on to go wrong. Murphy didn't become famous by passing a bum law. But when everything goes right, when a plan is executed to perfection, it is something to be cherished.

The voracious twenty-four-hour cable, Internet, blogging media is onto Yogi's story before Vince's paper even physically hits the newsstands. The idea of a dog taking refuge in the abuse-excuse defense is just the kind of thing to push more significant news to the side, and it certainly does exactly that here.

I wake up at six a.m. and turn the television on. There on CNN is Yogi's beautiful, pathetic mug, with the graphic across the bottom asking "Stay of Execution?" Their details are sketchy but accurate, having already gleaned from Vince's story the main facts, including our legal actions.

The phone starts ringing, as I knew it would, and I find myself fielding calls from what seems like every media outlet in the free world. My standard response is that I will have a great deal to say on this later, and I arrange late morning interviews to take place at the animal shelter with the main cable networks. I have appeared on all of them as a celebrity legal commentator at various times during the past two years, so my involvement with this case provides a level of comfort for them to cover it.

I finally make it into the shower, and I spend the endless minute waiting for the conditioner to sink in, by happily reflecting on how perfectly this is going. In less than a day, I've made an entire country, or at least the media of an entire country, sit up and take notice.

I am Andy, the all-powerful.

The phone rings as I'm turning the water off, and I decide to ignore it. I've already done enough to reach saturation coverage, and I'm not going to have time for any more.

I let the machine pick up, and after a few seconds I hear a woman's voice. "Andy, it's Rita."

The caller is Rita Gordon, the clerk at the Passaic County Courthouse, and the only reason that venerable institution operates with any efficiency at all. I once had an affair with Rita that could be characterized as brief, since it lasted only about forty-five minutes. But those were forty-five great minutes.

I pick up the phone. "Rita, sorry I screened the call. I thought you were Katie Couric."

I don't think Rita and I have ever engaged in a conversation that was not dominated by banter of some sort. Until now. "Andy, Hatchet wants to see you right away."

That one sentence renders obsolete all my gloating about the perfection of my legal and public relations effort. "Hatchet was assigned this case? Is that what you're telling me?" I ask.

"That's what I'm telling you."

Judge Henry Henderson has been called "Hatchet" for as long as I can remember. One doesn't get nicknames by accident, and they are generally quite revealing. You won't find demure librarians named Darla "the Sledgehammer" Smiley, or nannies dubbed Mary "the Exterminator" Poppins. And there won't be many professional wrestlers with names like Brutus "Little Kitten" Rockingham.

Legend goes that Hatchet got his name by chopping off the testicles of lawyers who annoyed him. My belief is that this is just urban myth, but that doesn't mean that if given the opportunity I would want to rummage through his desk drawers.

"How pissed is he?" I ask.

"I would say somewhere between very and totally."

"When should I come in?" I ask.

"Let's put it this way. If you're not here by the time I finish this sentence, you're late."

By that standard, I'm late for my meeting with Hatchet, but not by much. I'm down at the courthouse and ushered into his chambers within a half hour of receiving the call. Since the courthouse is twenty minutes from my house, that's pretty good.

Hatchet keeps his office very dark; the drapes are closed, and only a small lamp on his desk provides any light at all. If it's meant to disconcert and intimidate attorneys, it achieves its goal. Yet if the stories I hear are true, I am less afraid of Hatchet than are most of my colleagues. For example, I haven't pissed in my pants yet.

Hatchet etiquette requires letting him speak first, so I just stand there waiting for the barrage. Finally, after about thirty seconds that feel like three thousand, he looks up. "Do you know what time it is?" he asks.

I look at my watch. "Eight forty-five. I got here as soon as I—"

He interrupts. "Do you know how long I've been up?"

"I'm sorry, Your Honor, but I have no idea."

"Four hours. My wife woke me at four forty-five."

This is a stunning piece of news. Not that Hatchet has been up since early this morning, but that he has a wife. Someone actually sleeps with this man. I find myself picturing a female leaning over in bed and saying, "Hatchet, dear, it's almost five a.m.—time to get up." It's not a pretty image.

"I assume this is somehow my fault?" I ask.

"She woke me to say that I cannot kill some poor dog. I assumed she was talking about an attorney, until she showed me what she was watching on the television."

"She sounds like a very compassionate person, who doesn't sleep much," I say.

Hatchet takes off his glasses and peers at me. "Are you trying to turn my court into a circus? A sideshow?"

"No, sir. Never. Definitely not. No way."

"Then why are you representing a dog?"

"Because if I don't, he'll be killed. And that would be unjust. And it would make many people unhappy, including me and Mrs. Hatch—Henderson."

If he is going to kill me, this is the moment. He doesn't

say anything for about thirty seconds; it's possible he's so angry that he's unable to unclench his teeth. He finally speaks, more softly and calmly than I would have expected. "I can't believe I'm even saying this, but I'm going to issue a stay of execution. I am scheduling a hearing in this court tomorrow morning at nine o'clock. It is a hearing that I do not want to take more than one hour, and I will be conveying that view to certain city officials. Is that understood?"

It's completely understood, and I say so. I leave Hatchet's office, my dignity and testicles intact, and head down to the shelter to conduct the television interviews.

This won't be officially resolved until tomorrow, but I now know one thing with total certainty: Yogi and I have already won.

I say this because we have surmounted the only serious obstacle that was in front of us. Mostly through the use of media pressure, along with a creative defense, we have gotten the legal system to give us our day in court. In a normal situation, we would now have to defeat our legal adversaries.

But the reason we've already won is that we don't have any real legal adversaries. Simply put, we want to win, and there's no one who will want us to lose. Nobody gains if Yogi is killed in so public a fashion, and there isn't a politician in Paterson, in New Jersey, in America, or on the planet Earth who would want to be responsible for it.

The afternoon media interviews are a slam dunk; I'm not exactly bombarded with difficult questions. This makes for a great story, and the press will willingly help me promote it. Besides, all I have to do is keep pointing to

Yogi and asking as plaintively as I can why anyone would want to end his life.

The most interesting piece of information comes from one of the reporters, who asks if I've heard the news that the mayor of Paterson is at that moment meeting with his director of Animal Services to discuss this matter. I would imagine the "discussion" consists of the mayor screaming at the director to find a way out of this.

I'm not going to get overconfident and let up, but my guess is that by tomorrow, Yogi will be dining on biscuits at my house.

I wonder how Tara is going to feel about that.

• • • • •

KEVIN MEETS ME at the diner for breakfast to go over our strategy.

He also brings me up to date on his conversation with Warren Shaheen, the alleged owner and victim of the vicious Yogi. Shaheen told Kevin that he has been asked to be at court today by the animal control people, but Kevin doubts he'll show. Mr. Shaheen is apparently not enjoying his fifteen minutes of fame, and was clearly frightened when Kevin told him that when I latch on to his leg in court, it's going to hurt a lot more than when Yogi did it. Faced with that prospect, he was more than happy to go along with whatever Kevin said was necessary to make it end.

We head for the courthouse early, and it's lucky we do, because the media crush adds ten minutes to the time it takes to get inside. We still get to our seats at the defense table fifteen minutes before the scheduled start of the hearing. My testicle-preservation instinct is not about to let me show up late in Hatchet's court. I plan to make sure that my client remains the only neutered member of the defense team.

A young city attorney named Roger Wagner puts his briefcase on the prosecution table and comes over to shake my hand. He smiles. "Any chance we can make a deal?"

"What do you have in mind?" I ask.

"We keep Yogi and we trade you a German shepherd, a beagle, and a Maltese to be named later."

I laugh. "I don't think so."

I sit back down. It's an unusual feeling not to have my client present at a court proceeding, and I had briefly considered asking that Yogi be allowed to attend. The determining factor in my not doing so was my uncertainty whether Yogi was house-trained, or in this case court-trained. Taking a dump in Hatchet's court would not be a productive legal maneuver.

Hatchet starts the proceedings by laying out the ground rules. The city will get to call witnesses, which I can then cross-examine. I can follow with my own witnesses, should I so choose, and then we will adjourn. There will be no opening or closing arguments.

"And there will be no theatrics," he says, staring directly at me.

Wagner calls Stephen Billick, the Passaic County director of Animal Control. He starts to ask him about his education, work experience, and general qualifications for the job, but he barely gets two sentences out before Hatchet cuts him off. "That isn't necessary. Mr. Carpenter will stipulate as to the witness's experience and expertise. Isn't that right, Mr. Carpenter?"

I had no intention of so stipulating, but I have even less intention of arguing with Hatchet. "Your Honor, that's uncanny. You took the words right out of my mouth."

Wagner proceeds with his questioning, which basically elicits from Billick the rationale for the policy of putting down dogs with a history of biting humans. It's a public safety issue and one that is consistent in localities across the country. It would be irresponsible to send a dog like that back into civilized society, because of the likelihood that he could strike again.

Hatchet offers me the opportunity for a "brief" cross-examination, and I begin with "Mr. Billick, what happens if a dog bites someone, but the owner does not bring it to a shelter to be put down?"

"If someone reports being bitten and is treated by a doctor or a hospital emergency room, then the dog is quarantined either at a shelter or a veterinarian's office for ten days, in order to make sure the dog does not have rabies."

"So let's say I had a dog that bit someone. I could keep the dog at my vet for the ten days?"

"Yes."

"And after the ten days are up?" I ask.

"Assuming he didn't have rabies, you could bring him home."

"Wouldn't that put the public at risk of the dog biting again?"

He nods. "It would. But you would have signed a document accepting future responsibility."

"So I as the owner can have the dog back, simply by accepting responsibility for his future actions?"

"That is correct," he says.

"What does it mean to be the owner of a dog?" I ask.

"I don't understand."

"I mean, in the eyes of the animal control system, if I buy a dog, I then own it?"

He nods. "Yes."

"And then that ownership means I have responsibility for it?"

"Yes."

"What if I sell it?" I ask.

Hatchet cuts in. "Mr. Carpenter, do you remember my use of the word 'brief'?"

I nod. "I do, Your Honor. I committed it to memory. I'm almost finished here."

He lets me continue, so I repeat the question for Billick. "And if I sell the dog? Who owns it then?"

He seems confused. "Well, the person you sell it to."

I walk over to the defense table, and Kevin hands me two pieces of paper. I then bring them over to the bench. "Your Honor, I would like to submit these two documents as defense exhibits one and two."

"What is their substance?" Hatchet asks.

"Number one is a bill of sale, confirming that Warren Shaheen sold me the dog referred to as 'Yogi' yesterday afternoon for the sum of fifty dollars. Number two is my declaration of ownership and my intention to take full responsibility for Yogi as his sole owner."

"So you are now the dog's owner?" Hatchet asks.

"Yes, Your Honor. Under the terms of ownership as Mr. Billick has just defined them."

Hatchet thinks for a moment, then turns to Billick. "Give the man his dog."

"Yes, Your Honor." Billick says, smiling himself as the gallery breaks out in applause.

We've won, but I can't help myself. "Your Honor, a dog's honor was besmirched here. I would like to call a trainer to the witness stand, to testify that Yogi is a sweet and loving dog."

"Mr. Carpenter . . . ," Hatchet says. He usually doesn't have to say any more, but I'm having fun with this, so I continue.

"Your Honor, Yogi now has his freedom, but where does he go to get back his reputation?"

"Perhaps it would help if I held his lawyer in contempt," Hatchet says. I'm not sure, but I actually may see a twinkle in his eye.

"Have a lovely day, Your Honor."

With that, he slams down his gavel. "This hearing is concluded."

• • • • •

IT HAS TAKEN a while, but I finally understand the joy of sex, and I am now prepared to reveal it to the world.

The purest joy of sex comes from not having to think about it.

About a year ago the person who filled the double role of private investigator and undisputed love of my life, Laurie Collins, left to become the chief of police of Findlay, Wisconsin, her hometown.

We had no contact whatsoever for the next four and a half months, as I tried to convince myself that I hated her. It worked until she called me and asked me to come to Wisconsin to take on a case of a young man accused of a double homicide but whom she considered innocent.

I spent four months in the frozen tundra, won the case, ate a lot of bratwurst, and reconnected with Laurie. When it was time to leave, neither of us could bear the prospect of splitting up again, so we agreed to maintain a long-distance relationship, seeing each other whenever either of us could get away. It's worked fairly well; since then I've gone to Wisconsin three times, and she's come to Paterson once.

The point of all this is that I no longer have to think about sex or wonder if and when I'm going to have it. When I see Laurie, I'm going to, and when we're apart, I'm not. It's incredibly freeing, and pretty much the first time since high school that I've spent no time at all wondering whether sex was imminent or possible.

There are other, side benefits as well. For instance, I save gallons of water by cutting back on showers. I always want to be clean, but I don't have to be "naked in bed with someone" clean, when there's no chance that's going to happen. I don't have to wash the sheets as often; my mouthwash frequency is cut by at least 30 percent . . . The positives go on and on.

I haven't talked to Laurie since the Yogi thing began. We usually try to speak every night, but she's at a police convention in Chicago, and I've been pretty busy, so we've traded phone messages. I'm not the most sociable guy in the world, and most of the time when I call people I hope their machine answers. This is not the case with Laurie.

The phone is ringing as I walk in after returning from court, and when I pick up I hear her voice. It's amazing how comforting, how welcoming, how knowing one voice can be. Think Patsy Cline with a New Jersey accent.

I admit it. I may be a little over the top about Laurie.

"Congratulations," she says. "I just missed a panel on the use of Taser guns watching you on television."

"I'm sure it was stunning," I say.

"You were great. I was proud of you."

"I meant the Taser gun panel must have been stunning. It was a Taser gun joke."

"Now I'm a little less proud. What are you going to do with Yogi?" she asks.

"Find him a good home. He can stay here until I do, although I haven't quite discussed it with Tara yet."

"You think she'll mind?"

"I think I'll have to give her an entire box of biscuits as a payoff, but she'll be okay with it."

"When do you get him?" she asks.

"I'm supposed to be back at the shelter at three o'clock."

"Seriously, Andy, I thought what you did was great."

I shrug off the compliment, and we talk about when we are going to see each other. She has two weeks vacation owed to her, and she's coming in at the end of the month. It'll mean showering more, but it's a small price to pay.

After speaking to Laurie, I do a couple of radio interviews about our victory in court and then head to the shelter to secure my client's freedom. There is a large media contingent staking out the place, and it takes me ten minutes to get inside.

Fred is waiting for me, a big smile on his face. There aren't too many happy stories in his job, and he's obviously relishing this one. "I gave him a bath," Fred says. "Wait till you see how great he looks."

We go back to the quarantine section, and he gives me the honor of taking Yogi out of the cage. Yogi does, in fact, look great, freshly scrubbed and wagging his tail at the prospect of imminent freedom.

Yogi and I leave, having once again to go through the media throng to get to the car. I've said all I have to say, and Yogi doesn't even bother barking a "no comment." We both just want to get the hell out of here.

When we get home I lead Yogi directly into the backyard. I then go into the house and bring Tara back there as well, feeling that somehow the meeting will go better outside. It goes amazingly well; Tara doesn't seem to show any jealousy at all. My guess is, I'll hear about it later when we're alone, but right now she's the gracious hostess.

I grab a pair of leashes, planning to take them for a walk in Eastside Park, which is about five blocks from my house. We're halfway down the block, walking at a leisurely pace, when I hear a voice.

"Reggie!"

Suddenly, instead of holding two leashes, I'm only holding one, Tara's. Yogi has taken off like a track star exploding out of the blocks, surprising me and breaking out of my grip on his leash.

I panic for a moment, fearful that he will run into the street and get hit by a car. I turn to see that he is still on the sidewalk, running in the other direction toward a young woman, perhaps in her early twenties. The woman is down on one knee, waiting for Yogi to arrive. She doesn't have to wait long; for a middle aged dog, Yogi can really motor.

Yogi takes off about five feet from her, flying and landing on her. She rolls back, laughing, with him on top of her. They roll and hug for about fifteen seconds; I'm not sure I've ever seen a happier human or dog.

Tara and I walk back to them; Tara seems as surprised by this turn of events as I am. As we reach them, the woman is struggling to get to her feet, no easy job since Yogi is still draped all over her.

"I have a hunch you two know each other," I say, displaying my gift for understatement.

She is giggling and, apparently, incredibly excited. "We sure do. We sure do. God, do we ever!"

"I'm Andy Carpenter," I say.

She nods again. "I know. I saw you and Reggie on television," she gushes. "I followed you here from the shelter. I'm Karen Evans."

"His real name is Reggie?" I ask.

"Yup. He was my brother's dog. My brother is Richard Evans."

She says the name as if it's supposed to mean something to me. "How can you be sure it's him?" I ask, though from Yogi's—or Reggie's—reaction I have little doubt that she's telling the truth.

"The cut marks. My brother rescued him from a shelter when he was a year old. He had the marks then, and the vet had said that his previous owner had wired his jaw shut, maybe to stop him from barking. Is that the most awful thing you've ever heard?"

"How would the vet know that?" I ask.

"If you look, you'll see that there are faint cut marks under his mouth as well. It's from the wire being wrapped around."

I hadn't noticed that, but I look under his mouth, and sure enough, there they are. If there was any doubt she was telling the truth, that doubt has now been eliminated.

The Golden Retriever Formerly Known as Yogi starts tapping Karen with his paw, in an effort to get her to resume petting him. She starts laughing again and obliges. "Mr. Carpenter—"

"Andy."

"Andy, do you realize how unbelievably amazing this is?"

"It really is," I say, though that seems to be a little strong. She seems like the type who finds a lot of things to be unbelievably amazing.

"It's a miracle," she proclaims.

"Hmmm," I say cleverly, not quite wanting to sign on to the "miracle" description.

She looks at me strangely. "You don't know what's going on, do you?" she asks as she realizes that, in fact, I don't know what's going on.

"Maybe not," I say.

"My brother is Richard Evans. This is his dog."

"I understand that," I say.

"Mr. Carpenter . . . Andy . . . the State of New Jersey says that this dog has been dead for five years."

•　•　•　•　•

ONCE WE'RE IN my house, Karen reminds me why I should remember Richard Evans.

He was a U.S. Customs inspector, working at the Port of Newark, who kept his own small private boat at a pier near there. One evening more than five and a half years ago he went out on that boat off the Jersey coast with his fiancée, Stacy Harriman, and his dog, Reggie.

At about nine o'clock a significant storm was coming in, and word went out to the private boats in the area to get to shore. All of them did except for Richard's, which was off the coast near Asbury Park, and the Coast Guard sent out a cutter to escort it in.

When the Coast Guard arrived, no one on the boat responded to their calls, and they decided to board it. They found Richard alone and unconscious on the floor of the deck below, an empty bottle of sleeping pills nearby. There was no sign of a suicide note, and the coastguardsmen had no way to know that anyone else had been on board.

Richard spent three days in a coma while the police investigated the circumstances. Long before he regained consciousness, they were aware that Stacy and the dog had been on the boat when it sailed, and they had found traces of blood on the floor and railing of the boat. He was immediately arrested and taken into custody.

Three weeks later a woman's decomposed body washed ashore, soon identified by DNA as that of Stacy Harriman. Richard was tried for the murder. The scenario the prosecution posed was a murder-suicide, and there was no way for the defense to counter it effectively. The case was not a huge media event, but as a local defense attorney I had some awareness of it.

The dog's body was never found.

"This is the dog," Karen says. "Reggie. You saw how he reacted to me. There's no doubt about it."

"It certainly seems like it," I agree.

"So will you help me?" she asks.

"How?"

"Get my brother out of prison. You're a lawyer, right? Isn't that what you do?"

Even though I am Andy Carpenter, crack defense attorney, I can't see how she can go from Reggie's survival to her brother's innocence. "How would you suggest I do that?" I ask.

"Look, you don't know Richard. There's no way he could have hurt anybody."

"The people to convince of that would have been the members of the jury."

"But if Reggie is alive, then he wasn't thrown overboard. Then neither was Stacy."

"But they found her body. And her blood on the railing." It gives me no pleasure to point this out, but it does seem time for a reality check.

It doesn't seem to faze her. "I know. But Richard didn't kill her. Just like he didn't kill Reggie. If the jury was wrong about one thing, why couldn't they be wrong about another?"

"Karen, goldens are great swimmers. Isn't it possible that he swam back to shore?"

She shakes her head. "No, they were too far out. And there was a big storm; that's why the Coast Guard was out there."

She can see I'm not at all convinced, so she presses her case. "Andy, Richard loved this dog more than anything in the world." She points to Tara. "You love her, right? Could you throw her overboard to drown?"

Clarence Darrow never gave a better closing argument than Karen just did. "I'll look into it. But your hopes are way too high."

"Thank you. And it's okay. I've spent the last five years with no hope, so this feels pretty good."

We agree that I'll keep Reggie in my house, and I promise that until this is all resolved I won't do anything about finding him a permanent home. She thinks his permanent home will be with her brother Richard, as soon as I convince the justice system of his innocence.

As for me, this is not that big a deal, and pretty much a no-lose proposition. In the unlikely event that she's right, I will be attempting to help an innocent man get his freedom. If she's wrong, then I'll get the pleasure of seeing someone who could throw a golden into the ocean rot in prison.

Besides, what else do I have to do?

• • • • •

POLICE OFFICERS, WITH the notable exception of Laurie, can't stand me.

This is partly due to the natural antipathy between cops and defense attorneys, though it is also true that I am disliked by people of many occupations.

Actually, I do have one buddy in the Paterson Police Department, Lieutenant Pete Stanton. He's a pretty good friend, which means we drink a lot of beer together while watching TV sports, and when we call each other "shithead" we don't mean it personally. Professionally, ever since I helped his brother out on a legal matter about five years ago, it's become a one-way street. I often call on him for favors, and after endless grumbling he obliges.

This time I call him to see if he can set up a meeting for me with someone in the Asbury Park Police Department. I tell him that in a perfect world it would be with someone who was involved in the Richard Evans murder case five years ago.

"You're representing Evans?" he asks, with evident surprise.

"Not yet. For now I'm looking into it for a friend."

"What's the matter?" he asks. "You run out of scumbag murderers to help in North Jersey?"

"Only because of your inability to arrest any."

"You call for a favor and then insult me?" he asks.

"You know, I have some friends who would do me a favor without first putting me through the wringer."

"Is that right?" he asks. "Then why don't you call one of them?"

He finally agrees to make a phone call to a detective he knows down there, and within fifteen minutes he calls me back. "You're set up to see Lieutenant Siegle of Asbury Park PD tomorrow morning at ten."

"Does he know about the case?"

"She."

"Does she know about the case?"

"She ran the investigation."

"Did you tell her I was representing Evans?" It's something I wouldn't want Siegle to think; it might make her reluctant to be straight with me.

"All I told her was that you were an asshole," he says. "I figured that was okay, since if she was smart enough to make lieutenant, she'd figure that out anyway."

I'm on the road by eight in the morning for the drive down to Asbury Park. It's about sixty miles on the Garden State Parkway and, with traffic, can take almost two hours. In the summer it can be even worse.

Asbury Park has long been a key city on the shore,

which is how those of us from New Jersey refer to the beach. If you ever suspect that a person is posing as a Jersey-ite, ask him to describe the area where the ocean hits land. If he says "beach," he's an impostor. Of course, I have no idea why someone would fake New Jersey credentials, but it's important to be alert.

The drive invariably brings back memories of my misspent youth. My lack of success with girls throughout high school was just about one hundred percent, but at least I had a few "almosts" at the shore. An official "almost" occurred when one of my friends or I would get a girl to talk to us for fifteen minutes without saying, "Get lost, jerk."

Asbury has changed markedly over the years, and, I'm sorry to say, not for the better. It used to be a fun place, with restaurants, bars, and amusement rides and games, sort of a mini Coney Island. It has slipped into very substantial decline, and it makes me feel a little older and sadder to see it.

I arrive at the police station fifteen minutes early, and Lieutenant Siegle is out on a call. She arrives promptly at ten o'clock, and the desk sergeant points to me waiting in a chair at the end of the lobby.

She walks over to me, a smile on her face and her hand outstretched. "Andy Carpenter? Michele Siegle."

She's an attractive woman, about my age, and it flashes across my mind that she could have been one of the girls I got nowhere with back in my high school days. "Thanks for seeing me."

"I've actually followed many of your cases," she says, then notes the surprised look on my face. "I'm going to Seton Hall Law School at night."

"Really . . . That's terrific," I say. "Crossing over to the other side?"

"Not quite. I'm hoping to be a prosecutor." She smiles. "We need somebody to make sure evil golden retrievers aren't out roaming the streets."

She takes me back to her office, and as soon as we get there, she gets right to it. "So you want to talk about the Evans case?"

I nod. "I do."

"Are you representing anyone involved?"

"Not yet. Maybe not ever, but a lot will depend on what you tell me."

She nods. "Shoot."

"How far from land was the boat when the Coast Guard boarded it?"

"About four miles."

"Did you ever determine the route it took?"

"What do you mean?" she asks.

"I'm trying to figure out how close the boat came to shore before it was boarded. Especially when it was in the area that the body washed up."

"Various people had sighted it along the way. It was always pretty far out there."

"And it was stormy that night?" I ask.

She nods. "Yes. That's why it was boarded in the first place. If not for that, Evans would have died from the pills he took."

"And the theory was that he threw the dog into the ocean at the same point he threw his fiancée?"

"That was the theory, although it was never that important to the case. If anything, it got in the way."

"What do you mean?" I ask.

"Everybody who knew him talked about how much he loved the dog. Killing him therefore didn't make much sense."

"So how was it explained away?"

She shrugs. "This was a murder-suicide. Not the most rational of acts."

"Was the dog's body ever discovered?" I ask.

"Not that I know of."

I decide it's time to pose the key question. "Is there any likelihood that the dog, once it was thrown overboard, could have swum to shore?"

She thinks about it for a moment, considering the possibility. "No," she says. "No chance. Not from half that distance, not in that weather."

I don't respond for a moment, and she says, "You think the dog is alive?"

I turn the question back at her. "What if it was?"

She thinks again. "Then that would be a very interesting development."

Yes, it would.

• • • • •

FOR EVERY LAWYER, in every case, there comes the time to make a key decision.

It's usually strategic: how to plead, the thrust of the defense, or perhaps whether to have the defendant testify. Because of my bank account, and my aforementioned work-ethic deficiency, my key moment always comes much earlier. It's when I decide whether to take the case.

I think about this on the way home from Asbury Park. At the moment it's premature, since I don't know enough about the case, have never met the defendant, and, obviously, he has not sought my help. All that is keeping me interested is a devoted sister and a golden retriever.

For now that's plenty.

I call Kevin and ask him to assemble all the information and material he can find, and once again I'm pleased to learn that he is way ahead of me. He's already gotten his hands on the transcript of the trial, as well as the contemporaneous news reports. We don't yet have standing to get discovery information, but for now this will do fine.

Kevin meets me at my house with the material, and we go into the den to go through it. Tara sits with me on the couch, and Reggie sits at Kevin's feet under the desk. I have taken to calling the dog Reggie instead of Yogi, which reflects my confidence that Karen Evans was telling the truth.

A couple of the tabloids around the time of the murder have pictures of the dog, and the distinctive cut marks are very much in evidence. There is much less white in his face, which goldens accumulate as they get older, but the dog certainly looks like the one snuggling against Kevin's leg.

The newspaper stories at the time were informative but not terribly lengthy. This was not a murder that captured the public consciousness as a select few do. Ironically, the facts as stated were somewhat similar to the Scott Peterson case, yet that one became a media obsession, while this one stayed basically under the radar.

Richard Evans had met Stacy Harriman almost a year before the fateful night. She had just arrived on the East Coast from her Minnesota home, though there is no mention about why she had moved. At the time of her death, she and Richard had been engaged and living together for six months.

Most of the neighbors, when questioned by the local newspaper reporters, did not have any knowledge of problems between the couple. Of course, the most collectively oblivious group of people in the world are neighbors. "Gee . . . I had no idea he was a serial killer. He was always so quiet . . . All I ever heard from his house was the chain saw . . ."

One neighbor did testify that Stacy had confided in her that she and Richard were having some problems and that she was a little worried about his temper. It was damaging testimony, but not the evidence that carried the day for the prosecution.

The transcript of the trial provides little help. Evans was competently defended; his lawyer was simply up against too much evidence. He had no way to explain away Evans's suicide attempt, the bloodstains, or Stacy Harriman's body washing up on shore.

The prosecutor did not spend too much time talking about Reggie except in his opening and closing arguments, when he used him to portray Evans as particularly heartless. The point was clear: No matter what might have been the cause of the violence between Evans and his fiancée, the dog was certainly an innocent. Killing the dog, he pointed out, was gratuitous and indicative of the callous nature of the defendant.

Once we finish going through all the documents, we spend some time discussing what we've learned and where we are. The only thing that is in any way unusual is the fact that Reggie is very much alive, despite the certainty of Lieutenant Siegle that he could not have swum to shore. If she is wrong in that assessment, or if this dog and Evans's dog are not one and the same, then Evans has absolutely nothing going for him.

Looking at this from the other side presents a bunch of questions that we are nowhere near ready to answer. If Evans is not guilty, why try to commit suicide? And who murdered Stacy? If it was somehow an elaborate scam to fake her own death, she didn't do that great a job, since she wound up dying.

We don't have Evans's answer to any of these questions, since he did not testify at trial in his own defense. It was probably a wise decision.

So for now all we have is Reggie and the absolute impossibility, at least in my mind, that a dog lover could have thrown him into the ocean.

I find myself staring at Reggie until I realize that Kevin is staring at me as I do so. "So what do you think?" I ask.

Kevin smiles. "It doesn't matter what I think. You're going to keep going after this."

"Why is that?" I ask.

"Because of the dog."

"But I want to know what you think."

"I think there's nothing here, Andy. It's as airtight as you're going to find. But I don't see anything wrong with pursuing it a little further. What the hell else do we have to do?"

"That's a good point. I'll call Karen Evans."

"To tell her the good news?"

I nod. "And to tell her I want to talk to her brother."

• • • • •

Prisons and hospitals feel the same to me.

When I say "hospitals," I'm not talking about the maternity ward, the tonsillectomy section, or even the emergency room. I'm talking about the cancer ward or the intensive care unit, the places where hope is scarce and resignation and sadness are for the most part the order of the day.

That same feeling exists in every prison I've ever visited; it's a dreary world in which there is a tangible, ever-present feeling of life ebbing away. The surroundings, the people, the conversations are all etched in shades of gray, as if living in a black-and-white movie.

I am therefore not looking at all forward to this morning's visit to Rahway State Prison. Not too much good can come out of it. I'll likely determine that I can't or don't want to help Richard Evans, in which case I'll be delivering crushing news to Karen. Or I'll sink deeper into the quicksand that is sure to be this case, and I'll spend six months of frustration futilely trying to reunite Reggie with his owner.

I pick up Karen at her house on Morlot Avenue in Fair Lawn, and if she shares my pessimism and dread, she's hiding it really well. She is waiting for me at the curb and just about jumps into the car; if the window were open I don't think she'd bother opening the door.

I try to start a normal conversation with Karen, asking her what she does for a living.

"I design dresses," she says. "Then I make them myself and sell them to stores."

"That's great," I say. "Which stores?"

She seems uncomfortable with the conversation. "If you don't mind, I'd rather talk about Richard."

"You don't like to talk about yourself?"

"There isn't any myself," she says. "There hasn't been one for five years . . . ever since they put Richard in that cage."

"You think it helps him to deprive yourself of a life?"

"I checked you out a lot," she says. "I know you defended your girlfriend, Laurie, when she was on trial for murder. What if you had lost? You think you'd have much of a life right now?"

Point to Karen, fifteen–love. If Laurie were in prison, my life would be a miserable, unbearable wreck. "We won because she was innocent, and we were able to demonstrate it."

"And you're going to do it again." She smiles. "So can we talk about Richard?"

"If that's what you want. But right now I know very little."

"I know . . . That's cool," she says. "I spoke to Richard yesterday. I didn't tell him anything about you. He thinks I'm coming to visit like I always do."

"Why?" I ask.

"I want him to be surprised. Boy, is he going to be surprised."

"Karen, these things are by definition long shots."

"But they happen, right? Didn't it happen with you and Willie Miller?"

She certainly has "checked me out" and is aware that I successfully got Willie a new trial and an acquittal after he spent seven years on death row for a murder he did not commit. "They happen rarely, but far more often nothing can be done."

"I believe in you," she says. "And I believe in Richard. This is gonna happen."

There's nothing for me to say to that, so I keep my mouth shut and drive. I'm not going to be able to dampen her optimism now, and I'd rather try and borrow some. It could even make the next couple of hours more bearable.

We arrive at the prison and go through the rather lengthy process of signing in and being searched. The reception area guards all know Karen; they greet each other easily and with smiles. She's obviously been here a lot, and she brings an enthusiasm and energy that is much needed in here, and probably much appreciated as well.

We finally make it into the visitors' room, which is like every visitors' room in every prison movie ever made. We sit in chairs alongside other visitors, facing a glass barrier that looks into the prisoners' side. Prisoners are brought in once their visitors are seated, and conversations take place through phones on the wall. In our case there's only one phone on the visitor side, so we'll have to take turns.

Richard comes out, and it's no surprise that he looks considerably older than the pictures I have seen of him. They were taken five years ago, but those five years were spent in prison. Prison aging is at least two to one.

Richard brightens considerably when he sees Karen, then looks surprised when he realizes she is not alone. He picks up his phone and Karen does the same. I can't hear Richard, but I can tell that he says how great it is to see her. Then he says, "Who's that?" referring to me.

"His name is Andy Carpenter," she says. "He's a famous lawyer who's going to help you." It's exactly what I didn't want her to say, but I'm not calling the shots here.

In response to something Richard says that I can't make out, Karen says, "I will, but I want to show you something first. Wait'll you see this; you're not going to believe it."

She opens her purse and takes out the picture of Reggie, but for the moment holding it facedown so that he can't see it. "Are you ready?" she asks.

He nods, and she holds the picture up to the window. "He's alive," she says. "I swear, he's alive."

You can fill an entire library with what I don't know about human emotion, so I can't begin to accurately read the look on Richard's face. It seems to be some combination of pain and joy and hope and bewilderment that form the most amazingly intense expression I've ever seen on anyone.

Within five seconds Richard is crying, bawling unashamedly, and Karen joins in. Soon they're both laughing and crying, and I feel like an intruder. Unfortunately, Karen hands the intruder the phone.

"Richard, I'm Andy Carpenter," I say, not exactly the most enlightening thing I could have come up with. He wants to know what the hell is going on, and here I am telling him the one thing he already knows.

He composes himself and says, "Please tell me what this is all about."

I nod. "I rescued a dog . . . the dog in this picture. Karen found out about it and came to see me. She said it's Reggie . . . your dog."

He closes his eyes for a moment and then nods. "It is; I'm sure of it."

"Is there any way you can prove it?" I ask.

"To who?"

"To me, so that I can prove it to the authorities," I say. "At this point I need to be completely positive."

"And then what?" he asks.

"Then I'll try and help you. If you want me to."

"Can you bring Reggie here?"

I think about this for a few moments, though the possibility has occurred to me before. "I'm not sure if I could arrange it," I say. "But even if I could, it would take a while."

"Then how can I prove it to you?" he says, exasperation in his voice. "Karen knows him . . . She can tell you."

I nod. "She has."

"Wait a minute," he says. "Let me talk to Karen for a second."

I hand Karen the phone, and Richard talks to her briefly. Whatever he says is enough to make her light up. "I forgot about that! Will he do it for me?"

Richard answers her, nodding his head as he does so. She then hands the phone back to me, and Richard says, "Karen should be able to prove it. Then what happens?"

"Then you hire me, if that's what you want. What about the lawyer who handled your trial—"

He interrupts. "Forget about him."

"I read the transcript," I say. "He did not do a bad job."

He frowns. "I'm here, aren't I?" It's a point that's hard to counter.

"Okay. After that, I come back here and interview you, and I learn everything about your case. Then we figure out how to proceed, if we proceed."

"You think we have a chance?" he asks.

It's important that I be straight with him. "Right now we have absolutely nothing. Zero. But if you're innocent, then it means there's something out there to be discovered. Which is what we have to do."

"I'm innocent," he says; then he smiles. "Everyone in here is."

A sense of humor in his situation is a good sign, and he's going to need it. I tell him that he'll have to sign a retainer hiring me as his attorney, with the disclaimer that it could be a short-term hire, depending on what I find out.

"I don't have much money to pay you," he says.

"Let's not focus on that now."

"Karen got some money from the sale of the house. We never got the boat back, but the cabin is worth something, and—"

"We can worry about that some other time, or never," I say, getting up to leave. "I'll be back to talk to you soon."

"The sooner the better."

Karen asks me to take her back to my house so she

can prove to me that Reggie is, in fact, Richard's dog. She doesn't want to tell me exactly how she is going to do that, and I don't press her. I've got other things to think about.

I learned a long time ago that I can't judge a person's guilt or innocence based on a first—or even tenth—impression. I've got a fairly well developed bullshit detector, but it's far from foolproof, and my conversation with Richard Evans wasn't nearly long enough or substantive enough.

But the truth is that I liked him and that I may have done him a disservice by showing up this way. He would have to be super-human not to be feeling a surge of hope, and at this point any confidence would by definition be overconfidence. I could have—should have—learned much more about the case before springing it on him. That way, if I thought it was not worth pursuing, he wouldn't have the letdown he surely will have.

"How well did you know Stacy Harriman?" I ask.

"Pretty well," Karen says. "She and Richard only were together for less than a year, but I saw them a lot. Richard really loved her."

"What do you know about her background?"

"She was from Montana, or Minnesota, or something. She didn't talk about it much, and she didn't have any family. Her parents died in a car accident when she was in high school, so I guess there wasn't much to keep her there."

"What did she do?" I ask.

"She lived with Richard."

"I mean for a living."

"She lived with Richard," she repeats, and I think I detect some annoyance or bitterness or something.

"And you're not aware of any problems between them?" I ask.

"No," she says, a little too quickly.

"Karen, I'm going to try and learn everything I can about what happened to Richard and Stacy. It is the only way I have any chance of accomplishing anything. If you know something, anything, that you don't share with me, you're hurting your brother."

"I don't know anything," she says. "They just didn't seem to fit together."

"How so?"

"Richard is a 'what you see is what you get' kind of person. He always lets people inside, sometimes before he should. But that is just his way."

"And Stacy?" I ask.

Karen shrugs. "I couldn't read her. It's like she had a wall up. I mean, she was friendly and pleasant, and she seemed to care about Richard, but—"

"But something didn't fit," I say.

She nods. "Right. I kept waiting for a phone call saying they were splitting up. They were engaged, but I just had a feeling they wouldn't be together long-term." She shakes her head sadly. "But I sure never figured it would end this way."

If there's one common denominator among everybody that a defense attorney meets in the course of handling a murder case, it's that no one "figured it would end this way." But it always does.

"Richard mentioned a house, a boat, and a cabin. Did he have a lot of money back then?"

"No. Our parents left the house and cabin to us; they weren't worth that much."

"Where were they?"

"The house was in Hawthorne; we sold that to pay for his defense. The cabin is in upstate New York, near Monticello. We kept it, but I never go there."

"Why not?"

"I'm waiting for Richard to go with me," she says.

"And the boat?" I ask.

"Richard bought that. It was his favorite thing in the world . . . except for Reggie."

Karen asks if I'll stop and get a pizza on the way home, the type of request that I basically will grant 100 percent of the time. She orders it with thick crust; it's not my favorite, but pizza is pizza.

Tara and Reggie are there to greet us when we arrive home. I think Tara is enjoying the company, though she would never admit it. She's used the situation to extract extra biscuits out of me, but I'm still grateful that she's being a good sport.

We eat the pizza, and I notice that Karen does not eat the crust, instead tearing pieces off and putting them to the side. It surprises me because I always do the same, since Tara loves the crusts. She tells me that she's saving her pieces for Reggie, but asks if we can delay giving out these baked treats for a few minutes.

Karen lets me know that she is about to prove Richard's ownership of Reggie. She seems nervous about it and prefaces it with a disclaimer that what she is about to get him to do, he has only done for Richard. Karen expresses the hope I won't read any possible failure as evidence that she and Richard are wrong.

She grabs the empty pizza box and takes Reggie out the front door, and then comes back in without him or the box, closing the door behind her. She leads me over to a window from where we can see him sitting patiently on the porch, just outside the door.

Suddenly, Karen loudly calls out, "Pizza dog's here!"

As I watch, Reggie hears this as well, and he stands on his back legs, rocking forward to the door. He puts his paw up and rings the doorbell, then goes back to all fours. He picks up the pizza box in his teeth and waits patiently for the door to open. Karen laughs with delight that Reggie remembered his cue. She lets him back in, and then he and Tara dine on the crusts.

It's a good trick—not brilliant, but it totally supports Karen and Richard's claim. Reggie is Richard's dog, I have no doubt about that.

Now it's time to try to reunite them.

• • • • •

THE WAY THIS works is, I take new evidence to a judge, and if we convince him, he then orders a hearing to be held on whether Richard should get a new trial. It's generally an orderly process, though in this case it's complicated by the fact that we have no new evidence.

In addition to all the other obstacles we face, there is the additional hurdle presented by the case being five years old. It's not an eternity, but neither will it be fresh in the minds of the people we are going to have to talk with. We are new to the case, but for everyone else it's old news.

There's a whole section of New Jersey that has an identity crisis; it's not sure whether it's a suburb of New York or of Philadelphia. It occupies the area on the way to the shore and basically has little reason for being, other than to provide housing for long-range commuters.

The houses are pleasant enough, though indistinguishable from each other. Block after block is the same; it's suburbia run amok. I feel as if I am trapped in summer reruns of *The Truman Show*.

I am venturing out here today to meet Richard Evans's former lawyer, Lawrence Koppell. His office is in Matawan, a community that seems to fit the dictionary definition of the word "sprawling."

Koppell's office is in a two-story building that, according to the directory, is inhabited exclusively by lawyers. His office is in suite 206, though that doesn't distinguish him in any fashion, as all the offices are labeled suites.

I enter the small reception area, which contains a desk, two chairs, and an absolutely beautiful young woman— maybe twenty-five, with black, curly hair and a wide, perfect smile. She finishes typing something with incredible speed, then turns and welcomes me, offering me my choice of coffee, tea, a soft drink, or water.

This is a woman with whom Edna has absolutely nothing in common.

"Do you do crossword puzzles?" I ask, just to make sure.

She shakes her head while maintaining the smile. "No, I really don't have the time. Any free time I have, I go surfing or hiking or skiing—in the winter, of course."

"Of course," I say, trying to picture Edna on a surfboard. Once I successfully picture it, I wish I hadn't tried.

She leads me into Koppell's office, which isn't that much larger than hers. He is on the phone but signals for me to sit down and then holds up one finger, which I take to mean he'll be off the phone in a moment.

"I'm sure he is a good boy, Mr. Givens," he says into the

phone. "But the problem, as I told you, is that in the eyes of the law he is not a boy. He became a man two weeks ago, on his eighteenth birthday. Which makes the marijuana possession more difficult to deal with."

He listens for a moment and then says, "I didn't say impossible; I said difficult."

He concludes by setting a date for the man to come in with his son so they can discuss his legal options. It is a case that will be boring and of very little consequence, and I'm sure Koppell must handle a hundred of them every year.

I don't, which makes me one lucky lawyer.

Once he's off the phone, Koppell turns to me and says, "So I hear I'm out of a job." Then he smiles and says, "Not that it's been a full-time job."

"What are you talking about?" I ask.

"You're representing Richard Evans."

"He told you that?" I'm surprised; prison inmates don't have that much access to outside communication, and I don't know why he would have bothered to call Koppell.

"No, I heard about it on the radio coming in today. They said that you had registered with the court as his lawyer, and that you would likely be seeking a new trial."

It's amazing that this could be considered news. All I did was register, and the reporter must have assumed I would be seeking a new trial, since what other purpose could there be for me taking him on as a client? The media had barely covered the murder and the trial, and a lawyer change qualifies as a news event? I shake my head. "Must be a slow news day."

"Hey, man, you're a star. Tom Cruise gets headlines when he changes breakfast cereals."

I make a mental note to mention to Laurie that I've been compared to Tom Cruise, even if it's by a middle-aged, overweight male lawyer.

"Anyway, yes, Richard has hired me. I'm sorry you had to hear it on the radio."

He shrugs. "No problem. You didn't come all the way down here to tell me that, did you?"

"No, I wanted to talk to you about the case and to get access to your files."

"They'll be in storage, but I'll have them sent here, and then I'll send them on to you."

"Thanks. Did you see anything on television about the case I handled recently? Where I defended the dog?"

He smiles. "I thought that was great. I'm thinking of hanging around the local shelter to get clients."

"That was Richard Evans's dog," I say.

His surprise is obvious. "Are you serious?"

I nod. "There's no doubt about it."

He thinks for a moment. "Then that changes a lot. If I remember correctly, two witnesses saw the dog with Evans when he boarded the boat."

"That's the kind of information I need."

"It'll all be in the files," he says. "Damn, how the hell could that dog be alive?"

"That's what I need to find out. But things apparently did not happen on that boat the way the prosecution claimed."

"I'm going to be straight with you," he says. "There was nothing, not a shred, that pointed to Richard's innocence. I worked my ass off trying to find something."

"You think there was anything there to find?" I ask.

"I did when it started, but I didn't by the end."

"What about the forensics?" I ask.

He shrugs. "They seemed solid, but we didn't have much money to hire experts. That's an area you could pursue." He pauses, then shakes his head in amazement. "Damn, that dog is really *alive*?"

"Definitely."

"You know, I never could figure out why he killed the dog. I mean, everybody said how much he loved it, and what would have been the harm in letting it live? What the hell could he have been afraid of, that it would be an eyewitness? It just didn't make any sense."

I have been wrestling with this from the beginning; it's one of the major reasons I took the case. If Richard was planning to kill his fiancée, he would have left Reggie at home. That's what I would have done if I were a murderer. And suicidal. And engaged. And had a boat.

Koppell promises to get the files to me as soon as he has them, and I thank him and leave. I make some wrong turns on the way out, and I feel trapped in a suburban maze. It takes me a half hour to reach the Garden State Parkway and the safety of a huge traffic jam.

I finally make it back home, though I'm there only long enough to get Reggie and put him in the car. We drive to the Teaneck office of Dr. Erin Ruff, as perfect a name for a veterinarian as you're going to find.

Karen Evans had told me that Dr. Ruff used to be Reggie's vet, and when I made an appointment, I explained that I was Richard's lawyer and I wanted to talk about the case. I asked her to have Reggie's medical records available, but I did not mention that Reggie might be alive.

When I get to Dr. Ruff's office, the receptionist is properly surprised when I have a dog with me, since I had said

I was just coming in to talk. She asks his name, and I say, "Yogi."

"And what are we seeing Yogi for today?" she asks.

"Just a checkup."

I'm ushered into a small room to wait for the doctor. It's pretty much like every small doctor's room I've ever been in, though this time I get to keep my pants on.

In about five minutes, the door opens and Dr. Ruff comes in, a smile on her face and a folder in her left hand. She reaches out her right hand to shake mine, when she sees Reggie.

"Oh, my God," she says. She looks as if she'd seen a ghost, and in a way she has. "That can't be . . ."

"That's what I'm here to find out."

She's not getting it. "Those cut marks . . . He's supposed to be dead."

I nod. "And someday he will be, but not yet."

I explain that the reason we are here is to find out if there is anything in Reggie's five-year-old records that would help identify him today.

"Is he the dog who was on the news the other day? The one you went to court about?"

"Yes. He's had his fifteen minutes of fame, but if he's Richard Evans's dog, he's going to get another dose."

Dr. Ruff goes over and pets Reggie, who wags his tail in appreciation. She gently lifts his head and looks to see if the marks are also under his chin, which, of course, they are. "It's as I remember it," she says.

I ask her if there are other factors she can point to that can help identify him, and she starts to look through his records. "We're in luck," she says. "When Richard rescued him, he had three bad teeth, probably from chewing on rocks. I extracted them."

She walks over to Reggie and opens his mouth. He obliges, probably because he thinks she'll fill that mouth with a biscuit. She looks into the mouth, then looks at the records again, then back in his mouth.

"This is Reggie," she says. "There's another thing I want to check—with an X-ray—but this is him."

"Are you sure?"

"Well, it's not DNA, but there's no doubt in my mind. The cut marks, the same three teeth missing . . . The coincidence would be overwhelming. But Reggie had a broken leg, and a surgeon put a metal plate in it. If that's in the X-ray, then you can be absolutely certain."

She takes Reggie to be x-rayed and brings him back about fifteen minutes later. "It's there," she says. "Between the cut marks, the teeth, and the X-ray, it's one hundred percent."

"You'd testify to that?"

"With pleasure."

She still has a bunch of questions about how Reggie survived whatever his ordeal had been, but I don't have the answers. Not now. Maybe not ever.

● ● ● ● ●

I PLACE A call to Sam Willis as soon as I get home.

Sam is my accountant, a role that took on an increased importance when I inherited my money. He's also a computer hacking genius, able to get pretty much any information at any time from anywhere. He sometimes crosses the cyber-line between legal and illegal information gathering, and I once helped him when he was caught doing so.

Sam has become a key investigator for me, using his computer prowess to get me answers that I might never be able to get on my own. It is in that role that I'm calling on him now; I need more answers than I have questions.

I call him on his cell phone, since that is the only phone he owns and uses. He cannot believe that I still use a landline in my home and office, likening it to someone tooling around Paterson in a horse and buggy. Wireless is everything, according to Sam, but the truth is, I'm barely starting to get comfortable with *cord*less.

I can hear a loud public address announcer as Sam is talking, and he explains that he's at Logan Airport in Boston. He's a Red Sox fanatic, a rarity in the New York area, and he goes up there about five times a year to see games. This time he's been there for almost a week.

His flight lands in an hour and a half, and I tell him that I'll pick him up at the airport because I want to talk to him about a job.

"On a case?" he asks, hopefully, since he loves this kind of investigatory work.

"On a case."

For some reason, I've always been a person who picks other people up at airports. I know that when I land I like someone to be there, even if it's just a driver. It's depressing to arrive and see all these people holding up signs with names on them, and none says "Carpenter." It makes me feel as if I have my own sign on my forehead—"Loser."

Sam flies into Newark rather than LaGuardia, which is where most Boston flights arrive. I share Sam's dislike for LaGuardia; it's tiny and old and so close to the city it feels as though the plane were landing on East Eighty-fourth Street. Newark is far more accessible and feels like a real airport.

Newark is far more accessible and feels like a real airport.

Sam is outside and in my car within five minutes of landing, because he did not check a bag. Sam wouldn't check a bag if he were going away for six months; he doesn't think it's something a real man should do.

Sam has some mental issues.

As Sam gets in the car, I realize I haven't prepared for the song talking game that dominates our relationship. The trick is to work song lyrics smoothly into the conversation, and Sam has so outdistanced me in his ability to do this that he has taken to adjusting the rules so he won't be bored. Now he will sometimes do movie dialogue instead of song lyrics, and I never know which it's going to be. Unfortunately, I have not prepared for either.

The good news is that Sam is so interested in finding out about the upcoming investigation that song or movie talking doesn't seem to be on his mind.

I brief him on what I know, and "brief" is the proper word, since I know very little. "For now I want you to focus on the victim, Stacy Harriman," I say. "There is very little about her in the record."

"You know where she's from, age, that kind of thing?" he asks.

"Some. What I don't have I'll get."

"Is this a rush?"

I nod. "Evans sits in jail until we can get him out. So it's a rush."

"I'll get right on it," he says.

"Thanks. I appreciate it."

He shrugs that off. "No problem. Someday, and that day may never come, I will call upon you to do a service for me."

He's doing Brando from *The Godfather.* It's a movie I know very well, so there's a chance I can compete, but right now my mind is a blank. "Sam, I want you to be careful, okay?" I say this because two people in my life have died because of material they have uncovered in this kind of investigation. One of the victims was Sam's former assistant.

"Right," Sam says, shrugging off the warning.

"I mean it, Sam. You've got to take this stuff more seriously. We could be dealing with dangerous people."

He looks wounded. "What have I ever done to make you treat me so disrespectfully? If you'd come to me in friendship, then these people would be suffering this very day. And if by chance an honest man like yourself should make enemies, they would become my enemies. And they would fear you."

He is incorrigible. "Thank you, Godfather," I say. "You want to work out of my office?"

He frowns. "You must be kidding. On *your* computer? It would take me a year."

"I can set up whatever system you want," I say.

He shakes his head. "No, I'll work at home . . . I've got wireless and a cable modem." Then all of a sudden he's yelling, "At my home! Where my wife sleeps! Where my children come to play with their toys!"

"Sam, can we finish this before you start making me offers I can't refuse?"

"Sure. What else is there?"

I'm about to answer when I hear a loud crashing noise and then feel a sudden rush of warm air.

"Holy shit!" Sam screams, and I realize that there is no longer a side window; it has just seemed to disappear. "Andy! To your left!"

I look over and see a car alongside us, with two men in the front seat. The man closest to us, not the driver, is pointing a gun at my head. He looks to be around forty, heavyset and very serious-looking. In an instant the thought flashes in my mind that he looks like a man on a mission, not a joyride. There have been some random highway shootings in the past few years, but I instinctively feel that this is not one of them.

I duck and hit the brakes just as I hear a loud noise, probably another shot. It doesn't seem to hit anything in the car, but I can take only momentary comfort in this. My fear-induced desire is to burrow under the seat, but I realize that my car isn't equipped with autopilot, and if I don't sit up and look at the road, we're in deep trouble.

I sit up and get the car out of a mini skid, staying on the road. The car containing the shooter is now ahead of us, and I start to think how I can get over to the side and off the road.

Sam has other ideas. "Get behind them! Get behind them!"

"You want me to get closer to people that are shooting at us? Why would I do that?"

"Come on, Andy, you can't just let them get away! Get behind them and put your brights on! We've got to get their license number."

Sam seems as if he knows what he's doing, and since I know that I don't, I do as he says, getting in behind the other car and putting the brights on. I get close behind, and then they speed up. There is no sign that they will or can shoot at us from this position. My heart is pounding so loudly that I can't hear myself think, although I'm too scared to think.

"We're on the New Jersey Turnpike, heading north about a mile past the Newark Airport exit. Two men in a black Acura have just fired a handgun at us and hit our car. Their license plate number is VSE 621." Sam is talking into his cell phone, apparently having called 911. "Yes, that's right. In the left lane, going approximately seventy-five miles per hour. Yes, that's right."

"What did they say?" I ask, when he stops talking. He still has the cell phone to his ear.

"They want me to hold on."

"But what did they say?"

"They said to hold on."

I'm not getting anywhere with this line of questioning, so I concentrate on driving. I'm now doing almost eighty and they're pulling away. Since I don't want to get killed by either a bullet or a crash, I don't speed up any more.

Moments later, we hear the sound of sirens, and police cars with flashing lights go flying by us as if we are standing still. "Holy shit, will you look at that!" Sam marvels.

It isn't long before the car we're chasing and the police cars are all out of sight, but I keep driving because I don't know what else to do. Sam has lost his cell phone connection with 911, so we're pretty much in the dark.

"Man, that was amazing!" Sam says. He seems invigorated; this is a side of him I haven't seen before, and he certainly does not seem shaken by the fact that a window inches from his face was shot out. Am I the only coward in America?

We drive for a few more miles, turning on the radio to hear if anything is being said about the incident. I'm aware that I need to report this in person to the police, but my preference is to drive to the Paterson Police Department and tell my story to Pete Stanton.

"What's that?" Sam asks, and when I look ahead I see what he is talking about. There's a large glow, far ahead and off to the right, which turns out to be the flashing lights of at least a dozen police cars. As we approach, there is no doubt that a car has been demolished, and another car is also damaged at the side of the road. The police are surrounding the smashed vehicle, which I believe is the one that had contained the shooters, but not seeming to take any action.

Two ambulances pull up as well, and paramedics jump out. If there is anyone in the car, it will be up to the paramedics to help them. Good luck; they haven't invented the paramedics who could help people in that car. It looks like a metallic quesadilla.

I pull over, resigned to speaking to the cops on the scene rather than to Pete. I park a couple of hundred yards away and turn off the car.

"We getting out?" Sam asks.

I nod. "We're getting out. Leave your carry-on and take the cannolis."

● ● ● ● ●

WE GET AS close as we can to the crash scene, which isn't very close at all. The police have set up a perimeter at least a hundred yards away and are in the process of closing all but the left lane of the highway to traffic. This is going to be a long night for drivers heading north to the city.

Sam and I approach one of the officers in charge of keeping people away. "That's as far as you can go," he says. "Nothing to see here."

"We're the ones who made the call to 911," I say. "They shot out a window in our car."

"Who did?" the officer asks. He probably is not even aware that there was a prior incident on the road; to him this must just be a crash scene.

"The two guys in that car," I say. "They shot at us, we called it in, and they must have crashed in the pursuit."

The officer considers this a moment. "Stay right here," he says, and then goes toward the crash scene to check with his superiors. A few moments later he comes back and says, "Follow me."

We do so, and as we get close to the crash, it looks as if the car containing the shooters smashed into a car parked along the side of the highway. It then flipped over, perhaps more than once, and came to rest as a complete wreck.

There is no doubt in my mind that no one in that car could have survived. The police have already set up a trailer, where they will spend the night as they investigate what they will consider a crime scene.

The officer takes us toward the trailer, and just before we get there, I whisper to Sam, "Do not say anything about the Evans case."

He nods. "Gotcha." Then, "This is so cool."

"Sam, you might want to get some professional mental help. On an urgent basis."

"You mean see a shrink?"

"No, I mean as an inpatient. A locked-in patient."

We are led inside the trailer, and I can't stifle a groan when I see that the officer in charge is Captain Dessens of the New Jersey State Police. I have had a couple of run-ins with Dessens on previous cases, and it would be accurate to say that we can't stand each other.

Dessens looks up, sees me, and returns the groan. "What the hell are you doing here?" He looks around. "Who let this clown in?"

The officer who brought us in says, "These guys are the ones I told you about."

Dessens shakes his head. "Well, so much for motive."

The officer standing next to him says, "What do you mean?"

"That's Andy Carpenter, the lawyer. I don't know anybody who wouldn't want to take a shot at him."

"Is the shooter dead?" I ask.

"Yeah."

"You'll still find a way to screw up the arrest."

Dessens starts an angry response and then seems to think better of it. He motions for us to sit down, then questions us on the details of what happened. Sam lets me do most of the talking; he just seems happy and content to be a part of it.

After we've given our statements, Dessens asks if I think the shooting was random or if I might have an idea who could be after me.

"Everybody loves me," I say.

Sam nods. "Me, too."

Dessens asks a few more questions and then tells us that they will want to check out my car and that an officer will drive us home.

"Did you ID the dead guys?" I ask.

He doesn't answer and instead calls out to one of the other officers, asking him to take us outside. He's apparently not into sharing.

It's not until I get home and have a glass of wine that I really think about what just happened. Word got out today that I was taking Richard Evans's case, and somebody tried to kill me tonight.

I don't believe in coincidences, and it wouldn't be productive to start now. I have to believe that the shooting is connected to Evans, even though I would much rather not. If somebody could react this quickly and this violently to my simply taking on Evans as a client, then he's got some very determined and deadly enemies.

Which means I now have them as well.

Laurie calls just as I'm about to get into bed, and I tell her the entire story. She believes in coincidences even less than I do, and I can hear the worry in her voice. Laurie is one of the toughest people I know, but she's well aware that toughness is a trait she and I don't share.

She's frustrated that she can't get away from her job to come back east until the end of the month, and cautions me to be extra careful. She also has one other piece of advice, the one I expected.

"Get Marcus."

• • • • •

MARCUS CLARK IS a terrific investigator, but that is not what initially comes to mind when one thinks of him. Focusing on his investigating talents first would be like somebody asking for your view of Pamela Anderson, only to have you respond that you hear she's a pretty good bowler. It may or may not be true, but it's not "top of mind."

Marcus is the scariest person I have ever seen, and there is no one in second place. He is cast in bronze iron, impervious to fear or pain, and possesses a stare that makes me want to carry around a piece of kryptonite, just in case.

He has been one of my key investigators since even before Laurie went to Wisconsin, and has displayed an uncanny knack for getting people to reveal information. They confide in him, operating under the assumption that they can talk or die. I, for example, would tell Marcus whatever he wanted to know, whenever he wanted to know it. And I would thank him for the opportunity.

Because I seem to have an involuntary knack for pissing off dangerous people, I sometimes employ Marcus as a protector, a bodyguard, rather than an investigator. That's why I've called him into the office this morning. I'll probably have a need for him to gather information at some point, but right now that takes a backseat to my need to stay alive.

I stop on the way in to drop my car off so that they can replace the window that's been shot out. They drive me to my office and promise to bring me the repaired car before the day is out.

I've had Kevin come in for this meeting as well. When I meet with Marcus, I like as many other people in the room as possible. It makes me feel safer, although if Marcus wanted to do me harm, the Third Infantry on their best day couldn't help me.

All I really need to tell Marcus is that some people tried to shoot me and that for whatever reason, it's very possible that I am a target. His job is to keep me safe and alive, pure and simple. But because I have respect for Marcus's investigative skills, and because I think he should have as much information as possible about whom he might be dealing with, I tell him all I know about the Richard Evans case.

My recitation of the facts takes about ten minutes, and Marcus is either silently attentive or asleep the entire time. His eyes are open, but that doesn't really mean anything one way or the other. Kevin sits as far away from Marcus as is possible while remaining in the same room.

When I'm finished, I wait for him to comment, and

after twenty long seconds it's obvious that is not going to happen. I prompt him with "So that's it. Any questions?"

"Unhh," says Marcus. Marcus is a man of very few words, most of which are not actually words.

"Will you need anything from me?" I ask.

"Unhh."

"Can you get started right away?"

"Yunhh."

I don't quite know how to end this, so I turn to Kevin. "Kev, you got anything you want to add?"

He shakes his head a little too quickly. "Not me. Not a thing. Nope."

Marcus gets up to leave, without my asking him how he will perform his protective functions. I've learned long ago that he will be there if I need him, and I won't see him if I don't. It's comforting to me, though I'll certainly miss our little chitchats.

As he reaches the door, it opens from the other side, and Karen Evans is standing there. She is one of the most talkative people I know, but the sight of Marcus stuns her into silence. Her eyes widen, and her mouth opens, but nothing comes out.

"Oh, my God . . . ," she says, once Marcus has left. "Is he on our side?"

I nod. "He is."

She breaks into a wide smile and smacks her hands together, generating more of her infectious enthusiasm. "This is gonna be great!"

I had not asked Karen to come to the office, and I'm not a big fan of unannounced visits. "What are you doing here, Karen?"

"I don't know . . . I'm just real nervous, and excited . . .

and I thought I could hang around and help. You know, run errands, get coffee . . . I spoke to Edna and she was okay with it."

"Edna was willing to give up running errands and making coffee? You must be quite the persuader."

I tell her that she can hang around now but that she should call before coming by in the future. I understand her excitement, and as a person who knows her brother and knew his fiancée, she can be helpful. However, I do not instantly share all information with my clients, and I can't have her rushing to him with constant updates.

I turn on the television to follow press reports about the shooting on the highway last night, and it's being treated as a pretty big story. They're calling it a random shooting, though the fact that I was one of the intended victims is duly noted, as is my recent representation of Richard Evans.

"You got shot at?" Karen asks, but I don't bother answering, since she's just learned the answer to her question from the television.

Instead I pick up the phone and call Pete Stanton in his office. Even though the state police are handling the shooting case, I'm hoping that Pete can use his police contacts to find out what he can about the dead shooters.

When Pete hears that it's me calling, he says, "Let me guess . . . You need something."

"That's amazing . . . How could you possibly have known that?"

"Well, we're already meeting at Charlie's tonight, so you're not just calling to say hello. And the last one hundred and forty-seven times you've called me in my office it's because you needed something."

"Do you have any idea how much you've just hurt me?"
I ask. "I've just been through a traumatic experience, actually a near-death experience, and I don't think I've ever
been so emotionally vulnerable."

He's unmoved. "Can we get to it already?"

"Well, you know I was shot at last night."

"That's the good news," he says. "The bad news is, they
missed." Then, "I've already put in a couple of calls."

"What does that mean?"

"To find out what I can about the shooters," he says.
"That is what you wanted, isn't it?"

"You are a goddamned legend, and just for that, I'm
buying at Charlie's tonight."

"You got that right."

I send Karen out to get some doughnuts and Necco wa-
fers, with specific instructions to try to find a package of
all chocolate Neccos, which are far superior to the multi-
colored kinds. It's about time to put her to the test.

I use the time for a quick strategy session with Kevin.
As I see it, there are three possibilities behind this case.
One is that Richard is guilty and the prosecution's position was completely correct. While that still may be true, it
doesn't help us to consider it.

The second possibility is that whatever is behind this
centers on the murder victim, Stacy Harriman. Among the
problems with this is that it doesn't make much sense that
the murderers would kill her and take Reggie off to safety.
If their goal was simply to kill Stacy, they would likely
have just left Reggie on the boat with Richard. Even if
they were somehow dog lovers, to have taken Reggie in
the midst of committing the crime seems very difficult to
believe.

The third possibility is that Richard was framed solely because of Richard himself. Either he had made an enemy or he knew or had something that could be dangerous to someone else. This seems to be the most fertile ground for us, especially because of his job with the Customs Service, and will first require an in-depth interview with Richard.

Karen comes back with a sack of doughnuts, jelly and cream filled, and three packages of chocolate Neccos, which she holds up triumphantly. I could send Edna out this afternoon, give her until a year from August, and she would not manage such a feat.

"Kid," I say to Karen, "I think you've got a future in this business."

● ● ● ● ●

I STOP AT home to feed and walk Tara and Reggie.

Tara really seems to like having him around, and it makes me far less guilty when I have to spend long hours away from the house. This morning I even saw them playfully tugging at opposite ends of a toy. I'm not sure how Tara will react if I get Richard Evans out of jail, so Reggie can go back to him. Of course, right now that is not exactly an imminent danger.

As we leave the house, Willie Miller pulls up in his car. I feel an instant pang of guilt on seeing him; I have recently been of no help whatsoever in our dog rescue operation. Willie and Sondra have been doing all the work.

I apologize for my uselessness, but Willie characteristically will hear none of it. "Forget it, man. You got another job to do; I don't. And Sondra and I love it. You know that."

He has come by to update me on the weekly events, and he does so as he walks with us. Our foundation—or, more accurately, Willie and Sondra—has placed twenty-one dogs in homes this week. We average about fifteen, so this has been a very good week.

"You did good saving Reggie," he says.

"Thanks."

"I hear you got shot at the other day."

"Who told you?" I ask.

"Laurie. She's worried about you. Getting out of the way of bullets wouldn't be one of your strong points, you know? I told her I'd look out for you."

"She knows I have Marcus."

Willie nods. "And you have me if you need me. Just pick up the damn phone, and I'm there."

"Thanks, Willie. I will."

Willie goes off to have dinner with Sondra, and I drop off Tara and Reggie at home. I then head down to Charlie's to meet Pete and Vince Sanders. Charlie's is a sports bar/restaurant that is truly my home away from home. Everything about it is perfect, from the large-screen TVs to the well-done french fries, to the ice-cold beer.

When people successfully make it through a terribly difficult emotional experience, they will sometimes credit their faith, their work, or their family for getting them through. When Laurie and I split up, Charlie's was my crutch.

Vince and Pete are at our regular table when I arrive. This particular table was chosen because of its proximity to four different TV screens, and it's large enough to handle the empty plates and beer bottles that often accumulate faster than the waitress can take them away.

We grunt our hellos, and they bring me up to date on the progress of the basketball games. They've placed bets that I've previously agreed to share, since I did not have time today to pick my own teams. We're losing three out of four, but each game is in the first quarter. Since it's the NBA, there is no way to predict how any of them will end up.

Once I've ordered my burger and beer, I turn to Pete. "Did you find out anything?"

He nods. "That I did. And you are not going to believe it."

He's piqued my interest; for Pete to say something like that means the information is going to be stunning. "Let's hear it."

"After you pay the check," he says.

"Come on, you know damn well I'm gonna pay. You want to hold my credit card?"

He shakes his head. "I can't. I'm allergic to platinum."

Vince says, "I'll hold it."

"No, you won't," I say.

"You think I'm going to steal your identity?"

"That doesn't worry me, Vince. What scares the shit out of me is, you'll try and trade identities. Come on, Pete."

Pete sighs and takes a couple of sheets of paper out of his pocket. He reads from them. "The driver was Antwan Cooper, a small-time hood from the Bronx. The shooter was Archie Durelle, ex-Army, served in the first Gulf war and Afghanistan. Hometown was Albuquerque."

I've never heard of these guys; their names mean nothing to me. "So what's the big news?" I ask.

"Well, it turns out that Durelle didn't just serve in Afghanistan. He also died there."

"What?" I ask, as penetrating and clever a retort as I can muster.

"His chopper went down, and all four guys on board died. He was one of them."

"There obviously has to be a mistake."

"No shit, Sherlock."

Pete grudgingly agrees to try to find out more about Durelle, but he retaliates for the imposition by ordering the most expensive beer on the menu. It's a small price to pay, and far smaller than the price I'll have to pay the bookmaker, since all our bets on the NBA games lose.

I head home and call Laurie before going to sleep. She pumps me with questions about the case, mostly motivated by the close call with the highway shooter. I can hear the relief in her voice when I tell her I've hired Marcus.

It feels strange to wake up in the morning and go to the office, but that's what I do. I get there at nine thirty, and waiting for me are Kevin and the files that Koppell had retrieved from storage. Edna walks in about an hour later, glancing at her watch in surprise at the fact that she's not the first to arrive.

Kevin and I spend most of the day going through the information. There's a huge amount to digest, and we'll be better prepared to gauge the value after we are more familiar with the case in its entirety. There are no exculpatory bombshells, but we didn't expect any. Koppell was looking for them, and if he'd found one, Richard wouldn't be in jail.

By late afternoon we are feeling confident enough in our knowledge of the case to set up another interview for tomorrow morning with our client. At least now we know what questions to ask.

• • • • •

THERE IS A noticeable spring in Richard's step when he is brought into the interview room. Since this is an official attorney's visit, Kevin and I don't have to talk to him through the glass in the visitors' area. We get to talk in this private room, a risk the state is willing to take because Richard is in handcuffs and leg shackles. Should this prove insufficient, two guards are stationed outside the room, probably armed with tactical nuclear weapons.

Despite the fact that our chances for success are remote, Richard's improved outlook is at least somewhat warranted. For the past five years he has had absolutely no reason to be hopeful; no one was working on his behalf to win his freedom or supporting his cause. Now we're doing that, and for the first time Richard can believe that things are happening.

I introduce Kevin, and then we get right to it. I start by giving the standard speech about how we can help him only if we know everything, and that he should leave nothing out when answering our questions. Any detail, however small or insignificant it might seem, can be the crucial one.

"Tell us about that night," I say.

"There was nothing unusual about it except for the way it ended," he says. "It was summer, and Stacy and I would go out on the boat most weekends, at least when the weather was good. When it wasn't, we'd go to a cabin I have in upstate New York." He pauses a moment. "That's the ironic thing. If we had known a storm was coming, we would probably have gone to the cabin. But it wasn't predicted."

"When you went out on the boat, did Reggie always go along?"

He nods. "Absolutely. Reggie went everywhere with us. Stacy loved him almost as much as I did."

"You slept on the boat?"

He nods. "Most of the time. It was a forty-footer . . . slept six."

"So there was nothing out of the ordinary about that night that you can remember?"

"Nothing. I've thought about it a thousand times. We went to bed at about nine o'clock. By then we had heard there was a chance of weather coming in, and I set the warning system up loud so I would definitely hear it."

"Warning system?" Kevin asks. He knows as little about boating as I do.

Richard nods. "If there are weather warnings, a general alert is sent out. We were only about four miles out, so we'd have plenty of time to get back if we had to."

"And you never heard a warning?" I ask.

"I never heard anything. I went to sleep and woke up in the hospital."

"Do you remember taking the sleeping pills?" Kevin asks.

Richard shakes his head vigorously. "I never took sleeping pills. Not that night, not ever in my life. I didn't even have any. They were not mine."

"Were they Stacy's?" I ask.

"I don't believe so. If they were, she never mentioned it. I never knew her to have trouble sleeping."

"So you have no idea how they got in your system?"

He shakes his head. "None at all."

We talk some more about the night of the murder, but he has little else to add. While the important things were happening, he was asleep. All he remembers is a pleasant night out on the water, dinner, some wine, and an early trip to bed since he was tired from working all day.

I turn the focus to his job, that of a senior customs inspector at the Port of Newark. I ask him if there was anything about his job that could have made him a target.

"No, nothing," he says. "It was a slow time."

The answer is a little quick for my tastes. "Richard, I want you to understand something. You may not have committed this murder, but someone did. Someone with a reason. Now, that reason could involve you or Stacy, or the two of you together. So you need to open your mind to anyone who could have possibly hoped to gain from putting you in this position."

"Don't you think I've done nothing but think about that for five years? If someone was trying to get rid of me because I knew something, they shouldn't have bothered, because I sure as hell don't know that I know it. Besides, if I was a danger to someone, why not just kill me?"

It's a good question, and one I eventually must answer. But for now I take him through a description of day-to-day life on his job. Border security in this era of terrorism has taken on an obviously extreme importance, and it was Richard's task to make sure that the Port of Newark was as free of contraband as possible.

Finally, I turn the conversation to Stacy, and even five years later, it's evident that his grief over her loss is still powerful. "How did you meet?" I ask.

"At a counter, having lunch. She was sitting next to me, and before I knew it we were having a conversation. We had dinner that night, and it just went from there."

"Where was she from?" Kevin asks.

"Minnesota . . . a town just outside of Minneapolis. Her parents were killed in a car crash when she was eighteen. She worked there and then decided to move east."

"What did she do?"

"She was a teacher, but what she really wanted was to be a chef. The things she made were incredible. She wanted to open her own restaurant."

He talks about Stacy for a while longer, answering every question but never getting much below surface platitudes. He makes her sound so perfect she reminds me of Laurie.

"Were you in the Army?" I ask.

He nods. "National Guard. Served three months in Kuwait during the first Gulf war."

"Do the names Archie Durelle or Antwan Cooper mean anything to you?"

His facial expression shows no recognition at all. "No, I don't think so," he says. "Who are they?"

I'm not ready to tell him that they took a shot at me on the highway. "Just some names I've heard; I'm checking out everything I can." ———

The last ten minutes of our visit are devoted to the obligatory questions he has about progress we might be making and strategy we might be employing. I fend them off because basically we're not making any progress and don't yet have a strategy.

Once Kevin and I are in the car, I ask, "So, what do you think?"

"I find myself wanting to believe him."

"Do you believe him?" I ask.

He shakes his head. "Not yet. His version is just too full of holes. The prosecution has it locked up airtight."

"Except for Reggie. Reggie says he's innocent," I say.

"He told you that?"

"Not in so many barks, but I got the message."

I like dogs considerably more than I like humans. That doesn't make me antihuman; there are plenty of humans I'm very fond of. But generally speaking, if I simultaneously meet a new human and a new dog, I'm going to like the dog more.

I'm certainly going to trust the dog more. They're going to tell me what they think, straight out, and I'm not going to have to read anything into it. They are what they are, while very often humans are what they aren't.

I say this fully aware that dogs cannot replace humans in our day-to-day lives. I have never met a competent dog airline pilot, short-order cook, quarterback, or bookmaker. These are necessary functions that we must trust humans to provide, and I recognize that. It's not that I'm an eccentric about this.

So for now I'm going to pursue this case, even though Richard has nothing going for him.

Except for Reggie.

• • • • •

JOEL MARSHAL IS on the front lines, protecting our country.

I can't say he looks the part. At about five eight and a hundred and fifty pounds, he's one of the few male adults under ninety that I would be willing to get in the ring with. As a protector of the country, he is not the type you would describe as someone "you want on that wall, you need on that wall."

Marshal is U.S. Customs director for the Port of Newark, and it's his job to ensure that the endless flow of cargo that comes in each year does not include things like drugs, guns, anthrax, and nuclear bombs. It is a daunting task, which is why I'm surprised it was so easy to get an immediate meeting with him.

It may have been a quickly arranged meeting, but it won't be a long one. He's looking at his watch almost as soon as I sit down. It's a common tactic; I think watches are more often used to demonstrate a lack of time than to tell time.

"Thanks for seeing me so soon," I say. "I won't take much of your time."

"I appreciate that," he says. "It's a busy day today." He glances at his watch again, though less than fifteen seconds have passed since the last time he looked. "What can I do for you?"

He says this with what seems to be a permanent smile on his face. If the smile could talk, it would say, "I am a political appointee, and this smile is government issue. It doesn't mean I am happy or amused."

"I'm representing Richard Evans."

"Yes, you mentioned that," he points out, accurately.

"I'm operating under the assumption that the evidence against Mr. Evans was deliberately faked. What I am trying to find out is why."

"What does that have to do with me?"

I explain that one of my theories is that Richard was targeted because of something involved with his work. He could have been removed from that work because of something he knew, or possibly to get him out of the way.

"It hardly seems likely," Marshal says. "But in any event, there's little I can help you with. I've only been assigned here for one year, and I had never even met Mr. Evans."

"So you're not familiar with his case?" I ask.

He shakes his head. "Should I be? It's pretty much ancient history, and my understanding was that it did not involve his job. It was a personal matter."

Murders usually are "personal matters," but I decide not to point this out. "Who replaced him?" I ask.

"I'm not sure. Roy Chaney is in the job now, but I'm not aware if he followed Mr. Evans, or if there was somebody else in the interim."

"Can you check?"

This prompts another look at his watch and, while not a frown, a slight weakening of the smile. Finally, he asks his assistant to get the information, but it proves to be unnecessary, as the assistant was working here five years ago. She confirms that Chaney replaced Evans.

I thank Marshal and leave. Rather than go straight to my car, I decide to display my awesome investigative prowess and walk aimlessly around the area. It's an enormous place, with endless, cavernous warehouses starting near the water and stretching well inland.

There are not many people around, just thousands of unattended boxes and crates. Security is either nonexistent or very subtle; I get the feeling that if one of the boxes had "ANTHRAX – IF YOU ARE WITHIN TWO MILES OF THIS CRATE, YOU WILL BE DEAD IN FOUR MINUTES" printed on the side it wouldn't attract attention.

After about twenty minutes of intensive investigating, all I've really managed to do is get lost, to the point that I have no idea where my car is.

I happen upon a small building that contains a few glass-enclosed offices. A woman sits behind one of the desks, so I lean in and ask if she knows where Joel Marshal's office is, since that's where I parked my car.

She smiles. "Just walk in the direction you were going, and after the second building make a right."

"Thanks," I say, and then decide to try another question. "Do you happen to know where I can find Roy Chaney?"

She smiles again, ever helpful, and calls out, "Roy! Somebody here to see you!"

All this time I thought I was lost, when in fact I was relentlessly zeroing in on Chaney's office. Within a few moments a man I assume to be Chaney comes out of a rear office and walks toward the doorway, where I am standing. He looks as though he's pushing 40, pushing 5'10", and has already pushed past 240 pounds. I wouldn't want to try to sneak any contraband chocolate cupcakes or potato chips into the country with this guy around.

"What can I do for you?" he asks.

"You're Roy Chaney?"

He nods. "Yup. Who are you?"

"My name is Andy Carpenter. I'm an attorney representing Richard Evans."

"Is that right?" he says as he walks past me and out the door, leading me to step out as well. It was a clumsy attempt to conceal that he does not want the woman at the desk to hear the conversation.

"Yes. I understand you replaced him when he went on trial."

"That's right. I didn't know him, though. I mean, we never met. When I got here he was already gone."

I'm not that great a judge of human behavior, but Chaney seems nervous. "But you took over his responsibilities?"

"Right."

"Was there anything unusual about any of the things he was working on? Or any of the people he was working with?"

"Unusual like what?"

"Unusual like something which would have made someone want to get him off the job and out of the way. Do you remember anything like that?"

"No." It's far too quick an answer; this was five years ago, and he would have had no reason to be thinking about those days until my question. This guy is hiding something and is not at all good at it.

"You didn't notice anything out of the ordinary with his work . . . anything that you might have reported to your superiors?"

"I haven't done anything wrong," he says. "I just show up and do my job." It's an answer completely unresponsive to my question, and when I get those kinds of answers, I usually assume they are both unresponsive and untruthful.

I give him my card and tell him that he should call me if he thinks of anything. As I'm leaving, he says, "You trying to get Evans out of jail?"

I nod. "I'm doing more than trying."

Laurie calls on my cell phone as I'm leaving the port area.

"Andy? Where are you?" is how she starts the conversation.

"Newark," I say.

"You're kidding," she says.

"I am?"

"Are you serious?" she asks.

"Why would I lie about being in Newark? And why are we having this inane conversation?"

"Because I'm in Newark, also. At the airport."

"Are you serious?" I ask.

"Why would I lie about being in Newark?" she asks, and then laughs. "I got someone to cover for me . . . We switched vacation times. There was a flight and I rushed to catch it; I tried your cell but it didn't go through. Can you pick me up?"

"Gee, I sort of had plans for tonight," I say as I race at high speed toward the airport.

"Okay, I'll hitch a ride with the good-looking guy I sat next to on the plane."

"Or I can change my plans."

I'm at the terminal within ten minutes, and Laurie is waiting for me outside baggage claim.

She looks fantastic, which does not come as a major surprise. A long flight is not going to affect that; she could go through three wash cycles at Kevin's Law-dromat and come out looking one corsage short of ready for the prom.

As I pull up, I'm faced with a choice. I can get out and help her get the suitcases into the car, or I can let her do it herself. My instinct is to get out, but it means that our hug and kiss hello will take place out in public, surrounded by travelers. If she gets in, we can do it in the car, in relative privacy.

It's decision making like this that is the reason they pay me the big bucks.

I get out, put the suitcases in the trunk, and we do the hug and kiss routine for all Newark Airport to see. It's not ideal, but it's not half bad, either. In fact, it's so not half bad that I briefly consider whether to take a room at the airport hotel.

Five minutes into our ride, Laurie says, "Is this where you got shot at?"

I was so focused on getting Laurie home that I hadn't even noticed that. "Just up ahead."

"Is Marcus around?"

I shrug. "You know Marcus. He'll show up if I need him." Then it hits me. "Wait a minute—you switched your vacation and came here early because you were worried about me. You don't think I can take care of myself."

She smiles. "You can't."

I laugh. "Then it's good you showed up."

We get home, and Laurie spends five minutes petting and hugging Tara, then another five meeting and petting Reggie.

"You want something to eat?" I ask.

She shakes her head. "I want to get these clothes off."

"Don't let me stop you," I say.

She smiles. "I was talking about your clothes."

"Don't let me stop you."

• • • • •

GETTING OUT OF bed early has never been my strong point.

It usually runs counter to my enjoyment drive; the bed is comfortable, right near my television, and an easy stroll to the kitchen refrigerator. All in all, not a good place to leave.

Leaving it when Laurie is lying next to me is positively goofy, and I am simply not going to do it. Unfortunately, Tara and Reggie have a different point of view, and at six thirty their scratching on the door tells me in no uncertain terms that they are anxious to take their morning walk.

I get up and grab the leashes, resisting the impulse to leave an "I'll be right back" sign on my side of the mattress. We walk for about twenty minutes, which is about nineteen minutes longer than I had planned. They just seem to enjoy it too much to cut it short.

Reggie has developed an interesting walking style. He keeps his nose close to the ground at all times, as if it were a metal detector. When he hears a sudden noise, like a car horn, his ears lift up but his nose stays down.

When we get back, my own ears alert me to an impending crushing disappointment. The shower is running, which means Laurie is out of bed, which in turn takes away my reason for getting back in. My day is officially starting, far too soon.

I grab a cup of coffee and head for the bedroom to get dressed. Laurie is already on the way out, in sweatshirt, sweatpants, and running shoes. It is one of her idiosyncrasies that she showers before and after exercising. "You want to go running?" she asks.

"I'd sooner go root canaling," I say, and she leaves.

She comes back maybe ten seconds later. "Miss me?" I ask.

"Let me have your cell phone," she says, her voice serious.

I get it off the table and hand it to her. "What is it?"

"There was a phone guy working on the line by the house. He was just leaving when I got outside, and when I called to him he drove off."

"So?"

"So it's seven o'clock in the morning. Has the phone company changed that much since I lived here?"

She calls a former colleague in the Paterson Police Department and asks him to send someone out to check the house for bugs. Then she says she'll wait for him to arrive, so I have to assume he's sending someone right away.

I think she's overreacting to this and is being overly

cautious. When she hangs up, I ask, "Do you want me to hang around? We could get back in bed."

"Have a nice day, Andy."

"I take it that's a no?"

"That's a no."

I head for the office and an early meeting that Kevin has arranged with Dr. Gerald King, a prominent criminologist. We had sent Dr. King the photographs, toxicology, and other reports on the physical evidence that we received from Lawrence Koppell. Koppell had admitted that he didn't have the resources to hire the top available experts to aid in the defense, so we decided to pay to get the best.

Dr. King is at least sixty years old, with degrees in everything from criminology to toxicology, to chemistry, and just about every other "y" I can think of. When I arrive he is drinking a cup of Edna's coffee—or, more accurately, looking at it. My guess is, he's anxious to take it back to the lab to find out what bizarre ingredients she puts into it to give it that lumpy texture and uniquely horrible taste.

I'm expecting a dry, tedious recitation of Dr. King's findings, but that expectation lasts for about three seconds. "Events on that boat were not as the prosecution described them," is how he begins.

Suffice it to say that he's gotten my attention. "How were they different?"

Dr. King takes out the pictures of the inside of the boat, and those of Richard. He points to a substantial bruise on the left side of Richard's head, which the prosecution claimed happened when Richard fell out of bed after being knocked out by the sleeping pills.

"This is not a bruise that could have been received from falling out of this bed." He proceeds to talk about the pattern of the bruise and how it could only have been caused by a blunt, rounded instrument. Then he goes over to the couch and demonstrates that the fall from that height, and at that angle, would have had Richard land on the right side of his head, not the left.

It's compelling but not overwhelming, and I'm hoping there's more. There is.

He takes out the toxicology reports, which show an overdose of Amenipam, the sleeping pills that almost killed Richard. His estimate is that Richard would have been dead if the Coast Guard medics had gotten to him fifteen minutes later. "But he did not take those pills; the drug was either ingested in liquid form or, more likely, administered by injection after he was unconscious."

This, if true and if it can be proven, is a blockbuster. "How do you know that?"

He points to a line on the toxicology report that shows Richard had traces of campene, a preservative used in test tubes. His theory is that liquid Amenipam was administered, that it was preserved in a test tube before that, and that that is why the trace was found in Richard's blood.

"Could it have gotten there any other way?"

He nods. "Yes, which is why it didn't attract much attention. It is found in shellfish."

Kevin speaks for the first time. "So where does that leave us?"

"In great shape," I say. "Richard is allergic to shellfish. I read it in the medical records."

Dr. King smiles as if his student had just made him proud. "Exactly. And it is a severe allergy. If he wanted to commit suicide, all he would have had to do was have a shrimp cocktail."

Dr. King leaves, and I have to restrain myself from giving Kevin a high five. This is a very substantial development and, if accurate, puts a major dent in the prosecution case. Coupled with Reggie's existence, it could well be enough to get us a hearing. Kevin agrees and sets out to write a brief to file with the court.

My euphoria is short-lived, as Laurie shows up with Sergeant Allen Paulsen, one of the technology experts in the Paterson Police Department.

She comes right to the point. "Allen found a tap on your phone."

He holds up a small, clear plastic bag with a device in it. "It looks new—no weather marks or anything. It could be a couple of weeks old, but based on what Laurie witnessed, my best guess is, it was installed this morning."

"Are you here to check the office phones?"

He nods. "Right."

"That's not all, Andy," she says.

I don't like the way she said that. "It's not?"

She turns to Paulsen, inviting him to explain.

He does, again holding up the device. "This device is state-of-the-art; I've never seen one like it. I would bet a month's pay it's government issue."

Oh, shit. "Local, state, or federal?" I ask, in descending order of preference.

"Federal," he says. "Definitely federal. Which agency, that I can't tell you."

Paulsen goes off to check the office and, after about fifteen minutes, tells me that the place is clean. He gives me the name of a guy and tells me that I should hire him to sweep my home and office for taps and bugs at least twice a week.

"They may not do it again," he says. "Because now that we've removed the first tap, they'll know you're on to them."

Paulsen leaves Laurie, Kevin, and me to ponder what all this means. In the brief time that I've been Richard's lawyer, I've been shot at by two hoods, one of whom was supposed to be dead, and had my phone tapped by a government agency.

"And I don't have a clue what the hell it's all about."

"It's all about somebody wanting Richard Evans to stay in jail," Laurie says.

I nod. "Or not wanting the case opened up. Kevin, as part of the brief you should include the attempt on my life, and the phone tap. Request that Richard be moved to a secure area of the prison, in solitary if necessary."

"You think he's in danger?" Kevin asks.

"If he's dead there's no case to open up," Laurie points out.

"On the other hand, then there would be no reason to kill his lawyers," I say.

I'm a glass-half-full kind of guy.

• • • • •

THERE IS NOT a very high standard for getting a hearing.

That's the good news. The bad news is, the standard for *prevailing* in the hearing, for being granted a new trial, is quite high. The defense needs to show that the new evidence would do more than just create reasonable doubt; it must show that an injustice is likely being committed by keeping the accused incarcerated.

Kevin's brief is terrific, which is no surprise, since he is probably the best I have ever seen at preparing them. The question we face is whether we should submit it now, since a hearing is likely to be held quickly if granted. By submitting the brief we are saying that we are ready to proceed, when in reality we are not.

Arguing for haste are the ominous things that have been happening to me, and the very real chance that Richard could be in jeopardy in prison. Without submitting the briefs, we have no chance to get him isolated, and therefore no way to get him out of grave danger.

After weighing all the factors, we send Kevin down to submit it while I meet with Sam Willis in his office, which is just down the hall from mine, to get a report on his computer investigation of the victim, Stacy Harriman.

I'm pleasantly surprised that he comes in all business, with no song or movie talking. He has her credit history, educational background, employment history, former addresses, birth certificate—the entire picture.

"Nothing unusual, Andy. Never in a lot of debt, never a late payment, straight B average in school, paid her taxes. If she lived, she would have had a house on Normal Lane and 2.2 children."

"Ever do any government work?" I ask.

"Not unless you consider teaching third grade to be government work."

He takes me through some more of her history, which further confirms my feeling that this is about Richard. Stacy was just in the wrong place at the wrong time.

"Thanks, Sam, you did a great job."

"It's nothing, Andy."

"No, really. You're terrific at it, you're fast, and you do it right the first time. And I just want you to know how much I appreciate it. You're a valuable member of the team."

"Andy . . . you had me at 'Hello.' "

Sam leaves, and I use this alone time to figure out what it is I know, or at least what I believe. It promises to be a short session.

I would bet that Roy Chaney was worried when I showed up. Couple that with the fact that some branch of the government was eavesdropping on me, probably operating without court authority, and it's a decent bet that whatever it is has to do with Richard's job with U.S. Customs.

Complicating matters is the incident on the highway. It's clearly not the government's style to send shooters after me like that. It's certainly not a random shooting or a coincidence, but it's just as certainly beyond my capacity to figure it out at this moment.

One question that will ultimately have to be answered is the one Richard raised. Why, if the bad guys wanted to get him out of the way, did they go to the trouble of killing Stacy and faking his suicide? Why not just kill him?

The only answer I can come up with is that by making the murder-suicide look to be about a personal, domestic problem, it would take the focus off Richard's work. If he were simply murdered, the police would start searching for motive, and they might look toward his job. That would likely have been dangerous for the real killers. If it's a suicide, there are no killers to look for, no further reasons to investigate.

When I get back to my office, I am treated, if that's the right word, to an amazing sight. A three-way conversation is taking place between Karen Evans, Edna, and Marcus Clark. Kevin is sitting off to the side, openmouthed at what he is seeing and hearing.

Karen's genuine enthusiasm for anything and everything has actually bridged the gap between Edna and Marcus. These are two people with absolutely nothing in common and nothing to say to each other, yet Karen has gotten them connected.

As Edna has her pencil at the ready, Karen asks Marcus, "What's a three-letter word for 'foreign machine gun'?"

Edna says, "Second letter is a 'Z.'"

Marcus thinks for a moment. "Uzi." For Marcus this is the equivalent of a Shakespearean soliloquy.

Karen practically leaps out of her chair in delight. "That's right! That's right!" Then she turns to Edna. "It fits, right?"

Edna smiles and writes it down. "Perfect."

Karen turns to slap Marcus five, but he clearly isn't familiar with the concept, and she hits him in the shoulder. He doesn't seem to mind at all.

I can't overstate what an immense diplomatic and personal accomplishment this is for Karen. Were I president, I would immediately appoint her secretary of state. It makes Jimmy Carter's achievement at Camp David seem insignificant. Compared to Edna and Marcus, Arafat and Begin were blood brothers.

It's a mesmerizing sight, and it's with the greatest reluctance that I pull Kevin away. I've arranged for another interview with Richard to discuss his former job in more detail, to try to learn what it might have to do with the murder.

The unfortunate result of my departure will be that Marcus will follow close behind in his bodyguard role, thus breaking up this threesome. I'm not sure that even Karen's wizardry can ever re-create it.

The drive out to the prison is becoming an all too familiar one, and it's not something I enjoy. The place always looks the same, the guards always act the same, and the depressing nature of the surroundings always makes me feel the same.

But Richard looks more upbeat each time I see him. It's understandable; he has spent five years being ignored, a ward of the system, whom nobody cared about, other than his sister. Now there is activity, his lawyers are frequently coming to talk about his case, and just that alone brightens his day.

I tell him my feeling that Roy Chaney was hiding something, but he cannot be helpful in that regard, because he never even met Chaney. He certainly hasn't kept up with developments at the Customs Service; there would have been no reason to. Moreover, 9/11-inspired protective measures have had an evolving impact on how the customs people do their jobs, and Richard would have no way to be familiar with many of these new procedures.

Kevin asks, "Do you know anyone who still works there that we could talk to?"

Richard thinks for a moment and then nods. "You could try Keith Franklin."

"Who is he?" I ask.

"He works down at the pier, same level as I was. I'm pretty sure he's still there."

"You haven't kept in contact with him?"

Richard shakes his head. "Not for a few years. We were good friends; he and his girlfriend went out with Stacy and me a lot. But . . ."

"He dropped you when this all went down?" I ask.

He shrugs. "He was supportive during the trial, and then visited me on and off for a short time after that, but then he stopped coming. I can't say as I blame him."

"Do you have his home address or phone number?" I ask. "I'd rather not talk to him at his office."

"Not anymore, but you could ask Karen. She knew

him pretty well; she was friendly with his sister." He smiles. "Karen, in case you haven't guessed, is friendly with everybody."

"I've picked up on that."

"Have you picked up anything else about her?"

The question surprises me. "Just that she designs dresses and would rather talk about you than herself."

He nods with some sadness. "She designs dresses so well that she has a standing offer to do a show in Rome. But she won't go, because she doesn't want to leave me. It's the same reason she left school."

"Where did she go to school?"

"Yale, majoring in English literature with a 3.8 average." He notices my surprise and then continues. "Then this happened. She's decided that if my life is going to be wasted, she'll join the party. She thinks she's helping me, but it makes it worse."

These are things about Karen that I never would have guessed. "You want me to try and talk to her?"

He shakes his head. "That won't help."

"What will?" I ask.

"Getting me out of here."

I nod and tell him that we have applied for a hearing and that it could take place within a couple of weeks. He is excited by the prospect, but it is tempered by concern. "What if we don't get the hearing?"

"Then we keep digging until we turn over more evidence, and then reapply," I say. "Nobody's abandoning you, Richard."

"Thank you."

"But it may feel like that for a while. I'm concerned for

your safety, so we're requesting that they put you into a more secure area."

"Solitary?"

I nod. "I'm sorry. I wouldn't be asking for it if I wasn't worried."

"Why would anybody want to go after me? I've been in here five years; who could I be a threat to?"

"Richard, when we answer that question, we'll know everything."

• • • • •

HAVING LAURIE WAITING for me at home
is as good as it gets.

Her pasta sauce is simmering on the stove while she's
in the backyard playing with Tara and Reggie. I see them
before they see me, and it's such a perfect sight that I almost want to hide and watch.

I try to be as positive a person as I can, but my logical
mind always forces me to see the imperfections in any situation. In this case, the fact that Laurie and I are together
maybe six or eight weeks out of the year is not exactly a
subtle imperfection, and it sure as hell doesn't fully satisfy
my enjoyment drive.

Laurie sees me and yells, "Daddy's home!" and the two
dogs run over to me, tails wagging, to receive the petting
that is their due. We grab a couple of leashes and go for
a walk in the park, and midway through, a thunderstorm

hits. It's one of those warm rains that feel great, and none of us is of a mind to let it curtail our walk. By the time we get home we're all drenched and happy.

After dinner we sit down to watch a DVD of *The Graduate*. For some reason, Laurie feels about movies the way most people feel about wines, that they get better with age. *The Graduate* is barely forty years old and is a little current for Laurie's taste, but she relaxes her standards because it's so good.

We sit on the couch and drink chardonnay as we watch, and Tara and Reggie are up there with us. It's such a wonderful moment that it's hard for me to concentrate on the film, but I try to focus mainly because I need dialogue lines to compete with Sam Willis. Unfortunately, it's going to be tough to get "Mrs. Robinson, are you trying to seduce me?" into a conversation with Sam. Maybe I'll just scream "Elaine! Elaine!" at him the next time I see him. That should throw him off.

When the movie is over, I realize I haven't called Karen to ask if she can put me in touch with Keith Franklin. When I do, she says that she hasn't seen him in a while, but still knows his sister and will do whatever is necessary to make this happen.

"I'll get right on it," she says. "I'm on the case."

Laurie's already in the bedroom, which is sufficient incentive for me to sprint there. She's lying on the bed, writing in a journal that she keeps, recording the day's events and her thoughts about them. Laurie has told me that she has kept a journal since she was nine years old.

If you supplied me with all the paper and time in the world and paid me in solid gold coins, I would still not keep a journal. I'm going to go back and read about my own life? To learn my own point of view? Why would I want to know what I think after the fact? I already know what I think during the fact. I've always felt that the purpose of reading is to find out what other people think.

Would I want to be able to refresh my memory of how miserable I was at being rejected by Linda Paige in high school? I don't think so. Or reconnect with my feelings about giving up a game-winning home run in the Lyndhurst game? Not in a million years. Journals make retroactive denial impossible, and that happens to be one of my specialties.

Yet there Laurie is, busily chronicling whatever the hell she is chronicling. After about fifteen minutes, during which I have looked at my watch maybe two hundred times, I ask, "Must have been a busy day today, huh?"

"Mmmm," she mumbles, not willing to be distracted from her literary efforts.

"Are you up to the late afternoon yet?"

"Mmmm," she says.

"You want me to write some of it? To save time? For instance, I know what you had for dinner, and what movie we saw. I can jot down stuff like that."

She puts down her pen and stares at me, an ominous sign. "Let me guess," she says. "You think we're going to make love tonight, and you're impatient to get started."

I put on a look of feigned horror. "You read my journal!"

She smiles, puts her journal on the night table, and holds out her arms to me. "Come here; I'll give you something good to write about."

And she proceeds to do just that, though it leaves me too tired to pick up a pen.

It also leaves me too tired to talk, and far too tired to stay awake. Regrettably, it doesn't seem to have had that effect on Laurie.

"Andy, when I'm here with you it feels like I never left. It feels like home."

I feel a twinge of hope through the fatigue; the possibility that Laurie will return here permanently is with me at all times. But I have recently become smart enough not to try to advance the idea myself. If she's going to decide to come back, she's going to reach the decision on her own.

"My home is your home," I say with mock gallantry.

"But when I go back to Findlay, that feels like home as well. I'm totally connected there."

So much for a seismic shift. "Why don't we see how you feel in the morning?"

"Andy, is this working for you? I mean, how we are together . . . when we see each other. Are you happy with how we're handling this?"

"It's not my first choice, but it's a solid second."

She thinks about this for a few moments, then seems to nod and says, "Good night, Andy."

Good night, Andy? Is that where we're going to leave this? I need to have a little more insight into her thinking. "Is there something else you wanted to say, Laurie?"

"I don't think so . . . maybe tomorrow. Good night, Andy."

I could pursue this further now, or I can wait until "maybe tomorrow." I think I'll wait.

Tomorrow actually starts earlier than I would like, as Karen Evans calls me at six o'clock in the morning. She apologizes for calling so early, but she wanted to get me before I went to work. She must think I'm a dairy farmer.

If there's any sleepiness in her voice, I can't detect it; my guess is, she's been up since four staring at the clock and resisting the urge to call. I wish she had resisted a little longer. But Karen is, in a very real way, fighting for her own life as well as her brother's, so I understand her impatience.

"I talked to Keith Franklin," she says. "He said he'd contact you."

"Good. When?"

"He'll call you at your office. He said he has to figure out the best time and place. He seemed a little nervous about it."

I have no idea what the hell I'm doing, yet everybody is nervous about talking to me. I guess ignorance can be intimidating.

I head for the office to wait for Franklin's call and do whatever other work I can think of doing. Hanging over our heads is the knowledge that the decision on whether to grant us a hearing can come down at any moment. If we don't get that, we're obviously dead in the water, and I'll start kicking myself for having pressed for the hearing so soon. It makes me nervous every time the phone rings, which isn't quite as bad as it sounds, because the phone hardly ever rings.

I place a call to Cindy Spodek, an FBI agent currently assigned to the Bureau's Boston office. Cindy and I were on the same side of a crucial case a while back, and she showed immense courage by testifying against her boss. Since he was a crook and murderer, it was the right thing to do, but it caused her considerable pain.

I consider Cindy a friend, and Laurie and I have been out with her and her husband a few times. As a friend she has the honor of my repeatedly asking her for favors, which is why I'm calling her today.

Her office tells me that she is currently at a conference in New York, one of the few breaks I've had lately. They promise to give her the message that I called, and she thus takes her spot alongside Franklin as a caller I am anxious to hear from.

Kevin and I spend some time going over our strategy for the hearing, in case it is granted. We've asked for a speedy resolution, and the prosecutor has not objected, so if we get the hearing, it will happen quickly. We have to be ready.

We're about an hour into it when Cindy Spodek returns my call. "Andy, it's such a pleasure to hear from you. Other people, when they call once every six months, it means they only want a favor. But in your case, it means you just want to express your friendship."

"How true that is," I say. "And so beautifully put."

"So how is everything?" she asks.

"Everything is fine, just wonderful," I say. "And that's all I wanted to say, besides expressing my friendship."

"I've got to be back in a meeting in ten minutes," Cindy says. "So this might be an appropriate time to cut the bullshit."

"Works for me. I need some information."

"What a surprise," she says.

"Somebody tried to tap my phone. The government. The government you work for."

"Are we getting paranoid, Andy?"

"It happened soon after somebody else tried to kill me."

Her tone immediately changes and reflects both personal concern and businesslike efficiency. "Can you meet me at three o'clock in the coffee shop of the Park Central Hotel, Fifty-sixth and Seventh Avenue? I have an hour between meetings."

"Thanks, Cindy."

"How's Laurie?" she asks.

"She's great. We still have the long-distance relationship, except right now it's not such a long distance. She's in town."

"Can you bring her? I'd love to see her."

I tell her that I'll try, and when we hang up I call Laurie. She likes Cindy a great deal and very much wants to come along. I pick her up at the house, and we drive into the city. I take the lower level of the George Washington Bridge, which always reminds me of the scene in *The Godfather* in which Solozzo's driver makes a U-turn in the middle of the bridge, so as to remove the chance of being successfully followed. If I ever tried that, I'd wind up in the Hudson River.

Cindy is waiting for us when we arrive, explaining that her meeting ended a little early. It's just as well, since the first fifteen minutes are taken up by her and Laurie talking girl talk, relationship talk, job talk, and talk talk. With a significant amount of laughing thrown in, this could go on forever.

Finally, I can't take it anymore. "Hello, remember me?"

They look at me as if trying to place the face. "Oh, right," Cindy says. "You're the guy who defends the scum balls."

I nod. "That's me." I take out the phone tap that was

removed by Sergeant Paulsen at my house, and I hand it to her. "Ever see one of these?" I ask.

Cindy takes it and looks at it from all angles. "This was on your phone?"

"Yes."

Cindy is no longer laughing, nor is she smiling. I'm not sure if the device is a phone tap or a mood changer. "Can I hold on to this?"

"Yes."

She puts it in her pocket. "Maybe you should tell me what's going on."

I lay out the whole story, starting with Reggie, right up to the present moment. She asks some questions, particularly about the shooting on the highway, and writes down the names of the dead shooters.

Cindy knows nothing about any of this; she had not even previously heard of Richard Evans. But something is clearly bothering her. "I'll ask around about this and get back to you as soon as I can," she says. "But in the meantime, be careful."

"Marcus is covering him," Laurie says.

Cindy nods. "Good."

"What is it you're not telling me?" I ask.

"I'll call you," she says, then says a quick good-bye and heads back to her meeting.

Laurie and I talk on the way to the car about Cindy's reaction to what I had to say. She agrees that it was strange and that Cindy seemed worried about something.

We don't have too long to ponder it, because my cell phone rings. I can see by the caller ID that it's my office.

"Hello?"

"Andy, its me," says Kevin. "You want the good news or the bad news?"

"Let's start with the good."

"We got the hearing."

"And the bad?"

"It's Monday."

• • • • •

SIX DAYS TO get ready for a hearing is not a lot of time, but in this case it's manageable. It's not as if we were preparing for an entire trial, and we don't have to anticipate and refute what the prosecution is going to say. We simply have to make our own points and demonstrate why, if those points had been available to be made in the first trial, Richard might well have been acquitted.

But there's still a lot to do, and Kevin and I have been in intense preparation for the past three days. Most of that time we've been at my house, which I've selfishly insisted on because that's where Laurie is. Kevin has no objections, because it's comfortable and because Laurie is cooking our meals. In fact, she has been helpful in every way, even sitting in on our strategy sessions and making suggestions.

Neither Cindy Spodek nor Keith Franklin has called, but I haven't really had time to worry about it. The hearing is more important than anything either of them could have to say; if it doesn't go well, then everything else is meaningless.

Half our time has been spent on witness preparation. Dr. King has come in, and we've gone over exactly what it is he will testify to. He is an experienced, knowledgeable witness, and I have no doubt that he will be very persuasive.

Our other main witness is more of a challenge, and a good deal of that challenge will be to get his testimony admitted at all. We are going to call Reggie to the stand, and let him testify to the fact that he is really Richard's dog, and thus survived that night on the boat. The prosecutor will fight like crazy to limit the testimony to human witnesses, and that will be a major battle that we must be ready for.

Today is a Friday that has felt nothing like a Friday. That's because there is no weekend coming up; tomorrow and Sunday are going to be full workdays.

Kevin leaves at seven o'clock, with a promise to be back at nine tomorrow morning. Laurie and I are going out to dinner, and we're almost out the door when the phone rings.

Laurie answers and, after listening for a few moments, hands me the phone.

"Hello?" I say, since I'm never at a loss for snappy ways to begin conversations.

The voice is Cindy Spodek's. "Andy, I don't have much information, but what I've got is not good."

"Let's hear it."

"Well, I went to our expert on electronic surveillance, and he told me that the tap is either CIA or DIA."

"What is DIA?"

"Defense Intelligence Agency. It's run out of the Pentagon. But about six hours later the guy comes back to me and says he was wrong, that it's just a run-of-the-mill tap, could be used by anybody."

"You don't believe him?" I ask.

"No, I don't. That device wasn't like any I had ever seen. And he hadn't taken it; I still had it. I just don't believe he did any research that changed his mind. I think he was instructed by someone to change his mind."

"Okay . . . thanks."

"I'm not finished," she says. "I asked around about the Evans case. I wasn't aware of any Bureau involvement, and the two people above me that I asked didn't seem to know anything about it."

"You didn't believe them, either?"

"Actually, I did. But later in the day one of them called me into his office and grilled me on why I was asking. I told him that you were a friend, and I was curious. He told me that it wasn't a door I should be opening, that I should not be involved in any way."

This is stunning news; it seems that the entire United States government is conspiring to keep Richard Evans in jail. "This doesn't fit with the facts of the case as presented at trial," I say. "It was supposed to look like a very personal crime—a distraught man kills his fiancée and himself."

"I don't know where or how deep this goes, Andy. But I do know it hits a nerve. The mother lode of nerves."

"Thanks, Cindy. I'm sorry I involved you in this."

"No problem. Just be careful, Andy. You may be dealing with people even more powerful than Marcus."

"Now, that is a scary thought."

We hang up and drive to dinner, though for a moment I'm nervous about starting my car. Laurie and I generally try not to discuss business during dinner, but the phone call from Cindy has pretty much blown that out of the water.

Laurie obviously has no more idea than I do about what is going on or why the whole world seems to have lined up against me. Nevertheless, it's important for me to come up with a theory, if only to give me something to test, to measure ideas against.

The flip side of that, however, is that once I come up with a theory, I have to guard against being married to it. I can't look at new information only through a biased prism; I have to let it take me in any direction, not guided by my preconceptions.

The only theory we can come up with is that Richard was the victim of a plot to get him out of the way, for something having to do with his work. I don't believe that the intent of the plot was to frame Richard for Stacy's murder; I believe that Richard was supposed to die as a "suicide" victim. The approaching storm was unexpected, and had it not appeared, the Coast Guard would not have boarded the boat in time to resuscitate him.

I can only assume that something was being smuggled into the country, and Richard's presence was considered a threat to the operation. If the CIA or DIA is involved in the case, then I doubt it was drugs; it was more likely something violent or military in nature. Probably a national security matter rather than a strictly criminal one. Try as I might, I cannot understand how this could still be an issue five years later, but based on the reaction to the reopening of Richard's case, it must be.

The other thing I want Laurie's opinion on is whether

to turn the hearing into a media event. Up until now, my handling of Richard's case has received modest coverage, nothing intense, and I've had no reason to change that. My involvement, and the fact that Reggie is so central to the case, can attract a great deal of attention, and I must decide if I want to go in that direction.

"There's no jury pool out there, Andy," Laurie says. It's a good point; the judge is going to make the final decision, so there are no potential jurors to influence.

The judge assigned to the case is Nicholas Gordon. The original case was tried in Somerset County, so that's where the hearing is as well. I don't know Judge Gordon, or any other judges from that county, since that is not where I usually practice.

"Do you know Judge Gordon?" I ask.

She shakes her head. "No, but I don't know too many judges who like excessive publicity. Or wise-ass lawyers."

It's another good point, even if she's not making it particularly gently. My normal trial tactics tend toward the flamboyant, and while they often work well with a jury, they tend to piss off judges. Pissing off the decision maker, which the judge will be in this case, is not a particularly logical thing to do.

"This hearing isn't going to be much fun," I say.

She smiles. "I'm not so sure about that. Watching you question Reggie is going to be a blast."

• • • • •

IT TURNS OUT that I am not Andy the all-powerful.

I had decided to keep the publicity level down, so as to dampen coverage and not annoy the judge. Unfortunately, it didn't work; the press is out in force in front of the courthouse when Kevin and I get there. The reporters on the court beat must have gotten a tip from the bailiff or someone else inside the system about what was going on, and the word spread.

Laurie will arrive later with Karen Evans and our star witness, Reggie. I'll be calling her when I have a better sense of when they will be needed; there's no sense having Reggie pacing, barking, and maybe even pissing in the witness room as he nervously awaits his appearance.

We're going to start the day in the judge's chambers. The prosecutor, Janine Coletti, has filed a motion to prevent Reggie from "testifying." We've certainly expected that and, hopefully, are prepared to defend our position successfully.

I'm not familiar with Coletti, but I've checked her out, and the prevailing opinion seems to be that she is tough and smart. Those are traits that I don't like to find in prosecutors; give me a mushy, dumb one any day of the week. The only slight positive is that she is not the original prosecutor and therefore might have less of a vested interest in protecting the original outcome.

Kevin and I meet Coletti and her team in the reception area outside the judge's chambers. We exchange pleasantries, but there is no discussion about the case. That will come soon enough.

We are led into Judge Gordon's chambers after only a five-minute wait. He looks to be in his mid-forties, though his hair is sprinkled with gray. Actually, I think gray hair may be a requirement to take a seat on the bench; prospective judges probably have to walk through some maturity screener that rejects pure black or brown hair as frivolous.

A court stenographer is also present, and Judge Gordon explains that this session will be on the record. He wanted to hold this particular argument in chambers because of "the large media contingent on hand," and he makes little effort to conceal the fact that he blames me for the turnout. It is particularly frustrating because this time it's not true.

"The question before us is whether to allow the golden retriever known as Reggie to appear in court," says the judge before turning to me. "What is the purpose behind the request?"

"We want to demonstrate that he is in fact Mr. Evans's

dog and that he did not die along with Ms. Harriman, as the prosecution claimed at trial."

"And how do you propose to do that?" he asks.

"Through testimony by his veterinarian and by the actions of the dog as he relates to Mr. Evans. We believe it is vital to establish ownership beyond a doubt."

The judge turns to the prosecutors. "Ms. Coletti?"

"Your Honor, as stated in our brief, the state feels that such a maneuver is completely out of bounds and likely to turn the proceedings into a circus. There is no precedent for a dog to take on the role of witness, and such testimony would be inherently unreliable."

I shake my head. "Your Honor, the reliability of canine testimony, as demonstrated through actions, has been amply demonstrated in many court proceedings, including those of Your Honor himself."

Judge Gordon looks surprised. "Would you care to explain that?"

I nod. "Certainly. In *New Jersey v. Grantham* you ruled that a search that uncovered drugs was reasonable, when the only fact presented to justify the search was the action of a DEA German shepherd who detected the drugs by his sense of smell."

"That dog was not a witness in court," the judge says.

"That's true. But you affirmed his reliability by allowing the search. He was, in effect, presented through hearsay testimony. If you'd like, we could conduct our own test outside of court, with you present or through videotape. Then the reference to *Grantham* would be exactly on point."

Coletti shakes her head in disagreement. "Your Honor,

that dog was trained in drug detection. It is an entirely different situation."

"No, it is exactly the same," I say. "We will demonstrate Reggie's training in court, training that could only have been done by Mr. Evans. And untrained dogs have testified as well, through hearsay. Even in the O. J. Simpson trial, endless testimony referenced the barking of a dog, and it was used to pinpoint the time of the murders."

"Obviously we disagree, Your Honor," says Coletti. "But we object just as strongly on the ground of relevance. Mr. Evans was not convicted of murdering his dog, and whether or not the dog is alive is of no consequence. He was convicted for murdering his fiancée, and her death has been confirmed by DNA."

"Mr. Carpenter?"

"Ms. Coletti was not the prosecutor at trial, so perhaps she is unaware that Mr. Steinberg, who did prosecute, referenced the deceased dog thirty-one times. He did so in his opening and closing arguments and through witness testimony. He used it to argue the facts of the case and to demonstrate Mr. Evans's 'extreme callousness.' The jury certainly considered it; he instructed them to. And this new evidence will prove that he should not have been able to reference it, and they certainly should not have considered it."

The judge continues questioning us for another fifteen minutes. My assessment is that he does not want to allow Reggie into the courtroom but is unable to come up with an adequate legal justification to prevent it.

"Your Honor," I say, "we think the evidence to be introduced by the dog will be compelling. But Richard Evans has not seen the dog in five years, and maybe we'll be wrong. Maybe it will blow up in our faces. But either way, what harm can come of it?"

"What do you mean?" he asks.

"There's no jury here to protect from being misled. You are the judge and jury, the sole arbiter. You can see it and assign whatever importance to it that you wish. If you think it has no value, you will ignore it. If you consider it valuable for either side, you'll assign it the appropriate weight. It will be significant or harmless, or somewhere in between, and only you will decide which."

The judge then asks how we would proceed, and I tell him that Karen Evans would bring Reggie in, that her presence as someone he knows would put him at ease. Then Richard would put him through some training paces, tricks that he had taught him, as a way to demonstrate familiarity.

The fact that the judge asks about process is a good sign; if he were going to disallow Reggie, then the process would not be important. Coletti seems to sense this as well, and she renews many of her objections to the testimony. I refute them, but we're going over the same ground.

"I'm going to allow it," the judge says, and then makes an unusual ruling. All other witnesses, for both sides, will testify before Reggie. His appearance will represent the finale. "See you in court," he says.

We take this as our cue to leave the chambers, and I immediately head for a phone to call Laurie. I tell her what time to have Karen and Reggie here, and that I will call her back if that changes.

"You're taking a chance," Laurie reminds me. "Reggie could go into court and bite your client, and your case, on the ass."

"You're right," I say. "You'd better ask Tara to speak to him."

She laughs. "Will do. See you later . . . good luck."

I take my place in the courtroom, and Richard Evans is brought in. I can see the nervousness etched in his face; he's experienced the wonder of hope this past couple of weeks, and he knows that it could all come crashing down today.

"You ready?" he asks.

I nod. "Ready."

He's searching my face for a clue to his chances, doesn't find anything particularly reassuring, so he finally nods. "Okay. Me, too."

• • • • •

WHEN THE JUDGE enters the courtroom and the bailiff calls the case, I get my own butterflies. This hearing represents not only a huge hurdle but also an unfamiliar one for a defense attorney like me. Usually we only need "reasonable doubt" on our side; the prosecution has to have a slam dunk, a unanimous verdict, to win. A hung jury is generally considered a defense victory.

Here the opposite is true. Richard is presumed guilty, and we must decisively prevail to give him another chance. In this case a tie doesn't go to the runner, and it doesn't go to the defense. We have to win decisively, and the judge must be persuaded that we would probably win in a new trial.

The first witness I call is probably the most important human witness I'll call all day. It's Dr. Gerald King, here to testify on the toxicology and medical reports. I start to take him through his credentials, which are as impressive as they come. Halfway through them, Coletti belatedly offers to stipulate to him as an expert witness.

"Your Honor, I would like you to hear his entire curriculum vitae," I say.

"It's not necessary," Judge Gordon says. "I'm very familiar with the doctor."

That's plenty good enough for me, and I don't push the issue. Instead, I take Dr. King through his description of how the bruise could not have been on the left side of Richard's head if he had fallen out of bed, and could only have been caused by a rounded, blunt instrument, not by the floor.

Dr. King has brought pictures and charts with him, some of which are identical to those used in the first trial and some which he has created from scratch. His presentation is reasonably compelling, and once I'm satisfied he's made his point, I move on to the toxicology.

It only takes a few questions before I lead Dr. King into dropping the bomb that the sleeping pills had to be injected or taken in a liquid form, because of the presence of campene. I could lead him even further, but I want to save some ammunition for when the prosecution puts on its rebuttal witness.

Coletti gets up to cross-examine, and she focuses on the bruise first. "Dr. King, you say that if Mr. Evans had fallen from the bed, the bruise would have been on the right side and not the left. Is that correct?"

"Yes."

"And you also conclude that the floor could not have caused the bruise. Is that correct?"

"Yes."

"Before the pills knocked Mr. Evans out, would they have made him groggy?"

"Certainly."

"Could he perhaps have staggered around the room, walked into a cabinet or something else, and then fallen to the floor? Could he have sustained the bruise that way?"

"That was not the prosecution version at trial."

"And there were, and are, experts and evidence to support that version. But if they were wrong, and you are right, could it have happened as I describe?"

He's trapped; Coletti is very good. "It's possible."

"Thank you," she says. "Now, to this mysterious campene. Are there other ways for campene to enter one's system? Is it contained in shellfish, for instance?"

"Yes."

"Could he have ingested it that way?"

I can almost see Dr. King salivate at this; maybe Coletti is not so good. "If he did, he would have been dead when the Coast Guard got there."

"Why is that?" she asks.

Here comes a great moment, and I envy Dr. King that he gets to say it. He waits a beat; his timing is perfect. "Mr. Evans is severely allergic to shellfish; it's in his medical records."

Coletti flinches; she had clearly not known this. She recovers quickly and gets Dr. King to agree that the campene could have been a preservative in another drug that Richard might have taken. Dr. King points out that there were no other drugs in his system, but has to admit that some drugs leave the body faster than others.

All in all, he has been a very good witness. He won't carry the day, but he's moved the day along nicely.

Next up is Dr. Ruff, Reggie's veterinarian. She shows the X-rays of the plate in his leg, as well as the missing teeth and the cut marks. Coletti establishes on cross that none of these issues could possibly be unique to Reggie, that the pulling of teeth and the repairing of broken legs in this manner are quite commonplace.

Dr. Ruff is a less accomplished witness than Dr. King, and she's too willing to concede facts to Coletti. The truth is that the combination of health issues would represent a mind-boggling coincidence if the dog is not Reggie, but Dr. Ruff doesn't come off as that certain.

Next up is Lieutenant Michele Siegle of the Asbury Park Police. I use her to recount the testimony of the witnesses who saw the boat at various times that night. This establishes the locations as far from the shore.

"So it's your opinion that Mr. Evans's dog could not successfully have swum to shore if he had been thrown from the boat?"

"That's correct, and it's not just my opinion. There was expert testimony to that effect during the trial."

I introduce the expert testimony from the original trial transcript as a defense exhibit and turn the witness over to Coletti. She gives only a cursory cross-examination, designed to elicit the fact that the murder case was ironclad with or without the dog's involvement.

Since Reggie's "testimony" will be kept completely separate, Judge Gordon invites Coletti to bring forward any rebuttal witnesses now. She calls Dr. Nicholas

Turner, a toxicologist of some renown who was not the prosecution expert during the trial.

She takes him through a point-by-point rebuttal of Dr. King's review of the blood work. He claims that Amenipam in liquid form is very hard to find, and that the empty bottle of pills showed traces of Amenipam, lending credibility to the theory that Richard overdosed on conventional pills.

He also talks about how quickly liquid Amenipam works, and that the Coast Guard would have had to appear very quickly after any injection, or Richard would have died.

Finally, Coletti takes him through Dr. King's testimony about the presence of campene. "Is campene used only to preserve Amenipam?" she asks.

He smiles a condescending smile. "Certainly not. It's used very commonly with all kinds of drugs. I've actually never heard it used with Amenipam, though it's possible that it would be."

I start my cross-examination by asking Dr. Turner if he has ever done any acting.

He seems taken aback by the question. "What do you mean by acting?"

"I mean playing a role . . . pretending. I don't mean professionally; have you ever been in a school play or anything?"

"In high school . . . once or twice," he says.

Coletti objects, asking where this could be going. Judge Gordon tells me to get to the point.

I nod. "Okay. Dr. Turner, I'd like you to act something out for me. Imagine you're sitting at a table, and you've decided to swallow a whole bottle full of pills. Show me how you would do it."

"How I would swallow the pills?" he asks.

"Yes. Do it like you're acting it out, or playing charades."

Coletti objects again, but Judge Gordon lets it proceed. Dr. Turner pours some imaginary pills from the imaginary bottle into his hand, then puts them as far back in his mouth as he can. Then he takes a drink from an imaginary glass and swallows the imaginary pills.

"Very nicely done," I say. "For the court reporter's sake, let the record show that you pretended to take pills out of a bottle, put them in your mouth, pretended to take a drink from a glass, and swallowed them. Is that accurate?"

He nods. "Yes."

"You weren't undecided about how to do it, were you? That was the obvious way?"

"It was the obvious way," he agrees.

"Except there was no glass," I say, taking some papers from Kevin. "Your Honor, here is an inventory of the boat that night. All the glasses were clean and put away in the cabinet. There were none on the table or on the sink. There were none anywhere except the cabinet."

"Maybe he cleaned it," Dr. Turner says, making the classic mistake of answering a question that wasn't asked.

I nod. "Right. He was willing to have someone find his own dead body, but a dirty glass would have just been too embarrassing."

"Perhaps he took the pills over the sink, cupping water in his hand." Dr. Turner is feeling trapped, even though he has no reason to be. He's a scientist, not a cop, and he shouldn't feel that he has to defend the investigation. But that's how he feels, and I'm going to take advantage of it.

"A whole bottle of pills?" I ask, not bothering to mask my incredulity.

"It's possible."

"There were no traces of Amenipam found in the sink. Do you find that desperate suicidal people who've just committed a violent murder are usually that neat?"

I move on to the pill bottle itself, which we have asked to be brought to court. I show it to Dr. Turner and ask him to read the label and tell me what pharmacy it came from.

"There is no label," he says. "It's been torn off . . . There are traces of the back of the paper."

"According to the police reports, the detached label was not found on the boat, and seventy-one pharmacies nearest to Mr. Evans's house were canvassed. None had provided the prescription. Can you explain that?"

He shrugs. "He didn't want anyone to know where he got it."

"Is it illegal for a pharmacy to dispense Amenipam?"

"Not with a prescription."

"Is it hard to get a prescription for it?"

"Depends on the doctor, and what the patient tells him."

I nod. "How about 'I'm not sleeping well'? Might that do the trick?"

"Depends on the doctor," he repeats.

"In your experience, is it likely that a suicidal murderer would care if people knew where he got his prescription?"

Coletti objects, and Judge Gordon sustains. I let him off the stand, having made enough points to satisfy myself.

In fact, all the morning witnesses have gone as well as we could have hoped, but the gallery and press in attendance have barely been paying attention. It is as if they have been watching the undercard before a heavyweight championship fight.

Our lunch hour is spent in an anteroom finalizing our plans. Karen will be bringing Reggie into the courtroom, and she will have a key role in our success or failure. She admits to being nervous but swears there is no chance she will screw things up.

I'm fairly confident, based on Reggie's pizza box trick at my house, but I'm still nervous myself. Lawyers don't call witnesses unless they know exactly what they will say, and I am violating that principal today. Reggie will speak through his actions, and I am far from certain what he will "say," especially in the new surroundings of the courtroom, with so many people watching him.

"Just try to keep him as calm as you can," Laurie says to Karen. "Keep petting him, and talk to him in a soothing voice."

Karen nods. "I will. We'll be fine. Right, Reg?" She pats him on the back as she talks, but he remains noncommittal about his testimony.

Karen and Richard will be the two humans with the

most responsibility in this afternoon's session. My role will be mostly to watch and hope, a situation guaranteed to leave me frustrated. But we all know on whom everything is riding.

Reggie is going to be the main event.

• • • • •

"THE DEFENSE CALLS Reggie Evans," I say, and everyone turns toward the rear of the courtroom.

The door opens, and Karen walks in with Reggie alongside her on a leash. She looks serious but relaxed, and he seems a little scared. I can tell this because his tail is down behind him, a sure sign that he is not comfortable. As Laurie instructed, Karen reaches down and pets him gently on the side of his head, and the net effect is to keep him amazingly calm.

Reggie handles pressure a hell of a lot better than I would.

Everybody in the gallery strains to get a look at them as they walk down the long aisle toward the front of the room. It reminds me of the footage I've seen of the Ali-Foreman fight in Zaire, as Ali and his entourage worked their way down to the ring.

Karen brings Reggie all the way to the witness stand. He has not seen Richard yet, because he's facing the other direction. This is how we planned it. I even had Richard wear aftershave to mask his scent. It's unlikely Reggie would have smelled him from this distance, with this many people, but I didn't want to take any chances. This had to be fully choreographed.

"Your Honor," I say, "with the court's permission, Mr. Evans will take over."

"Go ahead," Judge Gordon says, and Karen turns toward Richard, who is about twenty feet away from her. In the process, Reggie turns as well.

Reggie is looking in Richard's general direction, without reacting, for about five seconds, but it feels like five hours. The thud that can be heard in the courtroom is my heart hitting the floor, as my plan appears not to be working.

Suddenly, Reggie seems to focus in on Richard, and it is as if he had been jolted by electricity. He explodes toward Richard, and the leash comes out of Karen's hand. "Oh, my God, I'm sorry!" she lies, since letting him get away is exactly what I've instructed her to do. But her apparent distress is so real that even I almost believe it.

Reggie flies through the air and lands on Richard, knocking him backward over his chair. The three bailiffs don't have a clue what to do, and no apparent desire to try to restrain Reggie. I doubt that their handcuffs would fit on his paws, anyway. For now they are just content to watch.

Even Judge Gordon seems mesmerized by the spectacle, though he recovers fairly quickly. He starts to slam his gavel down, yelling for order, though none is forthcoming.

Richard, a look of pure joy on his face, finally makes it to his feet. "Sit, Reggie," he says, and Reggie immediately assumes a sitting position, as if waiting for the next command. The only sign to connect him to the chaos he has just caused is the fact that he is panting from the exertion.

It is a demonstration stunning in its simplicity; just by those two words Richard said all there was to say. No reasonable person could have witnessed what just took place and continue to have any doubt that Reggie is Richard's dog.

It turns out that Coletti is not a reasonable person. "Your Honor, may we approach the bench?" she asks.

Judge Gordon grants her request, and Coletti and I walk up for a private conference. "Your Honor, the defense should be admonished for that performance. It runs completely counter to what was agreed upon. The dog was supposed to be kept on the leash, under control."

I laugh. "Under control? It would have taken a marine battalion to keep him under control. He was seeing his owner for the first time in five years."

"That ownership is still to be determined," Coletti says.

"Were you in the courtroom just now?" Judge Gordon asks her. "Did you see what I saw?"

"I saw a demonstration that might well have been staged," she says.

I shake my head in exaggerated amazement. "*Staged?* He's a dog; he's not DeNiro."

"Ms. Colletti," Judge Gordon says, "if the state wants

to continue this, then the defendant can put the dog through whatever tricks they have planned. But I am telling you, as far as the court is concerned, this is the defendant's dog."

Coletti can tell that she has pushed this as far as possible. "We can end it here."

We both go back to our respective tables. Reggie is once again standing near the witness stand, held on the leash by Karen.

"No further questions," I say. "The witness is excused."

Karen and Reggie leave the courtroom, and both Coletti and I announce that we have no more witnesses. Coletti stands to give her closing argument.

"Your Honor, five years ago a lengthy investigation focused on the murder of Stacy Harriman. Hundreds of hours of work went into it by experienced, dedicated professional law enforcement officers.

"They determined that there was probable cause that Mr. Evans committed the crime. Their work was reviewed by the county attorney, who agreed with their conclusions and filed murder charges against Mr. Evans.

"A four-week trial then took place, during which Mr. Evans was ably defended. He entered that trial with the presumption of innocence and retained the right to challenge his accusers. At the conclusion of that trial, a jury of his peers deliberated for eight hours before unanimously voting to convict him.

"What has changed since then? We have now learned that Mr. Evans had infinitesimal traces of campene in his system. This might be significant, if we could be sure how it got there.

"And we know that a golden retriever seems to be the dog that Mr. Evans used to own. This also might be significant if Mr. Evans had been convicted of murdering that golden retriever, or even of dognapping. But no such charges were ever filed.

"Your Honor, the defense has not even come close to meeting its burden. To grant a new trial on this flimsy evidence would be to discredit the original trial, and there is certainly no reason to do that."

Coletti sits down, and as she does, I stand up immediately. She has presented a reasonably convincing argument, and I don't want it to stand unchallenged for a moment longer than necessary.

"Your Honor, I was not involved in Mr. Evans's original trial, but I have carefully read the transcript. Most of what I read was presented by the prosecution, since the great majority of the witnesses called were theirs.

"The prosecution contended back then that Mr. Evans sustained his facial bruise from falling out of bed. When Dr. King came in here and said that it could not have happened that way, they backpedaled and said it could have happened as he was staggering around the room.

"The prosecution contended back then that Mr. Evans swallowed a bottle of pills. Yet we find out today that they cannot find any pharmacy that prescribed the pills, and that Mr. Evans would have had to eat them dry, without using water. Such a technique would have been masochistic, in addition to being suicidal.

"The prosecution contended back then that Mr. Evans's dog was on board the boat; they presented eyewitnesses that were quite clear about it. They told the jury that he killed that dog by throwing him overboard, and then described the act as evidence of his depravity.

"Now we know with certainty that they were wrong. We know that Reggie is very much alive and that rumors of his death were, shall we say, exaggerated. There is nothing anywhere in all the hundreds of hours of investigative work, or anything presented at trial, that can come close to explaining what you saw in court here today. Reggie's very existence means that someone else was on the boat that night, and it is very likely that the same someone else was the murderer. Certainly, there is nothing in the record that says otherwise.

"Reggie is alive, and because of that, the prosecution's theories are dead in the water.

"Also revealing is what the prosecution didn't say in that trial back then. They offered no evidence of motive, and no claim that Mr. Evans had ever showed violent or suicidal tendencies.

"Now, I am aware that they were not obligated to present motive, but juries usually want to hear it. But back then it wasn't necessary, because the evidence as presented seemed so clear. Well, now it's not so clear, and the absence of motive and previous tendencies becomes far more significant.

"Your Honor, we are not talking about reasonable doubt here. We are talking about *overwhelming* doubt. If we knew then what we know now, only the most overzealous of prosecutors would have brought the case to trial. And there's not a jury in America that would have voted to convict.

"Richard Evans has spent five years of his life in prison for a crime he did not commit. The love of his life was murdered, and he was not allowed the space and freedom to grieve. He himself was nearly killed, and no one looked for, much less found, the actual guilty party.

"The truth, as always, will ultimately win out. It sometimes comes in strange shapes and sizes, and this time it came walking in on four paws. But it is the truth, and by recognizing it, you can start the process of giving Richard Evans his life back."

● ● ● ● ●

I'VE NEVER BEEN much of a fan of self-discipline.

It generally collides head on with my enjoyment drive and rarely survives the collision. It makes no sense to try to force myself to do something I don't want to do, since if there were a good reason to do it, I would want to do it in the first place.

But we are now entering a phase where self-discipline must rear its ugly head. It is going to take anywhere from a week to a couple of months for Judge Gordon to announce his decision about a possible new trial for Richard. We must work hard toward preparing for that trial, while knowing that if it's not granted, our efforts will be totally wasted.

The thing I can most liken it to is betting a parley, which is a bet that requires winning two games to be a winner.

If one of those games has already been played but I don't know the result, I would root for my team in the second game, knowing that it might be a waste of time because, if I lost the first game, the second one doesn't matter.

I'm going to have to work to develop a compelling case for Richard, but if we didn't win the hearing, then it won't matter.

At times like this I am particularly glad I have Kevin as my partner. He will keep me moving forward, both because he is a more dedicated attorney than I and because he is a more optimistic one.

Kevin thinks our performance in the hearing was a winning one—a "slam down," as he puts it. Kevin is not a sports fan in any sense, and what he means to say is "slam dunk." Or maybe "grand slam." Or "touchdown." With Kevin it's often hard to tell.

I arrange to meet him at the office at nine o'clock in the morning, which will give us an hour alone before Edna arrives. We spend only ten minutes rehashing the hearing; we did the best we could and just have to take it on faith that it was good enough.

So now we have to start investigating full-time, which would be easier if we had the slightest idea how to do that. All we know is that a supposedly dead Army guy tried to kill me and that the government tried to bug my conversations. The list of things we don't know could fill the Library of Congress.

"It has to involve Richard's job at customs," Kevin says, advancing his theory. "The bad guys who tried to kill you must be smuggling contraband into the country, and they're afraid you're going to find out something that screws up their operation. The government is tapping your phone to learn whatever it is that you come up with."

Neither Kevin nor I have any idea how to penetrate the customs operation at the Port of Newark. Keith Franklin, who told Karen he would call, has still not done so, and we'll have to get her to contact him again.

Edna arrives and dives into the *New York Times* crossword puzzle. She likes to get it done before lunch so she doesn't have it hanging over her head when she gets back. That way she can devote the afternoon to talking with family and friends on the phone. Her niece, Cassie, is getting married, which is creating more family controversy than was contained in an entire season of *Dallas*.

About twenty minutes later the phone rings, and when Edna shows no inclination to answer it, Kevin does. After saying hello, he listens for a moment and hands me the phone. "Keith Franklin," he says, a triumphant smile on his face.

"Mr. Franklin, I've been expecting your call."

"Yes . . . I'm sorry it took so long. I wanted to make sure this was serious."

"It's very serious. That much I can assure you."

"I know," he says. "I saw the coverage of Richard's hearing."

"I believe that Richard's work had something to do with the murder, but I need your help to find out exactly what."

"I really can't talk about it now . . . not here."

"Where do you want to meet?"

He tells me he'll meet me in Eastside Park at nine o'clock tonight, down by the baseball field. It is clear that he does not want to be seen or heard talking to me. That in itself may be very significant, somewhat significant, or of no significance at all. As with everything else involved with this case, I don't have the slightest idea.

I agree, and he says, "Will you be alone?"

"Why is that important?"

"Karen told me I could trust you, so I will," he says. "But only you."

When I hang up I tell Kevin what was said. "I'm not crazy about the sound of that," he says. "He could be setting you up."

"Why would he? We approached him; he didn't come to us. And Richard vouched for him; he said he's a friend. There's no reason to think he's on the other side."

"Except for the fact that so far everybody seems to be on the other side," Kevin says.

"You mean like hit men and the United States government?"

He nods. "That's what I mean."

"But we've got Marcus. Advantage, us."

Laurie's reaction when I get home and bring her up to date is the same as Kevin's. "Are you sure Marcus is watching out for you?" she asks.

I shrug. "He's never let me down before. But I must tell you, I resent the fact that you think I need Marcus for protection. I can handle myself when things get rough."

"Since when?"

"Since always," I say. "You may not know this, but when I was a kid, and the other kids were at the library or the ballet, you know what I was doing? I was at home watching boxing on television."

"Andy, you're a great lawyer and a wonderful man, and

I love you completely. But you'd be in major trouble if you got in the ring with the Olson twins."

"What does that prove? There's two of them."

The situation is becoming very stressful for Laurie. She has to go back home in three days and can't stand that she will be leaving me in what she considers a dangerous situation. In the old days, meaning last year, she would have been on the defense team and would be taking an active role. Now she's on the sidelines watching, and having trouble with it.

I spend the rest of the day hanging out with Laurie, Tara, and Reggie, as appealing a threesome as ever existed. I'm not feeling overly nervous about my upcoming meeting in the darkened park. Since I requested the meeting, there's little reason to consider Franklin a danger.

At nine o'clock I park my car by the baseball field and walk the few hundred yards across the field to the old pavilion. It's empty now, but when I was younger it had a snack bar with some of the best french fries in history. My father would take me there after my team lost a game or I played badly, to cheer me up. I went there a lot.

I stand in front of the pavilion as instructed, waiting for Franklin. There is some moonlight, but he is only ten yards from me before I see him. He came from the opposite direction and is so quiet he must be wearing moccasins.

"Hello, Mr. Carpenter."

"Thanks for coming."

"How is Richard doing?"

"He's okay, but he really needs your help."

"I'm not sure what I can do."

"I am operating under the premise that Richard was intended to be a murder victim, set up to look like he was perpetrating a murder-suicide. It could not have been to prevent him from revealing something he knew, since he would still be aware of it. It must have been to get him out of the way, so that he would not prevent something that was going to happen."

"Roy Chaney took over when Richard . . . left."

"I know. I spoke to him."

He seems surprised by this. "You did?"

"Yes. Is he a friend of yours?"

His response is instantaneous. "No." Then: "I don't trust him."

"You think he could be doing something illegal?"

"I'm not sure," he says. "But since he came in, guys have gotten transferred out of his section, and they brought in new people from the outside. They're a real tight group—not very friendly with the rest of us."

"So it's possible Richard was taken out to enable some people to do illegal business, with Chaney allowing it to happen?" I ask.

He answers my question with a question. "You think whatever it was is still going on?"

I nod. "Probably. A lot of people are nervous about what I might turn up. If it was over, they wouldn't be quite as worried."

"So what is it you want me to do?" he asks.

"I don't even know enough yet to be specific. I just want you to be alert to anything, maybe ask around discreetly. And carefully, very carefully."

He promises that he will and, before he leaves, asks

that I give his best to Richard. "I feel bad that I stopped going to see him," he says. "It's just that—"

"He understands."

Franklin leaves, and I head back for my car. It's gotten even darker, and I can barely find it. I'll be glad when I get out of here.

I reach the car, open the door, and get in. I turn on the car and flick on the lights at the same time, and when I look through the front window I get a jolt comparable to maybe six or seven million volts of electricity sent through my body. It doesn't kill me, but it makes me scream really loud.

There, lying on the front of the car, face pressed against the windshield, is a really large man. He's also really ugly, a condition made even more severe by the fact that his large nose seems to be bleeding, perhaps from the impact on the windshield.

I'm not quite sure what to do next. I can't drive like this, but neither am I inclined to get out of the car. The guy could be dead, and dead bodies freak me out. Even worse, he could be alive. Live bodies that look like this freak me out even more.

The next jolt is a tapping on the driver's window, which makes me jump so much that I literally hit my head on the roof of the car. I turn and see Marcus signaling me to roll down the window.

I do so, and Marcus sort of nods in the direction of Windshield Man and says, "Out."

"Him?" I ask, assuming that Marcus is talking about Windshield Man. "Is he just out, or dead?"

"He wants you to get out of the car, Andy. Which would

be a good idea, since we're going to be here a while." It's Laurie's voice, which represents still another surprise.

I get out of the car, but before I can say anything, Laurie says, "Let's take a walk. You can show me this part of the park."

"It's dark," I point out.

"That's okay," she says. "I've got a good imagination."

So Laurie and I go for a walk in the park, leaving Marcus behind with Windshield Man, whose moans indicate he is regaining consciousness. "Any chance you'll tell me what's going on?"

"It's pretty simple," she says. "Marcus was watching out for you, and he saw this guy following you. Marcus then put him on your car for safekeeping."

"Who is he?"

"That's what Marcus is in the process of finding out."

"Did he see who I was meeting with?"

"No," Laurie says. "Marcus intercepted him before Franklin got here."

"The amazing thing," I say, "is that you happened to show up in the same place and at the same time as Marcus and I. Talk about a small world . . ."

"Amazing," she admits.

"What exactly were you doing here?"

"I wasn't sure Marcus was covering you, so I figured I'd watch your back, just in case."

I could give Laurie grief about being here, but I won't. She was here to protect me, to make sure nothing bad happened. It turned out she wasn't needed, but she could have been. Besides, no matter how much grief I might give her, she'd still do it again in the same circumstances—not that she'll have the chance, since she'll be back in Wisconsin in three days.

"How long will Marcus need?" I ask.

"I wouldn't think very long."

We start walking back across the baseball field. "So this is the scene of your greatest imaginary athletic accomplishments?" she asks.

"Yup," I say. "Right over there is where I didn't hit the game-winning home run against Clifton. And the very spot we're standing on is where I didn't make a diving catch to beat Garfield."

"You must be very proud."

I nod. "I am. But as great as those fake moments were, I never dreamed that one day I'd be back here with a big ugly guy facedown and bleeding on the hood of my car, with my girlfriend here to protect me. You can't see it in the dark, but my eyes are filled with tears."

We head back to the car, and Laurie wisely calls out so that Marcus will know it's us. Suddenly the lights go on in the car, and we can see that Marcus has turned them on. Windshield Man is sitting on the curb, in front of the car. The headlights are shining right at him, but he doesn't seem to notice.

He looks thoroughly dejected and defeated. Marcus can do that to you.

Laurie asks Marcus to bring us up to date on what he has learned. Bringing up to date is not Marcus's strong point; he's not the most communicative guy in the world. But Laurie is better at drawing him out than I am, and before I know it, one- and two-syllable words are pouring out of him.

Windshield Man is a low-level member of the Dominic

Petrone organization. Petrone is a charming, intelligent man who just happens to control the most powerful crime family in New Jersey. I have had dealings with Petrone in the past; we have even helped each other on a number of occasions. It is not something I've been comfortable with, mainly because there's always a chance that he will get annoyed and have me killed.

Windshield Man has been assigned to keep an eye on me and report back on my actions. Marcus is positive that he was not sent to do me harm, and Marcus's instincts in the area of doing harm are usually quite accurate.

This conversation is conducted within earshot of Windshield Man, who seems to show no interest in it at all. He perks up a bit when Marcus inquires what I would like to do with him. The way he asks the question, I assume my options range from letting him go to dumping his dismembered body in the river.

I opt for letting him go, after Marcus and Laurie assure me that he will not go back and accurately report what has happened to his mob bosses. To do so would not be good for his job security, or his life expectancy.

We send Windshield Man walking off into the darkness. "I'm gonna miss his wit," I say. Laurie and I get into the car to leave, and Marcus declines a ride. I have no idea how he got here, but he's clearly going back the same way.

It's only a five-minute ride home, and Laurie and I talk about the situation while taking Tara and Reggie for their nightly walk.

"The list of things I don't understand keeps getting longer," I say.

"What do you mean?"

"Well, for instance, let's assume Petrone sent someone to kill me on the highway. Why would he then have Windshield Man just watching me? What have I done in the last two weeks that could have changed Petrone's mind about killing me?"

"I don't think you can make that assumption. Maybe it wasn't Petrone who sent the shooter on the highway," she says.

"You think there are other crime bosses out there sending hoods out after me? Maybe there's a competition to see who can kill me first."

She shrugs. "I don't know. But while it's obvious that Petrone has an interest in this, he clearly isn't the only one."

"Keep going . . . ," I prompt.

"Well, there's whoever planted the tap on your phone. Whether it's some secret government agency or just someone with access to their equipment, it wasn't Petrone. And don't forget, there is also the person who murdered Stacy Harriman."

"That could be Petrone," I say.

She shakes her head. "I don't think so—it's not his style."

"To set it up to look like a murder-suicide? If he was doing it so that he could get Richard out of the way, so he could smuggle something into the country, that was the best way for him. He left no reason for anyone to suspect it had to do with Richard's job."

"I understand that," she says. "But it falls apart with the pills—or the injection. Doing it that way was leaving it to chance. Petrone would have set it up to look like

Richard put a gun in his mouth and pulled the trigger. It removes the chance of survival."

It's a good point, and one I hadn't thought of. "So how do I find out what interest Petrone has in this?"

"You could ask him," she says.

Yes, I could.

• • • • •

VINCE SANDERS KNOWS pretty much every person in America.

And those he doesn't know, he can get to. He has a Rolodex slightly larger than Poland. It has always struck me as an incongruity that a person as disagreeable as Vince would connect himself to humanity in this fashion, but I've come to believe he wants to be able to genuinely dislike as many people as possible.

Vince has always had a relationship with Petrone, and he has occasionally served as a conduit between me and the crime boss. Now that I have decided to confront Petrone and question him about his connection to the Evans case, my logical move is to contact Vince and ask him to set it up.

"Why should I?" he asks.

"What do you mean, why should you?"

"Which part of the question didn't you understand? Why should I get you in to see Petrone?"

"Because we're friends and because it's important to me."

"You want to try again?" he asks.

"Because it's in connection with the Evans case, and if a big story comes out of it, you'll be the first to get it."

"Always happy to help a friend," he says. "You got a tuxedo?"

"I do."

"Then put it on; I'll pick you up at seven o'clock tonight."

I'm not understanding this. "I need to wear a tuxedo to meet with Dominic Petrone?"

"Tonight you do. Read my newspaper."

Click.

A quick check of Vince's paper reveals that there is a charity function tonight. The publisher of Vince's paper is on the board of directors of the charity, as is Dominic Petrone. It is characteristic of Petrone; when he is not peddling drugs, employing hookers, laundering money, and killing his enemies, he is one heck of a public-spirited guy.

To pass the time, I join Kevin as he leaves to interview Gale Chaplin, a former neighbor of Richard and Stacy's in Hawthorne. During the trial she proved to be a damaging witness, describing how Stacy had told her of difficulties she and Richard had been having in their relationship. She had also, according to Gale, expressed worry about Richard's "temper." She was the only witness to say anything like this, and it proved harmful to Richard's case.

Chaplin and her family moved a couple of months ago

to a town house complex just off Route 4 in Englewood. It's a very desirable location because of its proximity to the George Washington Bridge and, therefore, to New York City.

She seems quite proud of the place, and when Kevin makes the mistake of admiring it, she takes that as an invitation to give us what she calls the "grand tour." It is three stories high, and by the time we get to the top floor, I am too out of breath to give much more than admiring grunts. If I ever moved in here, the first thing I would do is interview elevator salesmen.

We finally settle in the kitchen, and Chaplin offers us coffee and cheesecake. Cheesecake is not something I understand. I consider the place for cheese to be on top of a pizza, and I reject any notion that a pizza topping can also be a cake. For instance, I would be similarly opposed to pepperoni cake.

I've planned to let Kevin take the lead in the questioning, but when she starts telling us in excruciating detail how much the value of the house has gone up in just the two months they've lived here, I feel compelled to intervene. "As I'm sure Kevin told you, we'd like to talk to you about your testimony at the Richard Evans trial."

She nods. "I read about what's happening; is it really Reggie? He was such a sweet dog."

"Yes, it's definitely him. That has been established."

"So there may be a new trial?"

"We certainly hope so," I say. "You spoke about Ms. Harriman confiding in you that she and Richard were having problems . . ."

"Yes."

"And that she was fearful of him, of his temper."

"Yes."

"Were you and she close?" Kevin asks.

"No, not at all. But she came over for coffee one day, and it just started pouring out. Like she had been holding it in and had to finally tell someone."

"Did it surprise you?"

She nods vigorously. "Very much; my husband, Frank, and I had liked Richard. He was always such a nice neighbor. But when the murder happened, I felt like I had to tell what I knew."

"How long before the murder was your conversation?"

"About two weeks," she says.

"And she never mentioned anything after that?"

"No, I don't think we even talked again. She was never really that friendly; most of the time she just seemed to keep to herself. I don't think she was a very happy person."

"Why do you say that?" Kevin asks.

"Well, for instance, we both grew up near Minneapolis, but she wouldn't talk much about it. She seemed well read and quite capable of talking about many subjects, as long as the subject wasn't herself."

"Any idea why that was?"

"Well, Richard mentioned one day that she had a difficult childhood. And then there were the problems with Richard. People from abusive households often enter into abusive relationships when they become adults. Don't they?"

I'm not really up for psychobabble now; I'm in my pre-tuxedo bad mood. "I'll have to get back to you on that," I say. "I TiVo'd *Dr. Phil.*"

Kevin and I leave, and I drop him off at the office before heading home. He's worried about my meeting with Petrone but agrees to my request to call Marcus and tell him not to interfere.

I had left a message for Laurie that I was going to a black-tie gathering, and told her she was more than welcome to come along. My investigative instincts help me anticipate her answer before she says anything; she is wearing sweatpants and has put my tuxedo out on the bed.

I don't know much about fashion history, and as an example, I don't know who invented the tuxedo. But whoever the father of the tuxedo might have been, he should have been neutered as a child. The tuxedo is as dumb an item as exists on the planet.

Actually, maybe the invention was a joint effort; maybe it was idiocy by committee. One dope created the bow tie, another the suspenders, another the iridescent shoes, and still another the ridiculous cummerbund.

As bad as each item is, when they are put together, especially on my body, they reach a perfect symmetry of awfulness. If you put me in Giants Stadium with sixty thousand men wearing tuxedos, I would still feel as though everybody were staring at me. I don't just *feel* stupid when I wear a tuxedo. I am by definition stupid, or I wouldn't be wearing one.

I go outside at 6:55 to wait for Vince to arrive, and he is characteristically late. That leaves me standing, penguin style, in front of the house, waving to smiling neighbors dressed in normal clothing.

Vince finally arrives, and I get in the car. He is dressed in khaki pants and a sports jacket with a shirt open at the neck.

"Well, don't you look snappy!" he says.

I'm about to take my cummerbund off and strangle him with it. "You told me to wear a tuxedo."

He laughs. "I was kidding. It's a casino night. Where do you think we're going, Monte Carlo?"

"So nobody else is going to be dressed like this?" I ask.

Another laugh. "You got that right."

I tell Vince to wait, and I go back into the house. Within ten minutes I'm dressed like a normal human being and back in the car. "That was your idea of a joke?" I ask.

"No, the way you looked in that monkey suit is my idea of a joke."

I'm so pissed at Vince that I don't talk to him for the twenty-minute ride to our destination. He spends most of the time whistling and listening to the Mets game; I don't think my silent treatment is bringing him to his knees.

The charity event is being held at a ballroom called the Fiesta, on Route 17 in Hasbrouck Heights. Vince parks in the general parking area rather than using the valet service, explaining that with the valet it will take too long to get out. The true reason is that this way there will be no one for him to have to tip.

We walk into the lobby, where we are required to pay for entry and to buy chips. It costs me five hundred dollars, plus another five hundred for Vince, who seems to have forgotten where his checkbook might be. Vince tells me that it's tax deductible, as if I should be grateful for the opportunity he's giving me.

Once I've paid we enter the ballroom, which is already quite crowded. There are bars in all four corners of the room, and blackjack, roulette, and craps tables

are set up throughout. The only people wearing tuxedos are the dealers.

Casino nights are among the more ridiculous inventions
of modern man. The chips we have purchased are merely
props that give us something to gamble with; they are not
worth any money. The only problem is that gambling is
one hundred percent about money; it is essential to the
process.

I glance over at a blackjack table where a woman is ag-
onizing over whether to double down with eleven against
a dealer showing nine. She just can't decide whether she
wants to risk five worthless chips or ten worthless chips.
Her children's college education might well be on the
line.

Gambling without money is like playing baseball without a bat and a ball. It's goofy. Yet everywhere I look, people are laughing and having fun. What kind of a world is
this? Why can't these people spend their time doing something productive, something worthwhile?

They need only look at me to follow my example. I am
here to meet with the leading crime figure in New Jersey,
to find out if he is trying to kill me. My mother would be
proud.

"Where's Petrone?" I ask Vince.

"How the hell should I know?"

"You said he'd be here and that he would talk to me."

"And he will. Just relax; play some blackjack."

I hold up the chips with disdain. "With these?"

"I'll take them," he says, and goes off to play with both
his chips and mine.

"I'll be at the bar," I say, and that's exactly where I
head.

I'm on my third Bloody Mary when two men, each ten years younger, four inches taller, and forty pounds heavier than me, walk over. Their very presence is menacing to me, and I instantly wish I were at one of the tables playing fake blackjack.

"This way," one of them says, and they start walking toward the back exit door. My mind decides to follow them, but my legs don't seem to be impressed, and I just stand there without moving.

The two men are out the door before they realize I'm not behind them, and they come back. "You coming, or what?"

I nod, and with an enormous effort, I actually start moving. I follow them out the door and down a corridor. They stop, and one of the men frisks me to make sure I'm not armed or wearing a wire.

I'm not a big frisking fan, whether I'm the frisker or the friskee. I prefer the honor system, but these two guys don't seem familiar with that system. They probably didn't go to West Point.

Satisfied that I'm not carrying an M-16 in my pocket, they then open a door and stand by it, waiting for me to enter. I do so, and they follow me in.

Petrone sits in an armchair, watching the Mets game on a large-screen television. It appears that we are in some kind of reception area where pictures are taken of wedding couples or Bar Mitzvah boys who have their parties in this facility.

Both men take positions, standing with their backs to the walls. "What's the score?" I ask.

Petrone doesn't answer or even acknowledge my presence. It's not until the end of the inning leads to a commercial that he looks at me. "I understand you want to talk to me," he says. "You have three minutes."

I nod; right now three minutes feels like two too many. "I am representing Richard Evans. He did not murder his fiancée."

Petrone doesn't say a word, just waits for me to continue.

"I need to find out what really happened, and I think the truth is tied into his job with U.S. Customs."

Still no response, which is not unreasonable, since I haven't asked a question.

"I've been followed, shot at, and had my phone tapped, and I have reason to believe that you know a great deal about what is going on, and why."

Still no response; he just stares at me. I don't think it's with admiration.

"You can jump in whenever you want," I say.

"I have not ordered that you be killed; it is not something that interests me either way," he says. "That is why you are still alive. But you have the potential to interfere with something that does interest me, and you would be well advised to be very careful."

"So you didn't have me shot at on the turnpike?"

He doesn't respond, and I assume it's because he's already answered the question by saying he didn't order me killed. Instead he looks at his watch. "Thirty seconds."

"Okay. I have no desire to interfere in your activities; all I want to do is get an innocent man out of jail. But to help me in my noninterference, can you tell me anything about the night of the murder?"

He thinks for a few moments, as if measuring his response. "You lawyers have a tendency to go from A to B to C to D. Sometimes A doesn't lead to D. Sometimes they are on two entirely different roads."

"That might be a little cryptic for me," I say. "Can I assume you have no interest in the Evans case? Is that what you're telling me?"

"That is what I'm telling you. But I am also telling you to be very careful."

He turns back to the game, thus announcing that my presence is no longer welcome. I turn and leave, and the two men follow me until I'm back in the main casino room.

I spot Vince at a craps table, his arm around the woman standing next to him. There is a large pile of chips in front of them. "Okay," I say. "I spoke to him. Let's get out of here."

He turns and looks at me, then at the woman he has his arm around, then back at me. Finally he picks up one of his chips and hands it to me. "Here, kid. Get yourself a cab."

● ● ● ● ●

I WAKE UP to the whirring sound of my exercise bike.

It is not a sound that I hear frequently, since I have long treated the bike as a piece of furniture. Of course, it has more than just aesthetic value; I use the handlebars as a place to hang shirts.

Once I am able to pry my eyes open, I look over and see Laurie pedaling furiously. Her energy level is now inversely proportional to my self-esteem. We made love last night, and it left me so exhausted that it feels as if it will take someone with a shovel to get me out of bed. Yet either I have been unable to remotely tire Laurie out, or she is in a desperate rush to get somewhere but isn't aware that the bike is stationary.

"What time is it?" I ask.

Laurie looks over at me, then at her watch, while continuing to pedal. "Four thirty."

I look toward the window. "And it's dark already?"

"In the morning, Andy. It's four thirty in the morning."

Tara and Reggie are paying no attention to this repartee; they are sound asleep on their beds. "Are you delivering newspapers or just out for a scenic ride?"

"I'm sorry, Andy. I exercise when I'm feeling stress."

"You exercise every day of your life."

"But I usually wait until six."

"Why so stressed?" I ask.

She stops pedaling, comes over and sits on the side of the bed. "Today is my last day here. I leave tomorrow morning."

I knew that, but it still hits me like a two-by-four in the head. I say this despite having no idea what a two-by-four actually is.

"How about if we spend it together?" I ask.

She smiles. "I'd like that. What did you have in mind?"

"Well, how about if we get dressed and go into the city?" I don't have to specify which city; any time someone in North Jersey mentions "the city," they're talking about New York.

Laurie reacts, surprised that I would say that, since she knows I'm not a big fan of driving into the city. "What for?"

"I thought maybe we could spend some time in the Bronx talking to people who knew one of the guys that tried to kill me."

She smiles again. "You really know how to show a girl a good time."

I shrug. "I'm just an incurable romantic."

Antwan Cooper, the driver for Archie Durelle the night they shot at Sam Willis and me, lived on Andrews Avenue in the Bronx. It is just across the street from the campus of Bronx Community College, which took it over from NYU in the seventies.

The campus seems like an idyllic oasis in the midst of what is a very depressed, run-down area. The people who live in houses like Antwan's have a hell of a lot more to worry about in their daily lives than chemistry homework.

Laurie and I pull up in front of the house, which seems to defy the laws of physical construction just by the fact that it is standing. There are holes in the structure where there should not be holes, and boards over where there should be holes, such as the windows. Above the front door there is the outline of Greek lettering, indicating that this was once a fraternity or sorority house.

Sitting on the stairs is a very large young man who looks frozen in time, like a statue. His 250 or so pounds are sort of folded over, his chin resting almost on his knees. His clothing is nondescript except for a Mets hat and outlandish new sneakers that probably set him back two hundred and fifty dollars. He gives absolutely no indication that he has even seen us pull up, or that he is alive.

We get out of the car, and I immediately realize that Laurie and I are about to reverse the traditional male-female roles, as we always do in situations like this. I am by nature a physical coward, and what I perceive to be dangerous surroundings intimidate me. She is a trained police officer, used to threatening situations, and if she is worried, she certainly does not show it. Laurie and I both know that I'm glad she's here.

I am still somewhat nervous about this. We are going to try to talk to people who were friends or family of a man who tried to murder me, who was killed in the process, and we are doing so in a place that does not exactly look open and inviting.

"We don't need to be doing this," I say.

"It'll be fine, Andy."

"We haven't even gotten the new trial."

Before she can answer, a car pulls up behind ours, and Marcus gets out. He most likely has judged this to be a time when staying in the background is not enough, and he wants to be present and accounted for if unpleasantness should break out. Suffice it to say that his presence changes my outlook somewhat.

I dare somebody to mess with Marcus and me.

Laurie and I approach the house, and Statue Man finally moves, albeit slightly. He tilts his head to follow our progress, and the look on his face is not particularly welcoming.

"Can you tell us what apartment Antwan Cooper lived in?"

"Get lost."

"We're looking for someone who knew him, maybe a family member that we can talk to."

"Get fucking lost," he says, slowly standing up. This is not going well.

"Tell him the number." It's Marcus's voice; he has approached and is standing just behind us.

Statue Man looks over and sees Marcus. He sizes him

up for a moment, then looks back at me. "Two B," says Statue Man.

We reach the front door and I attempt to ring the bell, though no sound can be heard. Laurie doesn't do or say anything, so I knock on the door a few times, but it doesn't seem to attract any attention. "We appear to be thwarted," I say.

Laurie frowns and turns the doorknob. The door swings wide open. I graciously let her enter first. The interior is predictably depressing, with a narrow, dark corridor with six apartment doors, and a staircase leading upstairs. Since Statue Man said we should go to 2-B, we head up the stairs. As we climb, I look back and see that Marcus has taken a position at the bottom of the stairs, thereby positioning himself as an impenetrable barrier between Statue Man and us. If the Alamo walls were that reliable, Davy Crockett would have spent his declining years in a condo in Boca Raton.

The second floor is identical to the first, and the B apartment is the second door on the right. Since I am apparently the designated knocker, I try my luck.

"Yeah?" a voice calls out from within the apartment.

"We want to talk to you about Antwan Cooper," I say through the door.

"You cops?"

That's a tough question to answer, and not just because Laurie is a cop and I'm not. It's tough because I'm not sure which answer will get whoever's inside to open the door and talk to us.

I decide to avoid the question. "Can we come in?"

"Nobody's stopping you."

I take that as an invitation to open the door, but Laurie motions for me to wait a moment. She has apparently decided that caution is called for, and she takes out her handgun, concealing it at her side. She gives me the okay, and I open the door.

The apartment is sparsely furnished but looks neat and cared for. Sitting at a small table is a teenager, maybe fifteen years old. He is obviously whom we were speaking with, but his voice sounds older. His eyes look even older than that.

"So, you cops?"

"I'm a lawyer," I say. "Did you know Antwan Cooper?"

"They want to talk about Pops," he says, and I realize he's talking to someone else. I look over, and there's a middle-aged woman standing in the doorway between this room and the kitchen. She is holding a kitchen towel in her hand.

She looks at us. "What about?"

"Was he your husband?"

She looks at me evenly and says with considerable pride, "He was. Now, who are you?"

"My name is Andy Carpenter. This is Laurie Collins. Just before your husband died, the passenger in the car he was driving tried to kill me."

"I'm sorry about that. I'm sure Antwan meant you no harm."

"Do you know why he was driving the car?"

"That man paid him five hundred dollars."

"Archie Durelle?"

"I didn't know his name," she says. "But Antwan knew him. He trusted him. Said when you fight next to a man, that was all you needed to know about him."

"Were they in the Army together?" Laurie asks.

"Yes. But Antwan didn't recognize him at first. I think 'cause he hadn't seen him in a long time. He just showed up one day, said he needed a favor, and that he would pay Antwan five hundred dollars."

"And Antwan didn't ask what the favor was?"

She looks at me as if I'm not the brightest bulb in the chandelier. "It was five hundred dollars."

"What happened to the money?" Laurie asks.

"He had it when he died. You think I'll ever see it?" It's a rhetorical question; she knows the answer all too well.

I reach into my pocket and take out a fistful of cash. I've taken to carrying a lot of it lately, ever since a cash machine ate my card a couple of months ago. I have a little over six hundred dollars, which I put on the table. "Thank you for the information," I say. "I'm sorry for your loss."

As we turn to leave, the teenager says, "How'd you get past Little Antwan downstairs?"

He must be talking about Statue Man, who could only be called "little" in comparison to the Chrysler Building. "You call him 'Little Antwan'?"

"Yeah."

"He's downstairs talking to little Marcus."

We leave, and once we close the door behind us, Laurie says with a smile, "Now you're paying for information?"

"Why not? Who am I, *Sixty Minutes*?"

● ● ● ● ●

LAURIE COMES BACK to the office with me for a meeting with Kevin.

These meetings are basically of dubious value, since all we seem to do is list the things we don't understand in our preparation for a trial we don't know will even take place.

It's the first chance I've had to tell Kevin about my meeting with Petrone. When I get to the part where Petrone denied trying to have me killed, Kevin asks, "And you believed him?"

"I did."

"Just because that's what he said?"

I nod. "As stupid as it might sound, yes. I've had dealings with him before, and he's always told me the truth, or nothing at all. And he had nothing to gain by lying."

"Andy, the guy has had a lot of people murdered. How many confessions has he made?"

"I think Andy's right," Laurie says. "If he admitted that he was behind the shooting, there's nothing Andy could have done about it. He could still easily have denied it later. And if he is trying to scare Andy off of the case, saying that he was out to kill him would have been more effective."

I nod. "You got that right."

"Okay," Kevin says. "Petrone wasn't trying to kill you, but somebody was. Unless it was a random shooting."

I shake my head. "No chance. Durelle specifically went to hire Cooper to be the driver for the attempt. He paid him five hundred bucks. Random shooters don't do that kind of thing."

"So the question is, who was Durelle and what did he have against you?"

"Right," I say. "And I'm betting the answer has to do with the Army. That's how Durelle knew Cooper, and Durelle was in the service when he apparently faked his own death. And it also might explain why the government was tapping my phone. Cindy Spodek said it could have been the Defense Intelligence Agency."

"This sounds like a job for my brother-in-law," Kevin says. "I'm glad I send him a birthday card every year."

Kevin's brother-in-law is Colonel Franklin Prentice, stationed at Fort Jackson, South Carolina. He was nice enough to help us on a previous case, and at the time he was only a lieutenant colonel. Now that's he's moved up a notch, maybe we can get him to solve the case for us.

Kevin will call him to learn all he can about Archie Durelle, the shooter who was killed in the helicopter crash and who came back to life. I'm particularly interested in whatever contact he and Antwan Cooper had in the service, and who else was on the copter with Durelle when it went down. If Durelle didn't die, maybe they didn't, either.

Laurie and I head home to enjoy our last night together before she goes back to Wisconsin. Wild and crazy pair that we are, we're going to spend it by ordering in a pizza and watching a movie on DVD. We each have our role to play. I order the pizza and she chooses the movie.

She chooses *Inherit the Wind,* which is one of the few lawyer movies that I can tolerate. I especially like when Spencer Tracy, playing Clarence Darrow, gets to crucify the opposing lawyer, William Jennings Bryan, played by Fredric March. I've wanted to cross-examine a few prosecutors in my day. The fact that the prosecutor then literally collapses and dies when making a speech in the courtroom is as good an ending as you're going to find anywhere.

We eat the pizza while watching the movie, carefully saving the crusts for Tara and Reggie. They have completely different eating styles. Tara virtually inhales the crusts in a matter of moments, while Reggie savors them, chewing slowly and carefully, then licking his lips clean after each one. The net effect is to have Tara finished and watching him, probably hoping in vain that he won't finish. It must drive her nuts.

Laurie and I share a bottle of Rombauer chardonnay, though the dogs don't get to sample it. Our drinking styles mirror the way the dogs eat. Laurie slips her wine slowly, while I chug it down like an ice-cold Pepsi on a hot day.

I know nothing about wine, but this tastes pretty good. Of course, in this setting I could serenely sip gasoline. "Mr. Carpenter, might I recommend an '88 Chevron? Or perhaps a '91 Texaco? Both are fruity and quite flammable."

Laurie doesn't say much all night, and it isn't until

we've made love that she decides it's time to talk. It's unfortunate, because I have already come to the conclusion that it's time to sleep.

"Andy, I'm going to tell you something because I think we should be open and honest."

Uh-oh, I think, bracing for what is going to come next.

"I'm taking a risk by saying this."

I don't say anything, because I find it hard to talk and cringe at the same time.

"Andy, I think that if you told me the only way to keep us together would be for me to move back here, I would move. That's how important you are to me."

This conversation just took a turn for the better. "I feel the same way about you," I say, and then worry that I may have just offered to move to Wisconsin.

If I made the offer, thankfully she doesn't pick up on it. "I love where I live, Andy, and I love my job, but I would give it all up if that were necessary to keep you."

My mind is racing for a way to appear understanding and generous and yet actually get her to move back here. "I would never want you to give that up," I say. My mind obviously didn't pull off the trick.

"And you'll tell me if that changes? Because right now I love you more than ever."

"I'll tell you," I say, knowing I won't, because then she'd love me less than ever.

In the morning we have a quick breakfast, and I drive Laurie to the airport. We don't talk about when we will see each other again, because we both know it might be quite a while. She's used up her vacation, and if we get the new trial for Richard, I'm going to be intensely occupied with it.

I'll still be jealous and worried about what she might be doing in Wisconsin, and who she might be doing it with. That usually begins about twenty-four hours after she gets on the plane to go home. She has never given me any reason to be concerned; my jealousy is more about my insecurity than her lack of trustworthiness.

"I wish I could stay and help you," Laurie says.

"You've got your own criminals to catch."

"You'll keep me updated on what's going on?"

She's feeling left out; she's not used to seeing me work a case without her having a role as my investigator. "I will."

"I'm sorry, Andy. I'm having a tough time with this."

"Move back here, Laurie. That's the only way I'll ever be completely happy." That's what my mind is thinking. What my mouth winds up saying is, "It'll be fine, Laurie. It'll be fine."

And maybe it will. And maybe it won't.

● ● ● ● ●

IN MY NEXT life I want to be an Army colonel.

Okay, maybe it's not my first choice. But if I can't be the starting quarterback for the Giants, or an all-star shortstop for the Yankees, then Army colonel is right up there on the list.

People listen to colonels. They follow their orders and don't ask questions. They don't ask if they can do it later or why it has to be done at all. Working for a colonel, Edna wouldn't last ten minutes. What's a five-letter word for "you're out of a job, woman"?

The second-best thing to being a colonel is having one on our side, and thanks to Kevin's sister's choice of a husband, we have a beauty. I'm sure Kevin would have preferred that she marry an internist, but this has worked out pretty well.

Kevin has explained to Colonel Prentice that we need

his help, and after asking a few questions, he made a phone call, and here we are at Fort Monmouth.

It's the second time we've been to Fort Monmouth, and the place still does not look like an army base. It looks more like a collection of civilian office buildings, which is probably what it is about to be. The Army is closing Fort Monmouth as part of their overall base-closing plans. The town, like other towns facing the same situation, is quite upset about it. The base is a source of jobs and revenue that is hard to replace.

Last time Colonel Prentice helped us, he did so by sending us down here to meet with Captain Gary Reid, and he's done the same thing this time. Captain Reid is now Major Reid, and he greets us just as crisply and politely this time. He informs us that he has already processed Kevin's telephone request and has copies of the documents we need. They cannot leave the post or be recopied, he says, but we are free to sit in a private office and study them as long as we want. We are also allowed to take notes.

Archie Durelle's Army record is relatively distinguished. He enlisted in 1994 and entered infantry training. He reached the rank of sergeant by the time he was sent to Afghanistan in 2001, and was a participant in the overthrow of the Taliban. He won a Purple Heart for his efforts, the result of a laceration from shrapnel.

It was about three months later that he was hitching a ride on a helicopter back to Kabul. The chopper crashed in a remote area, and Durelle was killed along with the pilot, a Special Forces officer named Mike Carelli, and two others. One was Captain Gary Winston, an Army surgeon whose tour of duty was up in just three days, and the other was Lieutenant Anthony Banks, a special services officer assigned to assist in Afghani reconstruction. It took a while for the American command to realize that the chopper had gone down, and another significant amount of time to find and reach the wreckage.

By the time search and rescue arrived on the scene, the enemy forces had been there first. The bodies and any-thing else of value had long since been carted off—at least, that's what the report said. We now know the truth is that Durelle's body was never there at all; if it had been, he wouldn't have made it to the New Jersey Turnpike with a gun in his hand—a gun that was shooting bullets at me.

There are pictures of all the victims in the file, but I never would have recognized Durelle. I got only a brief glimpse of him on the highway, and I'm sure I was paying more attention to the gun in his hand. Also, the picture is at least eight to ten years old.

If Durelle had a family, it's not listed in these reports, so instead we copy down the names of the others allegedly on the downed chopper, along with any family contacts they had. I have no idea if the others were involved with Durelle in anything criminal, but it's an avenue we need to pursue.

We leave the base, having gotten all the available in-formation, but disappointed with what we got. I had no reason to expect any kind of smoking gun, but it would have been nice to gain a little insight into what the hell is going on.

There isn't exactly a lot of insight waiting for us back at the office, either. Keith Franklin has left a cryptic message that indicates he has been keeping his eyes open but has not detected anything unusual about Roy Chaney's opera-tions at customs.

Karen Evans is also waiting for us, and I can tell that the stress of waiting for a ruling on the new trial is straining even her natural level of exuberance. She's been visiting Richard every day at the jail, which makes me feel a little better, since I haven't been getting there as often as I should.

"How's he doing?" I ask.

"Not great," she says. "I'm trying to keep him upbeat, but he knows everything's riding on this. Not knowing when the answer is coming is pretty tough, also. Even for me."

I nod. "How about the solitary confinement? How's he handling that?"

She smiles. "I think he likes it, at least for now. He hadn't made a lot of friends there anyway."

"I wish I had some news for both of you," I say.

She nods. "I know . . . and I don't want to be a pain, but is it okay if I hang around here more? It feels like if I'm here I'm closer to hearing the good news."

"What about your dress designing?" I ask.

She shrugs. "I've been working on that at night; I haven't been sleeping much. So what do you say?"

There's no reason to deny her that request, so I don't. "Sure. Come by anytime."

I hang around for a while longer and then head for home. That doesn't cheer me up a hell of a lot, either, since Laurie is back in Wisconsin. But Tara and Reggie are both there, tails wagging and smiles on their faces, and I reward them for their good mood with a two-hour walk in the park.

When we get back I turn on the television to the local news and then play the message on my blinking answering machine. In this way, the newscaster and the court clerk give me the message simultaneously: A decision has been reached in the Evans case, and it will be announced at nine o'clock tomorrow morning.

I spend the rest of the night fielding calls about the up-coming decision, from Laurie, Kevin, Karen, and an assortment of media types. I profess confidence to everyone outside our team; if we get the new trial, it is best if it appears we had expected nothing less. If we don't get the trial, then nothing else matters anyway.

Karen professes certainty that the news will be good, though I can't tell if she believes it or is trying to convince herself. Laurie is supportive and hopeful but really has no more idea about what awaits us than I do. Kevin is typically pragmatic, insisting that we plan our first steps after the new trial is granted. It's the right approach, because we will have to move quickly to be ready for trial. And if there's no trial to be ready for, then we'll still push toward another appeal.

In a lot of ways this is even worse than waiting for a verdict. When the jury reaches a decision, there is the possibility that the client will be free and exonerated. Here we're just hoping for the chance to *get to* a jury. So in a way, a bad decision is devastating, but a good decision is just the beginning.

Tara and Reggie seem to reflect my stress, getting close to me, as if being supportive. It's embarrassing to admit, but I actually feel as though I owe Reggie something, and I don't want to let him down. And not reuniting him with Richard would be letting him down.

Before I go to sleep I pet Reggie's head. "Big day tomorrow, buddy," I say.

He just looks at me, as if not willing to let me off the hook that easily. I look over and see Tara staring as well, supporting her friend against the hand that feeds her.

I pet him again. "No matter what happens, you've always got a home here."

Again he stares at me, the same way he stared at me that first day in the kennel.

I pet him a final time. "All right. Don't mention this publicly, but we're gonna win."

· · · · ·

"WHAT HAPPENS TODAY affects only the timing, not the ultimate result."

I say this as Kevin and I are meeting in a court ante-room with Richard and Karen. In fifteen minutes Judge Gordon is going to announce his ruling, and I'm trying to cushion them against the psychological devastation of a loss.

"We are going to find out the truth, and we'll prove your innocence in court. If Judge Gordon rules against us, it will only delay our victory, not prevent it."

Richard is in the process of establishing himself as unique among all the people I have ever defended. To this point he has not once asked me if I think we are going to win or lose. Usually defendants bombard me with the question, as if asking it repeatedly is going to unearth some secret truth that I am otherwise sworn to defend. Richard either senses that I have no idea what is going to happen, or thinks I have an idea and doesn't want to hear what it is.

At nine o'clock sharp we enter the courtroom, which is packed to capacity and has all the energy of a major trial verdict moment. I have been to some huge prizefights, including the first Tyson-Holyfield, and the electricity that courses through a courtroom at moments like these is similar to the feeling at those venues, albeit on a much smaller scale. One side is going to lose, and one will win, and nothing will be the same afterward.

Karen takes her seat directly behind us as Janine Coletti and the rest of her team occupy their places at the prosecution table. Coletti nods at me and smiles and doesn't appear at all nervous, which has the effect of making me nervous.

The five minutes that pass until the bailiff announces Judge Gordon's entry feel like five hours. Mercifully, he gets right down to it. "I'm going to make a very brief statement, and post the entire decision on the court Web site," he says.

Kevin looks over at me, a worried expression on his face. I know what he's thinking. The overwhelming percentage of people in the room want Richard to get a new trial. If Judge Gordon is going to deliver bad news, he might want to do it quickly and let the Web site do the rest.

This is the way nervous, worried lawyers think.

The judge then goes into all that led to his decision. It goes on for three or four minutes, leading me to start calculating whether my bad-news theory might be wrong.

It's an art form to give a lengthy preamble to a decision, listing the facts used to make the judgment, without giving away what the final decision will be. Judge Gordon has mastered it, and it takes me by surprise when he pauses and says, "Therefore . . ."

He pauses after the word, a delay that serves as a silent drumroll. I can feel Richard tense up next to me, and I can only imagine Karen behind me. She must have exploded by now.

Judge Gordon continues, ". . . it is the decision of this court that the defense has met its burden, and a new trial is hereby granted in the case of *New Jersey versus Evans,* said trial to commence on June fourteenth."

There is not an explosion of noise in the courtroom; it is more the sound of a hundred people exhaling at once. Richard lowers his head into his hands and keeps it there until Karen vaults out of her seat and starts pounding him on the back and shoulders in triumph.

He turns and hugs her and then does the same to Kevin and me. Judge Gordon is considerate enough to let this emotional scene play out for a brief while before gaveling order into the courtroom.

The judge has set a trial date for six weeks from today. It's rushed, but Richard has already told me that he doesn't want to wait a moment longer than necessary.

I pursue the matter of bail, but it is almost never granted in first-degree murder trials, and Judge Gordon does not make an exception here. Richard is disappointed, but I've prepared him for it.

The proceedings end, and the bailiffs come over to take Richard away. "You did great," he says to me.

"It's only the beginning, Richard. I know you know that, but I've got to say it anyway. The case starts now."

He smiles and nods, having expected me to temper his enthusiasm. "Give Reggie a hug for me," he says.

"That I can do."

Kevin and I head back to the office, rejuvenated by our triumph and by the certainty that we will now get our day in court. We both know that it will be like starting a six-week marathon; a murder trial takes total concentration and an incredible intensity.

Unfortunately, as soon as we start our meeting we have to face the fact that Judge Gordon's decision does nothing toward helping us understand what the hell is going on here. If we're going to tell a jury that Stacy was murdered and Richard was set up by some evil third party, we had better be prepared to credibly advance a theory of why it happened and who that third party might be.

The only two areas that seem to hold potential answers right now are the customs operations at the Port of Newark and the Army connection to Archie Durelle. There is little I can do about the customs area other than hope that Keith Franklin comes up with something, so I decide to focus on the Army and Durelle.

I make a couple of calls to set up meetings for tomorrow and then head for home. I give Tara and Reggie some celebratory biscuits, and then we go out for a long walk.

After I take them home I head for Charlie's to watch some baseball and drink some beer with Pete and Vince. "Congratulations," Pete says in a surprising burst of humanity.

"You gonna win?" Vince asks.

"Is this off the record?"

He nods. "Yeah."

I shrug. "I hope so."

He frowns his disdain. "You sure I can't use that? Because that's the kind of quote that sells newspapers."

I update Pete on what we learned about the chopper crash, and I give him the names of Mike Carelli, Dr. Gary Winston, and Anthony Banks, the other people on the flight, just in case he has anything on them. He says that certainly nothing comes to mind, but that he'll check.

"I called a friend in the State Police to see if I could find out any progress they're making on the highway shooting," Pete says.

"Thanks." I had asked him to do that; even though the shooters were dead, a full investigation would certainly take place. "You find out anything?"

He nods. "The case was turned over to the FBI."

This is a stunning development. "FBI? Are you sure?"

"Am I *sure*?" he asks with annoyance. "You think I get letters confused? Maybe they said they're turning over the case to the DMV? Or maybe LBJ?"

His sarcasm doesn't make a dent on me; I'm too focused on this news. "What the hell could the FBI have to do with an attempted murder on a New Jersey highway?"

"That, counselor, is something you might want to figure out."

• • • • •

IF YOU WANT to live thirty stories above New Jersey, the place to do it is in Fort Lee at Sunset Towers. It sits on the edge of the Hudson River and offers its upscale tenants spectacular views of the New York skyline. Its lobby and basement areas include a grocery store, cleaners, and drugstore, making running errands an easy jog. The place is so classy that the doorman is called a concierge.

I've come here to see Donna Banks, widow of Anthony Banks, the second lieutenant who, the records show, died in the same helicopter crash as Archie Durelle. I called yesterday and explained who I was, though I did not say why I wanted to talk to her about her husband. She agreed to see me this morning, though she did not seem pleased about it.

I left Kevin the job of trying to reach Cynthia Carelli, the widow of Mike Carelli, the chopper pilot listed as killed in the same crash as Durelle and Banks. She lives in Seattle, a rather long trip to make in person, considering the small likelihood that he has anything to do with our case.

I stop at the "concierge" and tell him that I am here to see Ms. Banks. He nods, picks up the phone, and dials her number. There must be hundreds of apartments in this building, and his not having to look up the number is impressive.

He receives confirmation that I am expected and sends me up to her twenty-third-floor apartment. The high-speed elevator has me there within seconds, and Donna Banks answers the door within a few moments of my ringing the bell. She is an attractive woman in her mid-thirties, but dressed and carrying a handbag as if ready to go out. Not a good sign if I'm hoping to have a long interview.

"Ms. Banks, thanks for seeing me on such short notice."

"Come in, but I don't have a lot of time. I'm quite busy," she says.

I nod agreeably as I enter. "We could do this some other time, when you're not as rushed."

"I'm afraid I always seem to be rushed."

"What is it you do?" I ask.

"What do you mean?"

I shrug. "I mean your work—what it is that keeps you so busy?"

She seems taken aback by the question. "Volunteer work . . . and I have many friends . . . You said you needed to talk about Anthony."

I sit down without being offered the opportunity and take a glance around the apartment. It is expensively furnished, and neat to the point that it doesn't even looked lived in. "Are you married, Ms. Banks?"

"No. I'm sorry, but I really am in a hurry, Mr. Carpenter. Can we chitchat a little less and get to why you're here?"

"Sure. How much did the Army share with you about the circumstances of your husband's death?"

"They said he was on a helicopter that went down in enemy territory. They weren't sure at the time if hostile fire was involved."

"And did they ever become sure?"

"I don't know. I didn't pursue it."

"Does the name Archie Durelle mean anything to you?"

"No." Her answer was instantaneous; she's not exactly racking her brain to remember.

"Antwan Cooper?"

"No."

"Have you ever had any reason to question the Army's account of the helicopter crash?"

"No. The circumstances are not important. Anthony was important, and his death was important. Whether they were shot down or had a mechanical failure doesn't change anything."

I ask a few more questions and get similarly unresponsive answers. When she takes out her car keys and stands up, it's rather clear that her volunteer work and friends can't wait another minute. I thank her for her time and leave.

There is nothing about this woman that I trust. She was completely uncomfortable talking to me, yet if that came from an ongoing grief over her husband's death, she hid it really well. There I was, asking what should have seemed like out-of-the-blue questions about the event that turned her into a widow, yet she showed no curiosity about where

I was coming from. All she cared about was when I would leave.

I don't believe she was rushed, and I test that by waiting at the elevator for five minutes. Even though she had her handbag and car keys in hand, there's no sign of her.

I go down and get my car out of the underground parking garage. I wait another half hour, positioned to see the garage exit and the front door of the building. It's my version of a stakeout, without the doughnuts.

She doesn't show up, which comes as no surprise to me. I head back to the office, calling Sam Willis on my cell phone as I drive. I tell him that I have another job for him.

"Great!" he says, making no effort to conceal his delight. He's probably hoping it results in another high-speed highway shooting.

"The woman's name is Donna Banks. She lives in apartment twenty-three-G in Sunset Towers in Fort Lee. I don't have the exact address, but you can get it."

"Pretty swanky apartment," he says.

"Right. I want you to find out the source of that swank."

"What does that mean?"

"I want to know how she can afford it. She doesn't work, and she's the widow of a soldier. Maybe her name is Banks because her family owns a bunch of them, but I want to know for sure."

"Got it."

"No problem?" I ask. I'm always amazed at Sam's ability to access any information he needs.

"Not so far. Anything else?"

"Yes. I left her apartment at ten thirty-five this morning.

I want to know if she called anyone shortly after I left, and if so, who."

"Gotcha. Which do you want me to get on first? Although neither will take very long."

"I guess her source of income."

"Then say it, Andy."

"Say what?"

"Come on, play the game. You're asking me to find out where she gets her cash. So say it."

"Sam . . ."

"Say it."

"Okay. Show me the money."

"Thatta boy. I'll get right on it."

I hang up and call the office, to make sure Kevin is around. I want to tell him about Donna Banks and my distrust of her. He'll think my suspicions are unfounded and vague, which they are, but he'll trust my instincts.

Kevin is there, and he tells me that his conversation with Cynthia Carelli yielded little. She has remarried and was reticent to discuss her previous husband with a stranger over the phone. Kevin did get her to say that she had no reason to question anything the Army told her about the crash, and he came down on the side of believing her. If we're going to pursue that further, it will have to be in Seattle.

I don't get a chance to tell Kevin much about Donna Banks, because we receive a phone call from Daniel Hawpe, the head prosecutor of Somerset County, and therefore Janine Coletti's boss. He would very much like to meet with me as soon as possible at his office. He has cleared his schedule for the day, so whenever I arrive will be fine.

It is an unusual development on a number of levels. Just the fact that Hawpe, rather than Coletti, made the call is a surprise, but the entire tone is strange. Prosecutors as a rule spend every free minute they have complaining that they never have a free minute. They wear their overwork as a badge of honor, and for someone on Hawpe's level to clear an afternoon's schedule for a defense attorney might well get him drummed out of the prosecutors' union.

Kevin is busy working on some pretrial motions, so I decide to drive down there myself. I arrive at about three o'clock, and Hawpe's assistant just about lights up when she sees me. "Mr. Hawpe said to bring you right in," she says. "Can I get you something to drink?"

I'm starting to let this feeling of power go to my head; I almost demand a pipe and slippers. But instead I let myself be led into Hawpe's office.

There are basically three types of prosecutors. The first group consists of those who love their work, feel that they are contributing to society, and are likely to do this for the rest of their working life.

Then there is the group that sees it as a launching point to the other side, the defense side, where there is more money to be made. Having spent time as a prosecutor gives a defense attorney some additional credibility. It's like hiring an ex-IRS agent to represent you in an audit. You feel that you're better off having someone who's been on the "inside."

The third group, and the one to which Daniel Hawpe belongs, consists of people who view the prosecutor's office as a stepping-stone to higher and greater political office. Hawpe is maybe thirty-five, tall, and good-looking and might as well be wearing a sign on his forehead that says, "One day you will be calling me Governor Hawpe."

But for now he starts off by telling me to call him "Daniel," and I, ever gracious, give him permission to use "Andy."

"Andy, I've been following your career; you've won some great cases. I told Janine Coletti you were going to be a handful at the hearing."

"Is she joining us for this meeting?" I ask.

"She's been reassigned. I'm going to handle this from now on."

This is a surprise, and probably unfair to her. She did a decent, albeit unspectacular, job. "She's a good attorney," I say.

He nods vigorously. "Damn good. Damn good. This is no reflection on her; we're just going to take this case in a new direction."

"Which direction might that be?" I ask, though I already know the answer.

"It's time to wrap this up, Andy. We don't need another trial, even though I think we'd win it. And Evans certainly doesn't need it. It's time to plead it out."

I'm not surprised that he's making the offer, though the speed with which he's making it is quite unusual. We only got the new trial yesterday. By doing it in this manner, he's looking more than a little anxious, and thereby hurting his negotiating position. He must know that but clearly isn't bothered by it.

"What's your offer?" I ask.

"Time served plus ten. He'll be up for parole in five, and we won't oppose it as long as he's a good boy in prison."

It's a shocking offer. In the original trial, the prosecution went for life without the possibility of parole and got it. Now we've got some new forensic evidence and a dog that didn't die, and Richard can be out in five years. It's generous to the point of nonsensical, and if we accept it, it will be an embarrassment for his office.

"I'll convey it to my client," I say. "But he's already been in prison too long."

He shrugs. "Just let me know."

My hunch is that the decision to make this offer was not his, and that he'd be happy if we turned it down. "I'll get back to you within a few days."

"Going up against you in court might be fun," he says.

I nod. "A real hoot."

● ● ● ● ●

I DON'T WITHHOLD information like this from a client one second more than necessary, which is why I have called this early morning meeting with Richard, Karen, and Kevin at the prison.

"The prosecutor has made an offer, which I will tell you now," I say to Richard. "But I don't want you to make a decision about it until I've described the entire situation."

He nods. "Fair enough."

"The offer is time served plus ten, with an agreement going in that you'll be paroled in five."

Richard nods thoughtfully, not saying anything. Karen says, "Oh, man . . ." Their outward reactions couldn't be more different, but I have no idea what each is thinking.

I proceed to lay out everything that I know about the case. He's already heard a lot of it, but I add my discussion with Petrone and with Antwan Cooper's family, what we learned from the Army files, and my recent visit with Donna Banks. I leave nothing out and, for the moment, do not give my subjective interpretations about it. There will be time for that later.

"I'm not sure what all this means," Richard says, a confusion that I unfortunately share.

"There is one consistent thread that runs through it," I say. "A lot of people, including some in the government, are concerned about what we are doing. Whether it's trying to kill your lawyer, tapping his phone, or offering an overly generous plea bargain, I think there exists a great desire on the part of a wide variety of people that this not go to trial."

"You think the plea bargain offer is overly generous?" he asks.

I nod. "I do, but that doesn't mean you should accept it. It's just very unusual for an offer like that to be made in these circumstances, and my guess—and it's only a guess—is that pressure from very high up was brought to bear on the prosecutor."

"Don't take it, Richard," Karen says. "Andy's gonna win this thing."

Richard smiles at his sister's confidence. He turns and, for the first time, asks me, "Would you really win this thing?"

"I think we'd have a decent chance. There's also a significant chance that we'd lose. Overall, fifty-fifty."

He turns to Kevin. "Is that how you feel?"

Kevin nods. "It is."

"I'm going to be very up front with all of you," Richard says. "I decided the other night, the night before we got the new trial, that I couldn't spend my life in prison. If we lose this, I'm going to take my own life."

Karen starts to cry softly, and Richard kisses her on the head.

"I'm sorry, honey, but it's just not a way to live, and the unfairness and waste just becomes too much to bear. Having all this happen—finally having a reason to hope—somehow, it's made that very clear to me." He turns back to Kevin and me. "So what we're talking about here is not five years versus life in prison. It's five years versus *my* life."

He says all this clearly and almost dispassionately, not looking to make an impact and not looking for sympathy. I think, in his situation, I'd feel the same way.

Richard continues: "The reason to accept the deal, even though it would include the horror of five more years in this place, is therefore pretty obvious. The reasons to turn it down are a little more complicated."

He goes on: "There's Stacy. Somebody killed her, and if I take the plea bargain, we'll never find out who, and that person will never be punished."

"We might never find out who anyway."

He nods. "I know. That's why it's complicated. And then there's the other reason."

I can't help but smile. "Reggie," I say.

He nods. "Reggie. He's not likely to live five more years. Not by a typical golden retriever's life expectancy."

"That's true," I say.

"He's the one who has given me this chance. I know it sounds stupid . . ."

"It's very stupid," I say.

"But you understand it."

I smile again. "I do."

Richard pauses a moment and then looks at Karen, Kevin, and me in turn before speaking.

"Let's kick their ass."

Ass-kicking in the justice system is done a little differently from ass-kicking in, say, the National Football League. They use bone-crushing blocks and devastating tackles while we use meticulously prepared briefs and probing questions. They need shoulder pads and helmets to protect themselves from harm; when we see danger coming we just stand up and object.

Kevin and I head back to the office to discuss exactly how we plan to kick the prosecution's ass. They are going to come in far more prepared than they were at the hearing. They'll have better answers for our forensics expert, and probably a bunch of canine lifeguards who'll swear that Reggie could have made that swim in his sleep.

We've been looking at three main areas: the customs operation in Newark, the Army connection from seven years ago, and the government's obvious, though surreptitious, interest in what we're doing. All three are still viable things for us to investigate, but I've been making the mistake of thinking they must be interrelated.

It would all tie together nicely if these Army guys had a scam to smuggle things, maybe arms or drugs, through customs and had to get Richard out of the way to accomplish it. The government could be onto them and be watching me out of worry that I might do something in the course of the trial to imperil their investigation.

Unfortunately, it falls apart because of the passage of time. If they were smuggling arms all these years, there would by now be a bazooka in every household in

America. And if the government has been watching all of it without acting, then they aren't asleep at the switch—they're comatose.

Edna buzzes in to tell me that Sam Willis is waiting to see me and says it's important. I tell her to send him right in, and he comes through the door about an eighth of a second later.

"Donna Banks is getting the money from Switzerland," he says. "The first business day of every month, a wire transfer from the Bank of Switzerland. The account is owned by Carlyle Trading."

"How much?" I ask.

"Twenty-two thousand five, every month."

With that kind of income, she can spend a lot of time seeing friends and doing volunteer work. "Can we find out who Carlyle Trading is?"

"I'm trying, but it's nobody. It's a dummy corporation; the bank wouldn't even know who's behind it."

"How long has she been getting the money?"

He smiles. "That's the best part. It started three months after her husband kicked off. *If* he kicked off."

This is exhilarating news, even though we don't yet know what it means. I believe it somehow ties into our case, but of course, I could be totally wrong. Donna Banks could be getting the money from some Swiss sugar daddy that she started sleeping with right after her husband died.

But that's not what my gut is telling me.

"What about the phone calls?" I ask. "Did she make any after I left her apartment?"

He nods. "She made four in the forty-five minutes after you left. All to the same number. The first three were only a few seconds long; my guess is, she got a machine and hung up. The fourth one lasted seven minutes."

"Who were they made to?"

Sam takes out a piece of notepaper and looks at it. "It's a company based in Montclair, New Jersey, Interpublic Trading. The only name I could find associated with it is a guy named Yasir Hamadi. I've got the phone number and address."

I dial the number that Sam gives me, and after four rings a machine picks up. It's a woman's voice, telling me that I've reached Interpublic Trading and suggesting that I leave a message. I leave my name and number and ask that Mr. Hamadi call me back on a personal matter.

Kevin and I spend the rest of the afternoon in pretrial preparation. In one sense it's easier to prepare for a retrial than a normal trial, since we know what the previous prosecution witnesses will testify to. They'll come up with a few new witnesses, mainly to counter us, but by and large we know their case. Additionally, everyone who has testified is now on the record, and if we catch them in an inconsistency, they can't back off it.

I'm about to leave for home when Karen Evans calls and asks if she can "buy me dinner." I had already planned a perfect evening; I was going to stop at Taco Bell, buy a couple of Crunchwraps, and eat them at home while watching the Mets game. But she seems to need to talk, so I agree to give it all up and have dinner with her.

We go to a restaurant in Paterson called the Bonfire, a place I've been going to since I was a kid. It's changed its decor and menu a number of times over the years, but the memories of going there with my parents have remained intact and unchanged.

Karen doesn't shake easily, but she's been rattled by Richard's revelation that he is contemplating, actually planning, to take his own life should he lose the retrial. "It makes me afraid that I talked him into going ahead with the trial," she says.

I shake my head. "You didn't talk him into anything. He knows exactly what he wants and what he's willing to tolerate."

"You know, these past five years, I've had hope, and now more than ever. But if we lose and he does what he says, then I won't have that anymore. *He* won't have it anymore."

"I don't think either of us can understand what it's like to be locked in a cage," I say. "And to be innocent at the same time . . . It must be beyond horrifying. To this day, Willie Miller won't talk about it."

She nods. "I know, but that same innocence is like a lifeline for Richard; it's all he has. And if he pleads guilty and takes the five years, he gives that up."

Karen's bubbly, irrepressible way has a tendency to make people like me underestimate her intelligence and maturity. She's tough and smart—easily smart enough to be scared of what could happen to her brother.

I manage to turn the conversation to less stressful matters, and she reveals in answer to my question that she has a boyfriend, a third-year law student at Columbia Law. He thinks that their relationship is more serious than she does.

"He's a nice guy," she says. "But there are a lot of nice guys in the world. I want what you and Laurie have."

"Then you should date guys who live thousands of miles away."

She shakes her head. "You know what I mean. You guys are connected; I can see that. Hey, anybody can see that. You could live on different planets, and you'd still be connected. That's what I'm looking for."

I know what she means, though I sure as hell didn't know it at her age.

We've just gotten the check when my cell phone rings. It's Keith Franklin, his voice barely above a whisper. "Mr. Carpenter, I found something."

"Where are you?"

"Down at the port."

"What did you find?"

He doesn't want to talk on the phone, and I tell him I'll be right down there. I hang up and describe the call to Karen. "I want to go with you," she says.

I shake my head. "I don't think so."

"Come on, I'll be like your sidekick."

"Karen . . . ," I say in a tone not nearly stern enough to carry the day.

"Here's the deal: If you don't let me go with you, I'll grab on to your ankle and won't let go, and I'll start screaming as loud as I can." She says all this with a smile on her face, but she's probably serious.

I have never been particularly successful at dealing with strong-willed people, or even moderately willed people, but I have reason to be hesitant to let her go. Last time I met with Franklin at night, Petrone had Windshield Man following me, and something similar or worse could happen this time.

I finally agree to let her come, but I take pains to look behind us as we drive, in case there's somebody following us. I even make a few quick, unnecessary turns as a way to detect unusual activity by any cars behind us. The problem is that my level of competence at tail detection is such that the entire Rose Bowl Parade could be lined up behind me and I wouldn't know it. I just have to trust that Marcus is the grand marshal.

Franklin is waiting for us in the parking lot in front of the main building. He gets right to the point. "I think I figured it out," he says, and leads us through a side entrance, down a darkened corridor and into a warehouse. There is a security guard at the entrance, but he just waves us in once Franklin identifies himself.

"There was a slowdown at the pier today, almost a work stoppage. So that's why some of these things are still here." He points to some huge crates and boxes. "Otherwise they would have been shipped out already."

I'm confused, which doesn't exactly qualify as a news event. "Shipped out? These things are leaving the country?"

He nods. "Right. Everything passes through here, but there is obviously less attention paid to what goes out."

He stands up on one of the crates and then climbs up toward another, which is farther back. He uses a small flashlight to help him on the trek. "Come on up here," he says. He's already pretty far off the ground, and what he is standing on seems rather precarious.

I turn to Karen. "You wait down here so that when I fall, you can call an ambulance."

I climb up after Franklin, though it takes me twice as long as it took him. He uses the flashlight to light my way, and when I get up there, he points it at a crate that has been partially opened.

"I opened a few of these. They went through Chaney's

department, and they were stacked so as to be hard to get to, so I figured I'd take a shot."

"What's in there?" I ask.

"Take a look," he says, and points the flashlight so I can see inside.

The crate is filled with maybe the last thing I'd expect. Money.

I can see twenties, tens and fives, but I have absolutely no idea how much might be in there, other than the fact that it's a hell of a lot of money. "Damn . . . ," I say, never at a loss for a clever quip.

"What's going on up there?" Karen calls out, but neither of us is inclined to answer her just yet.

"The two crates back there are the same," he says. "We're talking serious money."

I climb back down while Franklin closes the crate so that it will not look as though it had been opened. Soon he joins me on solid ground, and the three of us head outside. On the way I tell Karen what was in the boxes.

"Somebody was sneaking money out of the country?" she asks. "Why?"

I've already figured out the answer to that, but I wait until the three of us are seated in my car before I voice it.

"It has to be organized crime; it's Petrone's money."

"Dominic Petrone?" Franklin asks, and if it weren't so dark in the car, I would see him turning pale.

"Yes, it all fits. Don't forget, people don't pay prostitutes or street drug dealers or bookies by check or credit card. They pay in cash, and often small bills. Not only does it add up, but it weighs a lot."

"But why ship it out of the country?" Karen asks.

"Because our banking system is tightly controlled. Get-

ting that amount of cash into it would draw big-time attention. Other countries are not as strict, and once the cash
enters any country's banking system, it's easier to send it
back here. Probably by wire."

"So Petrone owns Roy Chaney?" Franklin asks.

"I would assume so," I say.

"And he was getting rid of Richard so that he could run
this operation?"

"That remains to be seen," I say, although I don't think
it does. I don't believe this has anything to do with Stacy
Harriman's murder and the setup of Richard, but I don't
want to share this with Franklin. He doesn't need to know
our case strategy.

One thing this does explain is why Petrone had been
monitoring my movements. He was afraid that I would
uncover his operation while investigating the case, and
he was right about that. The question now is what to do
about it.

Franklin has no great desire to intervene in a situation
that gets him on Dominic Petrone's enemies list. He is
therefore receptive to my suggestion that we just sit on
this for a while. The country is not going to be irrepara-
bly harmed by this shipment going out; similar shipments
have probably been making the same trip for years. I want
to see if I can somehow use this information to our advantage rather than have it lead to our deaths. Franklin is fine
with that.

As Franklin is about to get out of the car, I ask, "Have
you ever heard of a man named Yasir Hamadi?"

He thinks for a moment. "I don't think so. Who is he?"

"Just a name that came up in connection with the case.

I've been trying to get in touch with him, but I think I'm going to have to pay him a visit."

"Can I go with you?" Karen asks. "Haven't I been a great sidekick?"

I smile. "You've been extraordinary."

●　●　●　●　●

THERE IS NO message from Yasir Hamadi waiting for me at the office this morning. I can't say I'm surprised, nor is it a sign that he is any kind of bad guy. People don't return phone calls from strangers all the time. He could think I'm a bill collector or, even worse, a lawyer.

Sam has used his computer magic to get the guy's home address, and I'm going to take a ride out there tomorrow. I generally like to interview people face-to-face when I'm working on a case, and I'm partial to surprising them by showing up unannounced. There's always the possibility that he won't be home or won't talk to me, but since I'll be going on a Saturday, it'll be a nice drive with little traffic.

Kevin and I spend the day going through the nuts and bolts of preparing for the trial. We discuss whether to ask for a change of venue but decide against it. It's not as if the murder victim were a local person or even that the case drew great attention. There's no reason for us to think we can't get a fair trial down there, and for that reason our request likely wouldn't be granted if we made it.

It's midafternoon when we start talking about the Petrone situation in detail. I do not think that the revelation of Petrone's sneaking money out of the country means that he's involved in the Evans case.

Kevin disagrees. "I don't understand," he says. "We've suspected all along that there might be something going on at customs that would have caused Richard to be set up. Now we find out that Petrone, the head of organized crime in New Jersey, is involved in an illegal customs operation with Richard's replacement. And because of this, we think Petrone is not involved?"

I understand his point; it makes perfect sense. I'm just not buying it. "It just doesn't feel important enough for Petrone to have gone to all this trouble. He'd be able to get the money out in other ways."

"Maybe, maybe not," Kevin says.

"And Petrone didn't hire Chaney. How did he know he'd be able to control Richard's replacement?"

"Maybe he owns Chaney's boss."

I shake my head. "Then he certainly wouldn't have gone to the trouble of setting up this elaborate operation. And you think Petrone's people rescued Reggie from the boat that night?"

Kevin grins. "It always comes back to Reggie."

Before I head home for the evening of Taco Bell and baseball that I didn't get to enjoy last night, I call Karen and deliver on my promise to let her drive with me tomorrow, to try to talk to Hamadi. I won't let her sit in on the interview if there is one, but she can keep me company.

She's quite pleased to join me, and we agree that I'll pick her up at ten a.m.

I take Tara and Reggie on a very long walk, and pick up the Crunchwraps on the way back. It's quite late when we get home, and I've probably already missed three innings of the Mets game.

I hadn't left any lights on, so when I open the door it's very dark inside. The first thing I see is the little, flashing red light on my answering machine, and I go over to press the button and listen to the message.

The voice is Karen's. "Andy, it's Karen. I just got a strange call from Keith Franklin. He said that he needs to talk to me and wants me to meet him behind school number twenty. He told me not to tell you, that what he had to say you shouldn't hear. I said okay, but you said we shouldn't keep secrets from each other, so I'm letting you know. Tomorrow I'll tell you what he said. If I'm doing anything wrong with this, I'm sorry."

I'm in the den, and as I listen to the message, it feels as if the walls of the room are closing in and crushing me. I am simultaneously hit by a feeling of panic and dread so powerful that I have to make a conscious effort not to fall to my knees.

My certainty of the horrible danger to Karen doesn't make complete sense; Franklin could really have something to tell her that he doesn't want me to know. But every instinct in my body doesn't believe it, and if my instincts are right, then the truth is too horrible to contemplate.

I grab my cell phone and run out of the house. I don't know Karen's cell phone number or even that she has one, so calling her isn't an option. Instead, I call Pete Stanton as I drive, and tell him what's going on. He promises to get himself and some officers there as soon as possible.

School number 20 is a grammar school less than five minutes from my house. I will certainly be there before Pete, and I try in these few moments to plan what I will do when I arrive. I don't come up with anything, but the act of thinking helps to lessen the feeling of panic.

The parking lot and athletic field are behind the school, and I drive around at a high speed, pulling to a screeching stop. I want to make as much noise as I possibly can; if a bad guy is there, I want it to sound as though the cavalry is arriving.

It's very dark back here, with no streetlights and little moonlight. I think I can make out Karen's car, but it could just be a shadow. I run toward the back of the school and see a small light above an exit door. Standing there, that light glancing off her, is Karen. The fact that she is standing means she is alive, and the fact that she is alive is extraordinarily wonderful.

"Karen!" I call out, though I am still at least seventy-five yards away.

She looks over in my direction, a little startled, but there is no way she can see me.

"It's Andy!" I yell at the same moment that I see a glimmer of light from the road, off to the right. There is another car there, and someone is in it.

"Run! Run!" I yell, but she is confused, and doesn't move. "Karen, start running!" It is not until I add "Now!" that she starts to run, though I'm not sure she even heard the word, because at the exact moment, there is another, very loud sound. I know what that sound is, and therefore, I know why Karen crumples to the ground. I'm running toward her, but the sight of her falling is so painful that it feels as if the bullet hit me.

I hear another shot, not as loud, that seems to come from a different direction. Karen doesn't look to have been hit again, and it doesn't appear that I was either, since I'm still running.

Karen's prone body is now shielded by the darkness, and for a moment I can't find her. I finally do, and I lean down to her, dreading what I am going to see.

"Andy?" she says, and if there has ever been a more beautiful rendition of my name, I've never heard it. Barbra Streisand couldn't sing it any more beautifully. Karen's voice is weak and scared, but she has a voice.

"Andy, somebody shot me."

"Where are you hit?" I ask.

"In my shoulder. Andy, it hurts so much."

I hadn't given any thought to whether the shooter is still out there, and the sound of a car screeching away answers the question. The reason for that is soon obvious, as Marcus comes running over. Clearly Marcus chased off the shooter.

In the dim light I can see that the upper right part of her body is soaked in blood, and another wave of panic hits me. I quickly call 911 on my cell and request an ambulance. I take my shirt off and wrap it around her. Maybe it will slow the flow of blood, or maybe it will keep her warm and ward off shock.

Or maybe it won't do shit.

It was probably a good idea, because Marcus takes off his jacket and does the same.

"Karen, hang on. Help will be here in a minute."

She doesn't answer, and I fear that she may have lost

consciousness. Within moments that seem like years, I hear the sound of sirens, and Pete and every police officer in the city seem to arrive simultaneously. The area is bathed in light, and soon paramedics have descended on Karen. Pete tries to lead Marcus and me away.

"No," I say, "I want to see how she is."

Pete nods and walks over to the EMT in charge. He talks to him for a moment and then comes back to me. "I'll be the first one they'll tell," he says.

Pete leads me toward his car and starts to question me. He has one of his colleagues question Marcus—as futile an exercise as has ever been attempted.

"Do you have any idea who did this?" Pete asks.

I nod. "It's got to be Keith Franklin. He works for U.S. Customs at the Port of Newark."

"Why do you think it was him?"

"Karen left a message on my machine, telling me that Franklin called her and told her to meet him here. She said he told her not to tell me about it."

Pete leaves me for a moment to tell one of the detectives to get Franklin's address, and in less than a minute he has it. "We're going to pick up Franklin," he says. "You want to come?"

I look over and see that Karen is being loaded into an ambulance. "Any word on Karen yet?"

Pete signals someone who comes over and talks softly to him. Pete nods and turns to me. "She took it in the right shoulder. She lost a lot of blood, but they think she'll make it. She won't pitch in the major leagues, but other than that she should be okay."

It is a feeling of such immense relief that I actually get choked up. This almost never happens to me; the last time

I got choked up was three years ago when I mistakenly tried to swallow a chicken bone. "Let's go," is all I say, and Pete and I go to his car. I'm not sure where Marcus is, but I suspect he'll be able to handle himself.

Pete has called ahead and sent other cars to Franklin's house. We are not going to be the first ones on the scene, but no one will move or do anything of consequence until Pete gets there. He is the ranking officer on the case.

There are few things that I'd rather see right now than Franklin getting taken away in handcuffs, but I have no idea if it is going to happen tonight. I don't know whether he just set Karen up for someone else to take a shot at her or, even if he did it himself, whether he would have gone home afterward. I don't know what the etiquette is for attempted murders; maybe there is a traditional postshooting party, at which the criminal regales his colleagues with stories about pulling the trigger.

We park about a block and a half from Franklin's house, and Pete has the operation well coordinated. Everybody moves in from various directions; if Franklin makes a break for it, he will find himself surrounded.

We're about six houses away when Pete gets a message that the front door to Franklin's house is wide open. Pete instructs me to stay behind as he and the other officers move in.

As I watch from a distance, the area around Franklin's house is suddenly, eerily bathed in bright spotlights, and the sounds of men shouting through the previously quiet street are deafening, even though they do not include any gunfire.

Ignoring Pete's admonishments, I start to walk toward the house. As I approach, I am stopped by an officer cordoning off the scene. "You can't go any farther," the officer says.

"I'm with Pete Stanton."

"That's fine, but you can't go any farther."

After about ten minutes, Pete comes out and walks over to me. "Franklin is dead," he says.

I'm surprised to hear this. "Suicide?" I ask.

"Only if he's a real bad shot. He had seven bullets in him."

"Any idea how long he's been dead?"

Pete shrugs. "I'm no expert, but I'd guess an hour or so. He sure as hell wasn't the shooter at the school."

Without a doubt, Franklin was the person who set Karen up to be shot, and without a doubt, he was not the one who shot her.

Pete verbalizes the questions that are forming in my mind. "You think he was forced to call her? Or did his partner turn on him after he did?"

"I don't know," I say. "I don't know who the bad guys are or what the hell they're trying to accomplish. The only thing I know for sure is that Richard Evans isn't one of them."

• • • • •

EVEN THOUGH I'M anxious to get to the hospital, my first stop in the morning is the prison. I don't want Richard hearing about his sister's shooting from his radio or a guard. I want him to hear it from me.

On the way there I get a phone call from Kevin, who has gone to the hospital to check on Karen's condition. She is weak but doing well, and her wound is not considered life threatening. She is very lucky, or as lucky as a completely innocent person who is suddenly shot by a high-powered rifle can be.

I spend most of the drive trying to deal with my guilt. I'm aware that it's illogical; I did little to involve Karen in the case or expose her to danger. She constantly begged to be included, and most of the time I resisted. Nor did I send her to the school; I didn't know about it until it was too late, and my arrival probably saved her life.

Yet the feeling of guilt is so heavy it feels crushing. I started a series of events that led to Karen Evans getting shot. If there were no Andy Carpenter, she would not be in a hospital, hooked up to IVs.

I get to the prison at 7:45, fifteen minutes before the prisoners can have visitors, even from their lawyers. By the time Richard is brought into the room, I can see by the look on his face that he already knows what happened.

"Please tell me she's all right," he says. "Please."

"She's going to be fine. She took the bullet in the shoulder, but she's conscious and doing well. She's not in danger."

Richard closes his eyes for maybe twenty seconds without saying anything, probably giving thanks to whoever it is he gives thanks to. Then he looks up and says, "Please tell me everything you know about what happened."

I take him through all of it, starting with Franklin showing us the crates of money at the port, right through to finding him shot to death at his house.

"Why would Franklin have showed you the money if he was part of the conspiracy to sneak it out of the country?" he asks.

"I don't think this has anything to do with that money. Maybe Franklin discovered it and used it to throw us off the track. Or maybe he was an innocent victim and was coerced into calling Karen."

"But how could anyone have anything to gain by killing Karen? Who the hell did she ever hurt? What the hell did she know that could hurt someone?"

These are questions I can't begin to answer, and my fear is that Karen won't be able to answer them, either. First Richard was gotten out of the way, and now an attempt has been made to permanently remove Karen. They apparently posed a mortal threat to someone, without knowing who or how.

Before leaving, I question Richard extensively about his relationship with Franklin. He's answered the questions before, though now they have gained far more importance.

"We met through work," Richard says, "but we became friends. Richard and his girlfriend would go out on the boat with Stacy and me pretty often, maybe ten or twelve times."

"Could he have had a relationship with Stacy that you didn't know about?"

He shakes his head. "Not possible." He considers this a moment. "Sorry, I answered too fast. Anything's possible, but I saw absolutely no evidence of that, and I can't imagine that it could have happened. But even if it did, what would that have to do with Karen?"

"Nothing," I say. "I'm just grasping at straws here. Was there anything about Franklin's work that might be viewed as unusual in the light of what has happened?"

"Not that I can think of. We each handled our own area, so we didn't interact at work that often."

"And he came to see you for a while after you were convicted?"

Richard nods. "For about a year." He starts to say something else, then hesitates.

"What is it?" I ask.

"Well, when Keith would come see me here, he'd talk about the job a lot. He'd tell me what was happening down at the port, what people were doing, and he'd ask me questions. I didn't want to hear about it. I mean, I was never going back, but he kept talking about it. I figured my being in here made him uncomfortable, so that gave him something to talk about. But it was strange."

"What kind of questions did he ask you?"

"Procedural things, how to handle certain situations. I had more seniority than him and knew more than he did."

"So he was pumping you for information?"

He shrugs. "I didn't think of it that way at the time, but I guess you could say that."

I leave Richard and head to the hospital to see Karen. She is already sitting up in bed and laughing with the nurses. Her upbeat attitude is truly amazing; by tonight she'll be leading the entire hospital in a rendition of "If I Had a Hammer."

She looks a little weak but far better than I expected. It's hard to believe that it was just last night that I saw her lying bleeding and unconscious on the ground. I look worse than this if I stay up late to watch a West Coast baseball game.

"Andy!" she yells when she sees me in the doorway. "I was hoping you'd come by. Are you okay?"

It's been twelve hours since someone fired a bullet into her body, and she's asking how *I'm* doing. "Well, I might be coming down with a cold," I say, and then smile so she'll know I'm kidding. Otherwise she'll jump up and offer me the bed.

She laughs and starts introducing me to the nurses. "Andy, this is Denise, and Charlotte, and that's Robbie. This is Andy Carpenter, a really good friend of mine."

We say our hellos, and then I prevail on them to give me a few minutes alone with Karen. I notice two books on the side table: *Jane Eyre,* by Charlotte Brontë, and *Wuthering*

Heights, by Emily Brontë. Richard had told me she majored in English literature at Yale.

"You're reading those?" I ask.

She nods. "Many times. They make me feel better."

"How?"

"I'm not sure. Just knowing that people wrote things like this, so many years ago, and that they could feel what I feel. I guess it makes me understand that life goes on and that what happens in the moment is not everything."

"I understand," I lie.

"Have you ever read them?"

"The Brontë sisters? No, but I dated them in high school. They were really hot."

She laughs, which I cut short by saying, "Karen, Franklin is dead. He was shot in his living room about an hour before they shot you."

Karen doesn't say a word; she just starts to sob. It's amazing to watch her navigate 180-degree emotional turns at warp speed.

I give her a minute and then push on. "When he called you, was there anything unusual in what he said, how he sounded?"

"He sounded nervous, but I thought it was because of whatever it was he had found. The thing that he was going to tell me."

"And he didn't give a hint as to what that was?"

"No. All he said was that I shouldn't tell you he had called. God, he seemed like such a good guy—how could anyone do that to him?"

"Karen, whether or not he was a good guy, the purpose of that call was to put you in a place where you could be killed. Now, Franklin may have been forced to make that call, or he may have made it willingly. The point is—and you have to face it—somebody wants you dead."

She looks devastated, shattered, as the truth of this sinks in. "But why? I've never tried to hurt anybody."

"You represent a danger to someone."

"How? If I knew anything important, I would have told you already."

I nod. "I know that. But you have to think about it."

She is frustrated, a completely understandable reaction. "I will, Andy. But it just doesn't make sense."

"I know. And until we can make sense out of it, I'm going to arrange for you to be protected. Both in here and outside when you're ready to leave."

"So they might come after me again?"

She knows the answer to this as well as I do. "They might," I say.

She thinks about this for a few moments, then nods. "So we need to get them first."

● ● ● ● ●

IF POVERTY IS your thing, you probably don't live in Short Hills, New Jersey.

The town projects a serene, upscale elegance, and as I drive through it I find it amazing that I am rich enough to live here, should I so choose.

I've tried twice without success to reach Yasir Hamadi at his Montclair office, so rather than alert him further, I've decided to visit him at his home. Hopefully he'll be home, but if not, I've lost nothing and had a nice drive.

When feasible, I like to interview potential witnesses where they live. People in their offices are more inclined to be brusque and uncooperative, while being at home seems to activate their hospitality genes.

There is no wrong side of the tracks in Short Hills; in fact, I don't see any tracks at all. The homes seem to divide into two camps, luxurious and spectacular, and Hamadi's is in the latter category.

I say this even though I can barely see it from the street. It is up a long driveway from the curb, and the well-treed property blocks the view of most of the house. What I can see, however, is enough to convince me that Hamadi is not anxiously awaiting his monthly food stamps.

There are at least six trucks parked along the road, all with side panels indicating they are affiliated with a local construction company. They must be working on Hamadi's house, since the nearest neighbor is probably a quarter mile away.

One of those workmen is standing next to the truck, looking intently at a large piece of paper, which seems to be a construction plan of some sort. "You working on the Hamadi house?" I ask.

He nods. "Yup."

"Building an addition?"

He nods. "And repairing damage from the storm. Tree crashed through the back of the house."

He's probably referring to a major storm that went through North Jersey about three months ago, sending trees and power lines toppling.

I nod and walk toward the driveway. I'm trying to decide whether to drive up or park down here at the curb, when a BMW comes around the corner and turns into the Hamadi driveway. The driver of the car is a woman, mid-thirties, and the quick glimpse I get of her says that she is quite attractive. She notices me as she pulls in, but doesn't stop. Since I'm driving an ordinary American car, she probably thinks I'm one of the workmen, or somebody here to case the joint for a future robbery.

I decide to leave the car on the street and walk up the driveway. Before I do so, I open the mailbox at the curb and see three pieces of mail. Two are addressed to Hamadi, and one to Jeannette Nelson.

The driveway turns out to be quite steep, and by the time I get to the house I'm hoping that the woman knows CPR. If not, there are plenty of other people who might. The large reconstruction operation is going on near the back of the house, and at least fifteen workmen are back there hammering away.

She has parked her car under the carport, making a total of three cars now positioned there, and is walking toward the front door, when she sees me near the top of the hill. She eyes me warily, and I've got a feeling that any moment she's going to have a mace dispenser in her hand. She also looks vaguely familiar to me, and I wouldn't be surprised if she's a model and I've seen her in magazines or television commercials.

"Hi," I say. I find that clever conversational gambits like that have a tendency to relax people.

"Can I help you?" she asks in a tone that indicates she doesn't want to be particularly helpful at all.

I nod agreeably, granting her request. "I'm here to see Yasir Hamadi. My name is Andy Carpenter."

"Is he expecting you?" she asks, not bothering to tell me her own name.

"Could be. We could ask him and find out."

"He's not at home," she says, and I confess I am doubting her veracity. It was something about the way she said it, and the fact that there are three cars in the carport. Somebody else must be home, and Sam said that Hamadi is not married and has no children.

"Oh," I say. "Then I'll wait for him. Are you Jeannette Nelson?"

She reacts with some surprise that I know her name, and seems a little uncomfortable with it. I can't say I blame her; as strangers go, I'm a little weird. "I'm sorry, but I can't allow you to come in," she says without confirming the name.

I nod agreeably. "No problem. But in case you find out that he is home, could you give him this?" I take out a sealed envelope that I brought for this situation if it arose. Inside is a note that says, "I'm going to be talking about you and Donna Banks on *Larry King* on Wednesday night."

She takes the envelope and goes in the house. I decide not to trudge down the hill, in case I'm summoned within the next few minutes. It's better than walking up the hill again, especially since none of the vehicles in the carport is an ambulance.

Within three minutes, Jeannette Nelson, if that's who she is, comes back out. She doesn't seem surprised to see me standing there. "Mr. Hamadi will see you," she says, apparently feeling no obligation to explain how he will do that if he's not home.

I follow her inside, closing the door behind me. The interior of the house is even nicer than I expected. I'm not a good judge of the value of paintings and furnishings, but it's a safe bet that none of what is here has ever been in a flea market.

She leads me through the house, toward the back, then ushers me into a large den, which seems to function as a private office. "He'll be down in a moment," she says, then turns and leaves.

Her prediction is accurate, as Hamadi soon enters the room, closing the door behind him. He is about forty, at least six feet and in excellent shape, with a demeanor that can best be described as polished. He fits in this house.

"Mr. Carpenter, I did not expect to see you here."

"I tried calling you at your office."

"As do many people. But few come unannounced to my home"—he holds up the note that I wrote—"with so cryptic a message."

"I hoped it would get you to see me, and in fact, it did."

He nods and says, "State your business."

"I'm a criminal defense attorney representing a client in an upcoming trial, and Donna Banks has emerged during my investigation as a person of some interest. In checking into her background, I've learned that she receives a very substantial monthly stipend from you." I say this even though I don't know this to be true; all I know is that she receives money from a company in Switzerland called Carlyle Trading, and that she called Hamadi after I left her apartment.

My hunch pays off. "And you are wondering why?" he asks.

"Correct."

"Ms. Banks is an old, very close friend of mine. She was in dire financial straits when her husband passed away. As you can see, I have been blessed with considerable success. So I have made her life easier without causing any hardship to my own."

"That's quite generous of you," I say.

"I am a strong believer in friendship."

"Does your wife share that belief?"

He smiles patronizingly. "Jeannette is not my wife; she is an employee of my company. She's here to deliver some documents for my signature."

He's lying. She may not be his wife, but she's a hell of a lot more than an employee. Employees don't get their mail delivered at their boss's house.

"So you have no desire to keep your relationship with Ms. Banks secret?"

"There is no relationship, not the way you envision it. But if you feel the need to go on television and tell your suspicions to the world, that is your prerogative."

"Did you know Donna Banks's husband?"

He shakes his head. "I did not. I believe he was killed while in the service. Very tragic."

"What kind of business are you in?" I ask.

"Is that important to your investigation as well?"

"I like to collect information and figure out how it can be helpful later. Is yours a secret business?"

He smiles, though without much amusement. "I am what could best be described as a facilitator. If your business needs something that is difficult to find, perhaps produced in an obscure part of the world, I find it for you and arrange for you to receive it. For that my company receives a fee. Or I purchase it and resell it to you."

"What kinds of things?"

He shrugs. "Could be anything. An unusual fabric, metal alloy, high-speed computer chips, whatever is needed."

"And it all passes through U.S. Customs?"

"Everything that enters this country passes through U.S. Customs."

I ask a few more questions, and he deflects them with ease. If he's worried that I'm uncovering some significant secret, he's hiding it well. Ever agreeable, he tells me that if I think of any more questions, I should call him at the office.

I head back to the city, having learned very little. Hamadi is either a very accomplished liar and villain, or a rich guy taking care of a woman with whom he had an affair. I'm suspicious, especially since his work involves U.S. Customs, but I have nothing concrete on which to base those suspicions.

I call Sam and tell him that I want him to learn everything he can about Interpublic Trading, Hamadi's business. I want to know who he does business with and just how lucrative that business is. He promises to get right on it.

Before heading home I stop off at the hospital to see Karen again. She's not in her room, having gone next door and made friends with her neighbor. If she stays in here much longer, she's going to organize a block party.

The doctors have told Karen that they want her to stay three more days for observation, but she has negotiated that down to two. I'm going to have to make arrangements to protect her, and since Marcus is already covering my ass, I'll need to recruit someone else.

"Do you like all dogs?" I ask. "Or just Reggie?"

"Are you kidding? I love them all."

I'm thinking Willie Miller would be a perfect choice to watch out for her, and since he spends his time at the foundation, maybe she can help out down there.

"I'd really like that," she says when I broach the idea. "Taking care of dogs, finding them homes—I can definitely get into that."

"But you'll need to listen to Willie and do whatever he

says. It will be his responsibility to make sure that you're safe."

"Is he cool?" she asks.

"He's even cooler than me," I say.

"Andy, nobody's cooler than you."

Aw, shucks.

● ● ● ● ●

THE WEEKS LEADING up to a trial are unlike
any others.

For one thing, they are much, much faster. A pretrial
month feels like about two days. The preparation is so intense that every moment is precious, and those moments
just seem to fly by.

The intensity during this period is also without parallel, at least in my life. Every witness, every word that is
spoken, will have the potential to change the outcome, and
the lawyers must be completely ready to deal with every
eventuality. It is the pressure that comes from the need to
cover absolutely every base that is so exhausting.

The period leading up to *New Jersey v. Richard Evans*
has gone even faster than most. A lot of that has to do
with the lack of progress we have been making; it has been

frustrating and has created a feeling, of if not desperation, then of very significant concern.

Kevin and I have looked at our mission as twofold. First there is the need to mount an effective defense for Richard, to punch holes in the prosecution's case and thereby create a reasonable doubt. Just as important is our goal of coming up with a possible villain, someone we can point to and say or imply, "He did it, not Richard." Juries, like movie audiences, like to have a story reach a resolution. They want to blame someone for the crime, and the easiest place to lay that blame is on the defendant. If they can't do that, then they at least want to be given a theory of who the bad guy really is.

It is in this second area that we have the most problems. Hamadi has so far been a dead end; Sam's report is that he has substantial, apparently legitimate business relationships with at least six other companies. We have also been unable to learn any more about Archie Durelle or the significance of his apparently faked death on that helicopter.

Equally puzzling is the government's role in all this. They tried to tap my phone, and the FBI mysteriously took over and put a lid on the investigation of the highway shooting. Perhaps it has to do with Franklin and his job with the Customs Service, but we haven't made the connection with any certainty whatsoever. And juries like certainty.

To complete the circle to nowhere, Pete Stanton has reported no progress on the investigation into Karen's shooting and Franklin's death. There are no leads at all, leading Pete to believe that they were professional hits.

One thing I don't like to overprepare for is my opening statement. I just figure out the points I want to make, without writing a speech or doing much rehearsing. I also like to relax and get away from the case the day before the trial starts, and since tomorrow's the big day, I'm taking today off.

I stop down at the Tara Foundation to see how things are going. It gives me a peaceful feeling to hang out with the dogs, all of whom would have been killed in the animal shelter had we not intervened. They're now well fed, warm, and safe as they hang out in what is a halfway station on their way to really good homes.

Karen's influence on the place has been remarkable. She's added a grooming station, decorated the visiting area in which potential adopters hang out with the dogs, and brought an overall warmth and enthusiasm that had been in short supply. Willie and Sondra are crazy about her, and she about them. Fortunately, no further attempts have been made to harm her, but Willie is ever vigilant.

"What are you doing here?" Karen asks. "Don't you have to get ready for tomorrow?"

"Andy'll be ready," Willie says. "He'll have the prosecution idiots for lunch."

Willie has an overly generous assessment of my legal abilities, but I make it a point never to correct him.

"Tomorrow's just jury selection," I tell Karen. "There won't be much excitement."

"Andy, every single moment of that trial is going to be exciting. And you are going to be great."

I spend about an hour there soaking up the compliments and then head down to Charlie's so Vince and Pete can insult me back to reality. And reality is where I need to be, because starting tomorrow, Richard Evans will be counting on me to save his life.

• • • • •

"THIS IS A very simple case," is how Daniel Hawpe begins his opening statement to the jury we have chosen together. I don't think that either side achieved any real advantage in the jury selection process; we're both going to have to win it on the merits.

"We are going to simply present to you a series of facts, many of them uncontested even by the defense. You will then look at those facts and decide whether or not Richard Evans killed Stacy Harriman, and I believe your conclusion will be that he did so.

"The evidence you hear will be mostly circumstantial, and I'd like to discuss what that means. There is no eyewitness to this crime, no one who saw Mr. Evans kill Ms. Harriman and throw her body overboard. This is true in many, many murder cases. Most murderers don't want to commit their crimes while others are around to observe them. So they do it when they are alone with their victims, when there is no chance for anyone to intervene and stop them."

Hawpe has a smooth, conversational style of speaking, of connecting with his audience. It will serve him well in politics, and I have no doubt he's thinking that achieving a guilty verdict in this trial will serve him equally well.

"But circumstantial evidence can be far more powerful than eyewitness testimony. The most common way to illustrate this is the snowfall example. If you go to sleep at night and the ground is not snow covered, and you wake up in the morning and it is, you know circumstantially that it snowed that night. You weren't an eyewitness to the event, but you know it well beyond a reasonable doubt.

"The same thing can be true of crimes. Eyewitnesses, in the excitement of the moment, can make mistakes. Facts do not make mistakes.

"So we will present you with facts that prove conclusively that Richard Evans went out on his boat one night with his fiancée, Stacy Harriman. Those facts will prove that he crushed her skull and threw her body overboard, then attempted to kill himself by taking a bottle of sleeping pills. Her blood was on the floor and the railing of the boat, and her body washed up on shore three weeks later. She was telling us her story even in death, and we must in turn bring her justice.

"The defense will paint a different picture, but instead of facts, they will use fantasy and wild theories. They will base their defense on a magical dog, and unseen villains who came out of the water like pirates, armed with clubs and sleeping pills.

"None of it will make sense, and it could not be expected to, because it will be up against the facts. So if there is one thing I ask of you, it is to listen only to those facts. And if you do, your conclusion will be obvious."

As is customary, Judge Gordon gives me the option of presenting my opening statement now or at the beginning of our defense case. I would only defer it in the face of an inept statement by the prosecution, which isn't the situation here. Hawpe was effective in connecting with the jury, and he made points that cannot go unchallenged.

"Ladies and gentlemen, you are not the first jury of twelve citizens to consider the case against Richard Evans. Another group of people, just like yourselves, sat in this very courtroom and did the same. And they voted to convict Mr. Evans of the murder of Stacy Harriman.

"Yet we're back here, going through this process again, and there is a very simple reason why. Because in that trial the prosecution presented a series of facts to that jury, a number of which have turned out not to be true. I'm not saying they did so deliberately; in fact, I'm quite sure they did not. But they were wrong, and their facts were wrong, and they will admit to that. So when Mr. Hawpe stands and tells you that he is going to present you with facts, please remember that they are his new version of the facts. And once again, they are wrong.

"Richard Evans is not a murderer—not even close. The prosecution will not be able to tell you about a single violent act he has ever committed in his entire life, and believe me, they have searched for them. He had no reason to hurt Stacy Harriman; they were going to be married. If he had wanted to end the relationship—and he did not—he could have just broken off the engagement. He had no motive for murder, and you will not hear any from the prosecution during this trial.

"Nor did he have a reason to attempt suicide. He worked for the United States government for fourteen years, protecting our shores, and he was promoted four times. He had a great many friends, a loving family, and a bright future in front of him. To anyone who knew Richard Evans, suicide was inconceivable.

"Yet he sits before you today, an innocent man in the middle of an extended, horrifying nightmare. It is a nightmare that you can end by recognizing an obvious truth: Richard Evans has done nothing wrong. He himself has been the victim of a terrible crime, and basic justice deserves that he be set free to live his life.

"Thank you."

I turn back and sit down, noticing that Karen is giving me the thumbs-up from the front row. Richard whispers to me, "Good job," but I'm not comfortable with what I said, because I'm not comfortable with our case. All we have is reasonable doubt, and "reasonable" is certainly in the eyes of the beholder. And these jurors seemed to want to behold Hawpe a lot more than they did me.

Hawpe's first witness is Coast Guard Captain Ron Ferrara. He was in charge of the cutter that boarded Richard's boat that night, and Hawpe will use him to set the scene, and other witnesses will provide background to it. But it is the scene itself that is probably the most incriminating factor against Richard.

"We received the warning at approximately twenty-two fourteen," says Ferrara, using military time and demonstrating that he does not have a great understanding of the word "approximately."

"And then you passed it on to the private and commercial boats in the area?" Hawpe asks.

Captain Ferrara shakes his head. "No, those warnings are sent out over the alert frequency from land-based positions. Our responsibility is to make sure that the boats leave the area and assist those in difficulty."

"How bad was the approaching storm?"

"It was a significant system, but survivable. We've experienced far worse."

Hawpe takes him through the process by which Ferrara determined that Richard's was the only boat not to heed the warnings, and then did not answer Ferrara's radio call. When Ferrara could not see any activity on the boat, he made the decision to board it.

"Please describe what you found when you boarded."

He paints a picture of a placid scene, normal except for the lack of passengers. It was when one of his men went down below that Richard was discovered, lying on the floor, a small amount of blood oozing from his head.

"Was there anything on the floor near Mr. Evans?" Hawpe asks.

Ferrara nods. "There was. An empty bottle of pills."

Ferrara then goes on to describe the emergency medical attention that Richard received. A decision was made to evacuate him by helicopter—risky because of the approaching storm. But it was accomplished, and then the boat was brought back to port to be examined, though at that point no one knew about Stacy Harriman's disappearance.

"At what point did you consider this to be a crime scene?" Hawpe asks.

"From the moment I saw Mr. Evans."

Hawpe turns the witness over to me. There will not be much I can do with him; both his actions that night and his testimony today were straightforward and basically correct. But I consider it important to make points with every witness; the jury has to know that there are two sides to this fight.

"Captain Ferrara, when did you learn of the possibility that there had been someone else on the boat with Mr. Evans that night?"

"I read about it in the papers; I think it was two days later."

"So you found Mr. Evans lying unconscious, with an empty pill bottle nearby and a wound on his head?"

"That's correct."

"And you testified that you immediately considered this a crime scene?"

"I did."

"Suicide being the crime?"

"Yes."

"Would another possibility have been that Mr. Evans had a heart attack and had just taken pills, perhaps nitroglycerine, to counteract it?"

"I never considered that."

"Was there a label on the pill bottle so that you could determine what was taken?"

"No, there was not."

"Any way for you to have known how many pills had been in there?"

"No."

I hand Ferrara a transcript of his radio conversation with Coast Guard command on shore. "Please read the passage where you say that you are treating the boat as a crime scene."

He looks at it but knows the answer. "I did not mention that."

"You didn't think it was important?"

"I considered Mr. Evans's health to be my first priority."

"And mentioning that this might be a crime scene would in some way jeopardize his health?"

He doesn't have an effective answer for that, so I move on. "Please read the passage where you instruct the people on shore to have forensics ready to check out the boat."

"I did not so instruct them."

I feign surprise. "Do you have training in forensics?"

"No."

"Do you at least watch *CSI*?"

Hawpe objects, and Judge Gordon sustains. I then take Ferrara through the process by which Coast Guard personnel boarded the boat. A total of nine people did so, including Ferrara.

"Nine people? How big is this boat?" I ask.

"Forty feet."

"And you and your people had your eighteen feet tromping all over it?"

"We were very careful not to contaminate the scene." I frown with disdain at the very thought. "A storm was approaching, so you were in a hurry; your first priority was the man's health; you had virtually no reason to suspect a crime, but you and your army of men were careful?"

"Yes."

"Did you stop what you were doing to put on booties?"

The jury and most of the gallery laugh at this, which is the reaction I was hoping for.

"No."

Finally, I take him through the bloodstains and ask him why they were not washed away by the rain.

"One was under cover, and the other was on the bottom of the railing."

"That was convenient for you and your crack forensics team, wasn't it?"

Before Ferrara can answer, Hawpe objects and Judge Gordon sustains. I let Ferrara off the stand, having accomplished as much as I could with him. Kevin's nod as I head back to the defense table indicates that he is pleased with the result.

Judge Gordon adjourns court for the day, and I turn to Richard before they take him away. "You okay?" I ask. Sitting quietly and watching the State of New Jersey attempt to take your life away can't be easy, even the second time around.

He grins. "Are you kidding? Compared to what I've been doing every day for the last five years, I feel like I just saw a Broadway show."

• • • • •

TOMORROW IS STACY Harriman's day in
court.

Daniel Hawpe is going to parade a series of witnesses
in front of the jury who know nothing about the night of
the murder but who will talk about Stacy. It is Hawpe's
way of humanizing the victim and making the jury feel as
if they knew her.

It is a standard and perfectly logical strategy. Human
nature is such that the more the jury likes Stacy, the
more likely they are to exact revenge on her behalf. Unfortunately, the only one around to get revenge against
is Richard.

For me it should be a relatively easy day. All the witnesses on Hawpe's list for tomorrow were called during
the first trial, so I know what they are going to say.

The truth is, they aren't going to say that much. Stacy

may have been a wonderful person, but she was not yet well known in the community and seemed to live a very private life. The witnesses will talk about her in positive generalities, but it is clear from the transcript of the first trial that none of them counted her among their close friends.

As I do every night during a trial, I review every piece of information we have that in any way relates to the next day's testimony. So tonight I gather everything we have about Stacy, including information from the first trial, notes from my interviews with Richard and Karen, and the material that Sam came up with when he checked her out.

Sam had described her as relentlessly normal, and there's nothing here to contradict that. Actually, she seems disconcertingly normal. I'm reading page after page about her, but I don't have a real sense of who she was.

Sam's background check provides some of the facts of her life but not much more. It tells me where she lived before coming here, where she worked, what credit card accounts she had, and how much she owed on them.

I've gone over these things at least five times, but this time something about the credit card records strikes me as strange. Her credit report shows that she owed a total of about $4,500 on three different cards, which is certainly not unusual. The strange part is that the accounts are not listed as closed.

I call Sam, who, as always, answers on the first ring. I think he keeps his cell phone clipped to his ear so he can be ready. "Hey, Andy," he says. "What's up?"

"I need to talk to you about some of the things you dug up on Stacy Harriman."

"Shoot."

"I'd rather do it in person; then we can have the reports in front of us."

"Charlie's okay?" he asks.

"Well, my office has more privacy, but Charlie's has better beer. Meet you there in fifteen minutes?"

"You got it," he says.

He's waiting for me when I get there, and once we order I spread out some of the Stacy Harriman pages in front of him.

"I've been going through these reports," I say, "but they don't seem to list her credit card accounts as closed."

He takes a quick look at them to refamiliarize himself, and then he shrugs. "So maybe nobody called and told them she was dead. That's not unusual, especially since she wasn't married. Nobody else was going to be responsible for her debts, so why bother? And Richard wasn't home to receive the bills; he was in the hospital and then jail."

"But these records are current?" I ask.

"Sure, I got them . . . ," he says, and then pauses. "Holy shit." He has just come to the same realization that hit me a few minutes ago, and he looks at the pages more thoroughly to confirm that realization.

"If nobody reported to these companies that she died, then the accounts would be listed as delinquent," I say. "By now they would have been closed for nonpayment."

He nods his head vigorously as he continues to look at the pages. "And if they pursued it and found out that she had died, they would have closed the accounts anyway. There's no way they would just be sitting there like this."

"Here's a riddle for you," I say. "When does a credit

card company show no interest whatsoever in money that is owed to them?"

He looks up. "Never."

"Right. Which means that she didn't owe them a dime. The accounts can't be real."

I ask Sam to look into Stacy's background again but this time to go much deeper. "I don't just want her college transcript; I want to know who her teachers were and how often she cut class. I don't just want her previous address; I want to know where she got her café lattes in the morning."

"I'm on it, boss," he says, getting up. "I'll start right now."

I tell him we can finish our meal and have a beer or two, and he sits back down. I can tell he's anxious to get going, and I want to get the information as soon as possible, so we eat quickly.

When I get to the parking lot, I call Laurie in Wisconsin from the car. It takes her five rings to answer; apparently my calls aren't as important to her as they are to Sam.

"Andy, I just walked in the door," she says.

"You first walk in the door at eight o'clock at night? Where were you? Nightclubbing?"

"Actually, I was doing paperwork in the office. I just came home to change before going back out. I hate dancing in my uniform."

"Before you go, I need your opinion." I describe to her what I've learned—or, more correctly, what I haven't learned—about Stacy Harriman's background.

She listens without interrupting until I finish. Then, "Can you check the other records besides the credit reports more thoroughly?"

"Sam is starting on that right now. But can you think of an explanation for the credit reports never being updated or closed?"

She thinks for a moment. "It could always be some kind of mistake. Maybe some computer glitch that froze her records in time. But she is not just anyone; she is a murder victim."

"That she is," I say.

"So coincidences and mistakes are not to be trusted."

"No, they're not. So what's your take on it?"

"If Sam keeps hitting dead ends—and I've got a feeling he will—then her background has been created as a deception. And it's not a deception that she could have pulled off herself."

"Right," I say. "People don't get to write their own credit reports."

"But there are people who can write them for you."

"Government people," I say. "Witness protection program people."

"It all fits, Andy. The government has been looking over your shoulder on this from day one. If the victim was someone they were protecting, they would absolutely be interested."

"Not if they thought Richard did it," I say. "If Richard killed her, they'd just cross her off their list and move on."

"The strange thing is the time that's passed, Andy. It's more than five years later. I don't know what they could be trying to find out from you or why they took over that highway shooting investigation."

I can feel my anger starting to build. "And if we're right about this, then those bastards let Richard Evans get sentenced to life imprisonment for a murder they damn well knew he didn't commit."

"Let's first find out if we're right," she says, ever logical. "Call me after Sam reports back to you, and I'll talk to a detective I know in LAPD."

In an instant my anger turns to childlike jealousy. "You know a detective in Los Angeles? What's her name?"

"His name is Matt Wagner. We worked together on a case about five years ago. We've kept in touch."

"You've kept in touch?" I ask. What could that mean? Physical touch? Emotional touch? There is no level that I can't sink to.

"Andy, give it a rest. He's worked on a couple of witness protection cases. He knows how they operate. I'll give him the broad picture, no specifics and no names, and see what he says."

"Make sure he doesn't repeat any of it to his wife and six children."

"I will," she says.

"Good night, Laurie."

"Good night, Andy. I love you."

"Then come home," I say, but she has already hung up. I knew that she had, which is the only reason I had the guts to say it in the first place.

I'm on the way home when my cell phone rings. "Andy, I'm at your house." It's Pete Stanton calling, and his tone of voice sends me into an instant panic. "It was broken into, and the alarm company called—"

"Is Tara all right?"

"She's fine. I'm actually petting her while we're talking. How far away are you?"

"About ten minutes. What about Reggie?"

"That's the other dog?"

"Yes."

"What about him?" he asks.

"Is he okay?"

"He was staying at your house?" Pete asks, and the feeling of panic returns.

"Yes. Isn't he there?"

"Andy, there's just one dog here, and that's Tara. I'm reading her name off the tag."

Within thirty seconds of my getting home, it's obvious that this was a straight kidnapping.

Unfortunately, that's the only thing that is obvious. Pete considers it a professional job, yet they took no money, no possessions, and left Tara alone and unharmed. They came here for Reggie, and they got what they came for. They either knew exactly what he looked like, or read his tag.

I think this might be the angriest I have ever been, and it takes an extraordinary effort to put aside the anger temporarily and try to understand what could be behind this.

Based on Pete's feelings about the professionalism of the thieves, and the precision of the operation, I discount the possibility that it was done by teenagers or vandals. Knowing how important Reggie has been to our case, and the publicity he has received, it's conceivable that we will get a ransom demand. That is my hope.

More worrisome is the idea that somehow, Reggie could represent a threat to someone. I don't want to think about the implications of that.

I call Laurie and tell her what has happened, though there is no way she can comfort me. The fact that Reggie is out there and I can't protect him is a constant agony that starts in my head and travels to my gut. And back to my head. And back to my gut.

Next I call Karen to give her the bad news. She is just as stunned and upset as I knew she'd be, as I am. I promise to call her if I get any new information, but I'm not likely to for a while.

I'm not going to sleep much tonight. I'm going to think about what to do next, and hug Tara until she gets sick of it.

• • • • •

I CALL KEVIN at six a.m. and tell him about Reggie.

His reaction mirrors mine; he's angry, confused and helpless. I ask him to join me for a meeting with Richard before court begins.

I had planned this meeting even before Reggie was taken; I need to talk to Richard about what we've learned about Stacy. I don't usually like to spring things on clients until I have all the facts, but we're in the middle of trial, which means we don't have the luxury of time.

If Stacy was in the witness protection program, then by definition there were very dangerous people after her. Exactly the kind of people I can point to in front of a jury and say, "They did it, not my client." So what we will have to do is figure out a way to prove it, and get it admitted as evidence. That will be a difficult assignment, and Kevin is already trying to develop a strategy.

Richard is stunned and disbelieving when we tell him our theory. What is important is not his skepticism but rather his inability to prove it wrong. He cannot come up with a single fact that would give credibility to Stacy's supposed background. He never met any of her previous friends, never visited where she had lived, and never knew her colleagues from work. She had always been vague, and Richard hadn't pressed her, because he suspected emotional trauma from which she was trying to escape.

Her need to escape may well have been more urgent than that.

As we are preparing to go into court, I make a decision. "Kevin, you need to go to Minneapolis."

He's obviously surprised. "When?"

"First flight you can get. You can check out Stacy's background personally, go to her high school, talk to her neighbors . . ."

He's obviously not thrilled with the prospect. "Well, I could do that . . . but . . . I've got sinus issues," he says.

"Sinus issues?"

He nods. "They're inflamed. Taking off and landing could be a problem."

"A serious problem?" I ask.

"Definitely. It could lead to an ear infection. Everything is connected."

I turn to Richard, who has been listening to Kevin's hypochondria with an open mouth. He should be careful about that, because something could enter his mouth and head straight for his ears, since everything is connected.

"Richard," I say, "Kevin has a sinus condition that could

lead to an ear infection if he takes off and lands. So are you okay spending the rest of your life in jail?"

He smiles. "No problem."

I turn back to Kevin. "Richard is fine with it."

Kevin sighs; the battle is lost. "I'll call you when I get there."

Kevin leaves; I think he'd rather be on the way to Minneapolis than have to be here when I tell Richard about Reggie. I debated keeping it from him, since there's nothing he can do anyway, but I believe in being as honest as I can with my clients. Besides, with the police searching for Reggie, it's likely to come to the media's attention. If Richard is going to find out, I want it to be from me.

"Richard, something has happened, and I don't have an easy way to tell you. There was a break-in at my house last night, and they took Reggie."

He looks as if he has been hit with an emotional baseball bat, and it takes him a few minutes to recover enough to ask the obvious questions about who and why. I wish I had the answers to give him; all I can do is tell him that every effort will be made to find Reggie. He doesn't seem comforted by that, and he shouldn't be.

I head into court, though Richard has to be brought in by the bailiffs. I'll miss having Kevin next to me; he often sees and points out things that I've missed. But we need to get a handle on who Stacy really was, in a hurry.

The testimony about Stacy that Hawpe elicits from his witnesses is no more impressive than in the first trial. He starts with two neighbors and two people from Stacy's gym. All speak highly of her, though it is only the last woman, Susan Castro, who describes herself as Stacy's "dear friend." She had not described herself in that way during her testimony in the first trial, so unless she's been attending a lot of séances, she's been influenced by the publicity surrounding this one.

My questions for the first three witnesses are perfunctory, designed to elicit that they really didn't know what was going on in Stacy's life, that they were shocked by her death, and that they knew and liked Richard.

I decide to go further with Susan Castro, since I may need to point out later in the trial that Stacy deliberately avoided having any "dear friends," because she was living a lie. I also do it for the childish reason that I don't like Ms. Castro; she is essentially making this friendship up to draw attention to herself. The fact that Richard's life is on the line is clearly not her first priority.

"You and Stacy Harriman were dear friends?" I ask.

"Yes, we certainly were," she says.

"What does it mean to you to be 'dear friends' with someone?"

She seems taken aback by the question but then says, "I suppose it's a willingness to share innermost feelings, to confide in a person and have them confide in you. To provide and receive comfort and support."

"I see. Let's go through a list of innermost feelings that your dear friend Stacy may have confided in you. Where was she born?"

Castro looks stumped by the first toughie of a question. "I'm not sure; I believe Kansas . . . or Wisconsin."

I nod sympathetically. "I always get those two confused myself. How many siblings did she have?"

"I'm not sure; she didn't mention any."

"Where did she go to college?"

"Objection, Your Honor, relevance."

"Your Honor," I say, "Mr. Hawpe took the witness through a speech about how close she and the defendant were. I have every right to demonstrate that her testimony was completely misleading in that regard."

Judge Gordon overrules the objection, but instead of telling me which college Stacy attended, she says, "We didn't talk about those kind of things."

"Right, you talked about more intimate, innermost stuff. Was she ever married before?"

"I think so . . . maybe not."

"Got it. Previous marital history—yes and no." I have a little more fun with this and then let her off the stand. Hawpe calls Gale Chaplin, the neighbor I had visited in her house to discuss her testimony in the first trial.

Chaplin's recounting is once again damaging. She talks about Stacy's admitting that she and Richard were having problems, and her concern about his temper. She comes off as credible because she makes no claims of great friendship. In fact, she says that she was surprised that Stacy confided in her at all.

Chaplin's testimony is troubling to me on two levels. Most important is the negative impact it can have on the jury. But I'm also puzzled about why Stacy would have had this conversation with someone who was not a close friend. Why make your whole life a secret and then pour things out to a relative stranger?

In my cross I press Chaplin on the level of friendship she and Stacy had, as a way of diminishing the credibility that Stacy would have opened up like that. I'm not very effective, because Chaplin openly and repeatedly admits that they weren't close.

"Did Stacy tell you where she was from?" I ask.

Chaplin nods. "Outside of Minneapolis, which is not far from where I'm from as well."

"So you two discussed your hometowns, maybe common friends and experiences?"

"No, she didn't seem to want to talk about that at all," Chaplin says, consistent with what she told me at her house.

I brought this up in case I am able to bring before the jury that Stacy's background was fabricated. Her reluctance to talk about her supposed hometown will fit in well with that.

It's a small point, the only kind I seem to make these days.

• • • • •

WEEKENDS ESSENTIALLY DO not exist
during a trial.

While court is closed, I still treat Saturday and Sunday
as full workdays, unless, of course, it's an NFL Sunday
and the Giants are playing.

Since this is a non-NFL Saturday, I'm reading and re-
reading my case files within a few minutes of returning
from the morning walk with Tara. It's weird, because he
was here only a short time, but the house seems empty
without Reggie. Even Tara seems depressed about it.

But I have to force myself to focus. The trial is going to
kick into a higher gear on Monday, and even though I feel
that I'm ready for it, there are different levels of "ready."

Kevin calls at about eleven o'clock from Minneapolis.
He gets right to the point. "She never lived here, Andy."

"Tell me about it," I say.

He hesitates. "You'll have to speak a little louder; since the landing I've lost most of the hearing in my left ear."

I yell, "THEN MAYBE YOU SHOULD HOLD THE PHONE TO YOUR RIGHT EAR!"

It's not the answer Kevin was looking for; he was hoping I'd ask sympathetic questions about his sinus issues. When it's obvious I won't, he gets down to business.

"I went to the home address listed. It's a garden apartment complex, and the specific apartment has been lived in by a married couple for thirty-one years. Neither they nor the superintendent of the complex ever heard of Stacy Harriman, and they didn't recognize her picture."

"How many people did you ask?"

"At least two dozen," he says. "All people who have been here for years. She never lived at this address, Andy."

"What else did you find out?"

"She never went to the high school, either. No teachers ever heard of her, and she's not listed in the yearbook."

"But she has a transcript," I say.

"The school administration wouldn't talk to me about it; they said the records are confidential."

"That's bullshit."

"That's what I told them, but they weren't impressed. But the bottom line is that unless she was invisible while she was here, then her background is faked."

"Have you got documentation?" I ask, knowing that he must.

Kevin confirms that he has a folder full of documents and sworn declarations that we can use in court as evidence for what he has found out, if we get the opportunity. "Andy, I never thought I'd say this, but I think Reggie was right."

"What do you mean?"

"Richard is innocent."

"Absolutely. And you should get back here fast so we can figure out how to get him out of prison," I say.

"I'm on a two o'clock flight."

"Take care of that ear. And keep an eye on your nose and mouth; everything's connected."

"Wise-ass," he snarls, and hangs up.

It doesn't pay to be concerned about people.

I hang up and call Sam Willis, who says that he had just been ready to call me. Sam presents more of the same; the further he digs into Stacy's background, the more obvious it is that her real history has been completely concealed.

"And this isn't run-of-the-mill stuff, Andy. "We're talking driver's license, voter registration card, passport, social security number—all issued in fantasyland."

"Let me ask you this," I say. "You've been able to access all this stuff on the computer. Could somebody as good as you, or even better—"

"Better?" he interrupts. *"Better?"*

"If such a thing were possible, could somebody as good or better have created all of this? Some citizen with a computer?"

He thinks about it for a few moments before answering. "No. Maybe some of it, but not all the stuff that I'm looking at. The effort involved would be unbelievable, and even then it wouldn't be this thorough. This has to be bigger than that."

This seems to be the prevailing view, and it's one I share. Another factor that also supports this conclusion is that as far as I can tell, Stacy Harriman never went around trumpeting her background. She was always pretty quiet about it, speaking in vague generalities. If she had gone to all the trouble of creating it, she would have held it out there more.

It's not until nine o'clock at night that Laurie calls to add her voice to the chorus. It's a sign of how exciting my life is that I'm already in bed, watching television.

Laurie has spoken to her friend at LAPD, though she gave him only generalities, not specifics. "He says it has to be WITSEC," she says.

She's talking about the government agency that handles witness security. Contrary to common perception, it is not run by the FBI but rather by the U.S. Marshals Service.

I tell her about my conversations with Kevin and Sam, which only reinforce her conclusion.

"Is your friend familiar with any cases in which they've been forced to provide information about one of the people they're protecting?" I ask.

"As far as I know, that never happens."

"You doubt my powers?"

"Never. But you might want to utilize Kevin's powers on this as well."

"Good idea." I had already planned to meet with Kevin tomorrow, and I'll leave him a message to that effect when I get off the phone with Laurie.

"Any word on Reggie?" she asks.

"No. Pete says every cop in the area has been notified, but no sign of him."

We commiserate about this for a few minutes, and then she asks, "What are you doing tonight?"

"I can't decide. I was thinking maybe a movie and then stopping for a drink, or there's a terrific new jazz club that just opened."

"You're in bed watching television," she says.

"How do you know that?" I ask.

"Because I know you better than you know you."

"You make me feel naked," I say, in mock protest.

"If I were there you would be."

Kevin is over at ten in the morning. He brings his own tissues, since occasionally in the past I've only had paper towels to give him when he needed to blow his nose. He blows his nose a lot.

Kevin also brings some case law research he did last night after getting my message. It relates to previous rulings that the courts have made concerning efforts to penetrate WITSEC; that is, to get them to reveal specific information about people in their program.

The agency has been notoriously loath to provide anything, which in most cases makes perfect sense. Their protection efforts depend on total secrecy; it is by definition a matter of life and death.

The crucial difference here is that the death has already occurred. There is obviously a logical problem in protecting someone who has already been murdered, and we need to use that as a wedge to find out what we need to know.

Kevin could find no specific case law directly on point. Just as it makes little sense to try to protect a dead witness, there has been little reason over the years for people to want to learn who those already dead witnesses might be.

We kick around our options, and though it's obvious that we must go to Judge Gordon, our key decision revolves around timing. The prosecution presumably knows nothing about this, and anytime we know something that they don't, it is a distinct advantage that is not lightly discarded. Once we go to the judge, then Hawpe will know what we know.

Which is not such a big deal, because we don't know a hell of a lot.

Kevin and I come to the same conclusion: We need to go to Judge Gordon immediately. If we can get definitive information that Stacy Harriman was in the witness protection program, the impact on our case will be immeasurable. If such dangerous killers were after her that she had to start a new life to escape them, then reasonable doubt about Richard's guilt can't help but kick in.

We've had two days' worth of witnesses, but this case really starts tomorrow.

• • • • •

"YOUR HONOR, STACY Harriman was not Stacy Harriman."

That is how I start the meeting in Judge Gordon's chambers. Present are only the judge, Hawpe, a stenographer, and myself.

"What does that mean?" he asks. "Who was she?"

"That's what we need you to find out," I say, and then lay out chapter and verse of what we have learned about Stacy's faked background. I leave out the other areas of government intervention, like the phone tap and the FBI's taking over the highway shooting case. To me that stuff adds credibility to our argument but might take the case on an unnecessary tangent.

I conclude with "I have consulted an expert in the field, and the only reasonable explanation that I can come up with is that she has been in the WITSEC program."

"And you're asking me to subpoena the information from the U.S. marshals?"

I nod. "Yes, Your Honor. And to hold a hearing if they refuse to comply."

"Mr. Hawpe?"

"Your Honor, first I would like to assure you that this is the first I've heard of this, so my reaction is an initial one. But I do not believe that the court should become an arm of the defense, to be used to conduct what seems on its face to be a fishing expedition."

I shake my head in disagreement. "If it is a fishing expedition, all evidence to the contrary, then no harm is done, and only a little of the court's time is wasted. If, on the other hand, it is true that Stacy Harriman's life was being protected by the U.S. marshals, then that is of monumental importance to Richard Evans's defense and to the search for the truth."

Judge Gordon nods slightly and turns back to Hawpe. "And your objection is merely a desire to be protective of the court's time?"

Hawpe says, "That and the possible impact of unfounded speculation like this on the jury."

Judge Gordon makes his decision. "I'll contact the U.S. Marshals Service immediately and, if necessary, issue a subpoena."

He goes on to impose a gag order, prohibiting either side from mentioning this to the press. I have no problem with that now, but if we don't get the information, I'll press to have it lifted.

Judge Gordon delays the start of the trial for one hour so that he can attend to this. I'm very pleased with his reaction; he completely understands the importance of the issue.

When the trial resumes, Hawpe's first witness is Lou Mazzola, the night manager of the pier where Richard kept his boat. He was on duty the night that Stacy was murdered, and he testified that he saw Richard and Stacy on the boat as it was leaving.

Mazzola's sole purpose is to place Stacy on the boat, and I have no desire to refute it, because I know it to be true, and others will say the same thing. Nevertheless, it offends my defense attorney's sensibility to let him get away without my accomplishing anything.

"Mr. Mazzola, were Mr. Evans and Ms. Harriman alone that night?"

"They had their dog with them." It's a fact that Hawpe conveniently forgot to bring out on direct.

"Was that unusual?"

"No, he was with them pretty much every time."

"What kind of dog was it?"

"A golden retriever. It's the one I saw on television last month."

I can't help but smile; Mazzola has just made an important point for our side, that Reggie turned up alive recently. I can only hope that he still is.

Hawpe doesn't want to object, because the statement has already been made, and because he doesn't want a fight over Reggie's identity. The court has already made a ruling about that at the hearing.

"So you're certain the dog was with them that night?"

"Absolutely. I kept dog biscuits in my office, and I gave him one every time they were there, including that night."

"Did you notice anything unusual about their actions

that night? For example, were they unfriendly to you, or fighting amongst themselves?"

I know from the transcript of the first trial what his answer will be, and he says that he does not remember anything unusual at all.

"Could you see where the boat was docked from your office?" I ask.

"No. It was pretty far away."

"So you weren't watching the boat before they got there?"

"No. I had no reason to."

"Could somebody have boarded the boat before them, and maybe hidden somewhere that they couldn't be seen?"

Hawpe objects, but I say it's a hypothetical, and Judge Gordon lets him answer.

"I guess so," says Mazzola.

That's good enough for me.

Hawpe calls two more witnesses, mainly for the purpose of placing Stacy on the boat, alone with Richard out at sea. In both cases, I'm able to demonstrate that they also saw Reggie and did not notice anything strange about Richard and Stacy's behavior. Also, none of them were on the boat, so they would have had no opportunity to tell if someone was hiding.

I think Hawpe has made a mistake in calling these additional witnesses. Stacy's presence that night is not in doubt, and the points I am making are damaging him, at least slightly.

After a break in the afternoon session, Judge Gordon suddenly adjourns court for the day and summons

Hawpe and me into his chambers for another on the record session.

"The U.S. marshals have declined to provide any information about the woman we know as Stacy Harriman," he says. "They cited a long-standing principle of
confidentiality and cautioned that we not read anything
into their position concerning whether or not Ms. Harriman was in the program. According to them, their position would be the same whether or not she was in fact
under their protection."

I'm not at all surprised to hear this. "Your Honor, we
would request that you convene a hearing to consider an
order to comply."

He nods. "I already have. Ten o'clock tomorrow
morning."

• • • • •

W<small>HENEVER</small> SOMEBODY SAYS "U.S. marshal," I'm thinking Wyatt Earp or Tommy Lee Jones.

I'm definitely not thinking Captain Alice Massengale, the attorney within the agency who leads a contingent of four into court for our hearing. Captain Massengale is all of five feet four and a hundred and ten pounds, one of the few lawyers I have ever gone up against whom I would be willing to arm wrestle to settle our dispute.

The physical structure of the hearing is a strange one. Kevin, Richard, and I occupy the defense table, Hawpe and his team are in their traditional place at the prosecution table, and a third table has been brought in for Captain Massengale and her group.

Hawpe is in the middle between us, and he's uncomfortably in the legal middle here as well. When Judge Gordon petitions the U.S. Marshals Service for documents, he is doing so on behalf of the State of New Jersey. Hawpe is an employee of that state and therefore bound to advocate its position. However, as the prosecuting attorney, he is opposed to Judge Gordon's, and my, request.

Suffice it to say, I don't think we'll be hearing much from Hawpe today.

Judge Gordon sets the parameters of the hearing and summarizes the situation to date. He then asks Massengale to state the position of the U.S. Marshals Service.

"Thank you, Your Honor. For over two hundred years, the United States Marshals Service has served as the instruments of civil authority for all three branches of the U.S. government. It is easily the federal government's oldest and most versatile law enforcement agency."

She thus launches into a fifteen-minute speech, without notes, about the glories of the Marshals Service. It's a stirring rendition, and I'm sure I would be moved to tears if not for the fact that I doze off three or four times during it. I would object as to relevance, but I can use the snooze time.

She finally seems to be getting near the point by saying that the Marshals Service "provides for the security, health, and safety of government witnesses and their immediate dependents, whose lives are in danger as a result of their testimony against drug traffickers, terrorists, organized crime members, and other major criminals."

It's a false alarm, because she goes on talking about the tremendous importance of the program, the remarkable people that run it, and the extraordinary success it has had.

Finally she gets to the matter at hand. "Any breach in the secrecy of this program, no matter how small, can imperil the entire operation. It is for that reason that we must regretfully decline to comply with the court's request."

"Any documents you would hand over would be under seal," says Judge Gordon.

"Even to confirm that such documents exist—and I am not saying that they do—would be to breach confidentiality by revealing whether this particular subject was in the program."

"Mr. Carpenter?"

"Your Honor, no one is disputing the need for secrecy in this program. It is crucial that witnesses be protected. But it is considerably less crucial when the witness is already dead. For that reason, secrecy should in this case give way to the defendant's right to a fair trial."

Massengale comes back at me. "A precedent would be established."

I nod. "Right. The precedent would be that dead witnesses no longer need to be protected from the revelation that they were witnesses. I think our system could survive such a precedent. And if you are able to keep your future witnesses alive, it will never come up again."

"Our methods and procedures could be compromised," she says. "If it is known that someone was in our system—even after they are deceased—an enterprising criminal might be able to learn how we go about protecting our people."

It's a good point, and I don't have a great comeback for it, but I give it a shot. "Your method is to provide the witness with an apparently normal background. There is no way to penetrate that unless someone first identifies the person they suspect is in the program, as we did with Stacy Harriman. Additionally, everything you present will be under seal, and the court can protect your methods and procedures."

Judge Gordon gives Hawpe the chance to intervene, and he speaks for about a minute without saying anything of consequence. Then Massengale and I kick it around for a while more, without breaking much in the way of new ground.

Judge Gordon finally says, "It is the decision of this court to order the U.S. Marshals Service to turn over any and all documents relating to any period of time when the woman known in this trial as Stacy Harriman was under the control of the U.S. Marshals Service in the witness protection program. Because of the urgency created by this ongoing trial, I will suspend my order for forty-eight hours to allow time for appeal."

It's a victory for our side, and a surprising one at that. The downside is what Judge Gordon has acknowledged, which is the right of the Marshals Service to appeal up the line, all the way to the Supreme Court. It can be time consuming and could easily exceed the length of the trial.

Massengale's only response to the ruling is, "May I have a moment, Your Honor?"

Judge Gordon grants her the moment, and Massengale and her group huddle up and talk among themselves. After perhaps five minutes, she turns and addresses the judge.

"Your Honor, in the interests of justice, and with the promise of the court to keep the entire matter under seal, I am declaring to the court that the woman known in this trial as Stacy Harriman was never under the control of the U.S. Marshals Service, in the witness protection program. Therefore, the documents you are requesting do not exist. We will not be appealing your ruling."

It's not a bombshell, but close, and it certainly defines the term "hollow victory." We've prevailed in our efforts to force them to reveal what they have on Stacy, only to find out that they have nothing.

"What are we going to do now?" Richard whispers.

"We're going to find out who Stacy really was, and why she went to such lengths to hide it."

●　●　●　●　●

KAREN EVANS AND Willie Miller are waiting for us in the hallway outside the courtroom.

Karen has been going crazy at not having been allowed inside during the hearing, and her first question is, "Did we win?"

I nod without enthusiasm. "We won . . ."

Before I can get the rest of the story out, Willie interrupts. "See? I told you," he says to Karen. "My man don't lose."

"Unfortunately, there's more to the story," I say. I don't want to talk about it in this public hallway, so I tell Karen she should come back to the office and I'll fill her in. Willie will drive her because when he is protecting someone, he doesn't leave them for a minute. And he certainly wouldn't trust Kevin and me, since for some reason he doesn't regard us as physically intimidating.

We all meet back at the office, and I take a few minutes to bring Karen up to date on what took place. When I tell her that the Marshals Service denied that Stacy was under their control, she says, "Maybe they're lying."

I shake my head. "No, lying to the court is a felony; there's no way their lawyer would risk that. Besides, they had much more they could do legally to fight the judge's order. There would have been no reason to lie now."

"So Stacy was really Stacy?" she asks.

"No. That's no longer possible."

"So is this terrible news?"

I shake my head. "Disappointing but not terrible. We can still go to the jury with what we know about her faked background. It's very obvious she was hiding from something, which certainly helps our case."

What I'm saying is technically the truth, but the reality is that the ruling today is very disappointing. If Stacy had been in WITSEC, it would have meant that the U.S. government was essentially testifying for us, saying that dangerous killers were after Stacy Harriman and that she needed protection from them.

Willie says, "Can't you dig up her body and get some of that DNA stuff?"

"It wouldn't help," I say. "We already have her DNA; it's how her body was identified. But there aren't national DNA registries; it's not like she would have had her DNA on file before this."

"So it's not like fingerprints?" he asks.

Sometimes I'm so slow to see things right in front of my face that it frightens me. "Willie, you're a genius."

"You got that right," Willie says, though he can't have any idea what I'm talking about.

"Of course," Kevin says, realizing where I'm going. "Fingerprints."

I ask Karen, "Is there anything that Stacy touched, maybe that she handled a lot, that you'd still have?"

"You mean fingerprints can last that long?" she asks.

"Depending on the circumstances, absolutely."

Karen starts thinking out loud. "The house was sold . . . maybe some things in the basement, but I don't know what the new owners have done . . . the cabin! We were up there all the time!"

"Where is it?"

"Up near Monticello. I didn't want to sell it; I always had this picture of Richard getting out and going up there, and I wanted to keep something that was his."

"So it's been empty all this time?"

She nods. "There's a guy who maintains the outside, but he doesn't have a key. And I haven't been able to get myself to go there without Richard."

She goes on to say that Stacy was at the cabin many times. It was her favorite place; she liked it even more than the boat. She particularly loved cooking there, so any prints on the pots and pans would be hers.

I call Laurie and ask her to recommend somebody around here who would be competent to retrieve the fingerprints. She suggests George Feder, a forensics specialist recently retired from his position with the New Jersey State Police. She had heard that he was doing private work to supplement his retirement income.

I call Feder, but he says that he would be too busy to go up to Monticello for at least a week. I offer to double his fee, and his schedule experiences such a sudden clearing that I can't help but wonder if it would also work on

Kevin's sinuses. Kevin, Karen, Willie, and Feder will go up to the cabin tomorrow morning, while I'm in court.

I call Pete Stanton, figuring I might as well take the abuse in advance. He tells me that he had been in a panic; I hadn't called him for a favor in almost twenty-four hours, and his fear was that he had offended me.

"Don't worry," I say, "I am a man who believes in forgiveness."

"The bigger they are, the nicer they are," he says.

"And to show there are no hard feelings, I'm going to let you do me another favor. I need a fingerprint run through the national database."

"Where's the print?" he asks.

"I don't have it yet."

"Oh. Well, what I'll do is put a stop to all fingerprint work around the country, and then the system will be ready for you when you get your hands on the print."

"Works for me," I say.

He asks if I'm going to Charlie's tonight, and I say that I'm busy with the trial but that I'm thinking of stopping by for an hour or so.

"Make sure it's the hour that we ask for the check," he says.

I agree to the request; I could use the relaxation that comes with beer drinking and sports watching, and it will give me a chance to ask Pete for an update on the investigations into Karen's shooting and Franklin's death.

I head home to walk and feed Tara, and then go over some files I need to be familiar with for court tomorrow. Once I feel fully prepared, I drive over to Charlie's, getting there at about eight thirty.

Vince and Pete have not exactly been waiting for me to

start; the table is filled with empty beer bottles and plates. Once he sees me, Pete calls out to the waitress the request that she change the beers to more expensive, imported ones.

"Well," I say, "if it isn't my two favorite intellectuals. What have you two been discussing? Literature? Fine art?"

"Shit, yeah," says Vince.

It takes mere minutes for me to stoop to their level, which is not far from my natural state. Actually, because of the need to stay alert for tomorrow's court session, I don't fully match their behavior. So while I eat, drink, watch TV, and leer at women, I don't drool or spit up my food when I talk.

I'm also ready to leave before they are, so I attempt to turn the conversation to the Franklin investigation. "How close are you to making an arrest?" I ask Pete.

"How close are you to being an Olympic shot put champion?"

"I came in third in the nationals."

Pete goes on to tell me what he has told me before, that this appears to have been a professional job and that no leads of any consequence have come to light.

"What about Franklin's job at customs? Have they opened up their records about his work? Because I would guess that's where the answer is."

He says that in fact the records have been checked but that nothing seems to be amiss.

"What about since that night? Have you checked that?"

"What are you talking about?" he asks.

"Well, let's say Franklin was doing something illegal,

letting in material he should not have been. If it's tied into the Evans case, then that's been going on for a long time. If the pattern has changed significantly since Franklin died, then that would be important to know."

Pete looks at me for a few moments. His mouth is preparing an insult, but his mind has other ideas, so they compromise. "You may not be as dumb as you look."

"Stop, you're going to make me blush," I say.

Pete promises to get right on it the next morning, and I grab a final handful of french fries before heading home.

My work here is done.

• • • • •

I HATE COURTROOM surprises—unless I'm the one springing them.

The kind I hate most are witness list surprises, and that's what I'm greeted with when I arrive in court for the morning session. Hawpe has come up with a new witness, and the first thing on the docket is a hearing in Judge Gordon's office to decide whether he should be allowed to testify.

Hawpe informs Judge Gordon and me that a witness, Craig Langel, has just come forward with the revelation that he saw a golden retriever, apparently quite wet, on the night of the murder. The location was about a quarter mile from where Stacy's body washed ashore three weeks later.

Langel reported it to the animal shelter, who sent out someone to search for the stray dog and capture him but could not find him. Hawpe has just checked the back records of the shelter and located the call and dispatching of the shelter worker, to confirm that it was the same date. It was.

I argue that Langel should not be allowed to testify, because he was not on the list Hawpe provided, but it's a halfhearted argument with no chance of success. Hawpe represents to the court that he did not know about Langel until yesterday afternoon, and he hadn't confirmed it with the animal control department until early this morning.

Judge Gordon rules that Langel will be allowed to testify, and I enter a formal objection. He overrules me, and we head into court.

Hawpe's first witness is Gerald Daniels, head of the Somerset County crime lab. Five years ago Daniels was the technician who handled the forensics on this case, and his promotion since then probably gives him additional credibility.

Not that he needs it. He gives a straightforward, professional analysis of the evidence. He describes the evidence collection on the boat, most notably the bloodstains on the floor and railing, and the positive DNA match to Stacy, based on hair samples from her brush in Richard's house.

There isn't any doubt that Daniels is qualified to render these conclusions, and no reason to think he would be deceptive. It is not particularly harmful to me, since I have not contended that Stacy was not on that boat or that she was not murdered.

My cross-examination is therefore short and narrowly focused. "Mr. Daniels, I would like to explore the scope of your investigation. So I'm going to ask you some questions, and I'd like you to answer based on what you can say with a reasonable degree of scientific certainty. If you cannot speak with that certainty, please say so."

"Yes, sir."

"Thank you. Now, where on Stacy Harriman's body did the blood on the boat come from?"

"I cannot determine that with any degree of scientific certainty," he says.

"Who caused her wounds?"

"I can't determine that, either."

"Was Richard Evans conscious when Stacy Harriman was killed?"

"I don't know."

"Were the bloodstains placed where they were deliberately?" I ask.

"Questions like that are beyond the scope of my work."

"Now I'd like to present a hypothetical. With Richard Evans unconscious, someone who had been hiding on the boat, or who had boarded it after it set sail, murdered Stacy Harriman and threw her body overboard. Is there anything in your work which could disprove that?"

"No, but . . ."

"Thank you."

I made some rhetorical points with Daniels, but nothing that will stick. I still have not given the jury any reason to believe that someone other than Stacy and Richard was on that boat. Making the point that it is merely possible is just not going to do it.

Hawpe next calls Dr. Susan Coakley, professor of veterinary medicine at Cornell University. Dr. Coakley might be called a physical therapist for animals, and teaches the practice of physical rehabilitation through exercise. A lot of that is "water therapy" whereby the dogs swim under controlled conditions in a university pool constructed for that purpose.

Her basic testimony is that she believes it to be possible that a young, healthy golden retriever could have made the swim from the boat to shore that night. She does not claim to know it for a certainty but is quite adamant in considering it quite conceivable.

She reminds me of a few professors I had in law school. They considered their opinions to be incontrovertible fact and wore their arrogance proudly on their sleeves. I never got a chance to knock them down a peg, which is why I'm so looking forward to this cross-examination.

In truth, I need to go after her very hard, since if she cannot be shaken, then our "Reggie turned up alive" advantage no longer carries much weight.

"Dr. Coakley, when did you conduct your physical examination of Reggie?" Unless she's the lowlife that broke into my house and kidnapped Reggie, I know that the answer to this question is "never."

"I did not conduct an examination."

"Pardon me?" I ask, betraying my surprise. Oh, the shock of it all.

"I did not conduct an examination on this particular dog."

"Were you prevented from doing so?"

"No, it wasn't necessary for what I was called upon to do."

"I see. So you merely went over his medical records, X-rays, that kind of thing?"

"No, I did not have access to them," she says.

"You were denied that access?"

"No, the records were not necessary for my work."

"So the health of a dog is not relevant in determining if that dog could swim four miles in the ocean in a major storm?"

"I was operating under the assumption that he was healthy."

"So if he were not healthy, that might change your opinion?" I ask.

"It might, depending on what was wrong with him."

"If I told you he had a badly broken leg that was repaired by inserting a metal plate and that he was taking a drug called Rimadyl for the resulting arthritic pain, would that be significant to you?" I'm shading the truth a little here. Reggie is on that medication now; he was not on it then.

But Hawpe does not object, and Dr. Coakley answers, "I would have to examine the records."

"You mean the records that weren't necessary for your work?"

Hawpe objects that I'm being argumentative, and Judge Gordon sustains.

I move on. "Do you have any personal knowledge of a dog swimming four miles in the ocean during a substantial storm?"

"No, I don't," she says, trying to control her annoyance. "But I believe it is within their capability, depending on the circumstances."

"What is the furthest you have personally seen a dog swim in the ocean in the midst of this kind of storm?"

"I have never seen it personally, but it would not be necessary for me to do so."

"Could a dog do it while carrying a radar antenna on his back?" I ask.

"I don't know what you mean."

"Well, it was nighttime, and even though there may be lights in the specially constructed swimming pool that you use for your therapy, there aren't any in the Atlantic Ocean. How would Reggie have known where to swim?"

I think I see a quick flash of panic in Dr. Coakley's eyes. She should just deflect the question as not something covered in her work, but she doesn't. "Perhaps there was enough moonlight."

"Dr. Coakley, I don't know how much time you spend outside, but have you ever seen a major summer storm? Are you aware that there are a lot of clouds involved?"

Judge Gordon admonishes me for being argumentative even before Hawpe has a chance to object. I let Dr. Coakley off the stand, a little less arrogant than when she took it.

The day's last witness is Craig Langel, the man who reported seeing a stray dog matching Reggie's description very late on the night of the murder.

In the hands of Hawpe on direct examination, he comes across as a decent citizen who is telling the truth about what he saw that night. Perhaps trying to make up for the Dr. Coakley debacle, Hawpe nurtures the witness, taking almost an hour to bring out what he could have gotten in ten minutes.

The jury has to be bored and wanting to adjourn for the day, so I don't want to prolong matters. "Mr. Langel, you've testified that you saw a dog, possibly a golden retriever, running stray near the harbor that night?"

"That's correct."

"He appeared very wet?"

"Yes, sir."

"Is it unusual for a stray dog to get wet in the middle of a rainstorm?"

"I wouldn't think so, sir."

"Thank you. No further questions."

• • • • •

KEVIN CALLS WITH the news that they got plenty of latent fingerprints at the cabin.

Our expert, George Feder, will eliminate those that turn out to match Richard or Karen, and hopefully that will leave many of Stacy's prints. I'll then give one of those to Pete, who will run it through the system. Unfortunately, not nearly everyone in the country has their fingerprints in the national database, so there's a pretty good chance we won't get a match.

Even so, I'm putting a lot of stock in this process, because tomorrow Hawpe is going to conclude his case, and I haven't made a serious dent in it. This looks like a classic domestic murder-suicide, and when the jury starts to deliberate, that's what they're going to see.

I can talk all I want about campene and a golden retriever who survived, but it won't cut to what the jury will see as the core truth. They will see that Richard and Stacy were out there alone, she wound up dead in the water, and he wound up unconscious from an overdose.

It's unfortunately an easy call, no matter what the wise-ass defense attorney says.

Kevin says that Karen has something else to tell me, and he puts her on the phone so that she can do so directly. "Andy, I think someone has been in the cabin."

"When?"

"I don't know, sometime since I was there last."

Karen has told me that she has not been to the cabin since the murder, so that doesn't narrow it down much. But she's also said that no one had a key.

"Was there any sign of forced entry?" I ask. "A broken lock or window?"

"No," she says, "but I'm sure there were things missing. Mostly some of Stacy's stuff."

This is potentially very interesting. If Stacy represented a danger to someone, it could have been because of something in her possession. After her death, they may well have gone looking for it in the cabin, a natural hiding place.

Unfortunately, although it's interesting, all I can do is put it in the bag with the other information I don't know what to do with. At this point the bag is bursting at the seams.

Kevin comes over for an evening strategy session. We prepare for Hawpe's final witnesses, but they are not of great consequence. All he'll be doing is smoothing out the rough spots; he's already made his point.

Instead we focus on our own case. We'll once again establish that Reggie is Richard's dog, and that he survived that night. We'll also bring in Dr. King, who will present his version of the events of that night, as well as his contention that Richard did not take the Amenipam orally.

But the more I think about it, the more I feel we should focus on Stacy's faked identity. Even not knowing who she really is, the deception increases our chances of raising reasonable doubt. If we match her fingerprint, then everything changes, for better or worse, depending on that identity.

Kevin agrees with my assessment, though we both realize we're in an uncomfortable position. Much of our preparation depends on that fingerprint, and all we can do is wait.

Feder meets us in the morning before court begins, with a copy of what he is sure is Stacy's print. There were many just like it in the cabin, and a particular concentration of them on the pots and pans. He has also come up with a couple of other prints that do not match Richard or Karen, and he's brought them as well.

To save us time, Feder agrees to bring the prints to Pete Stanton, since they have worked together many times in the past. Kevin and I head into court, where Hawpe proceeds to do us a favor by making his final four witnesses last all day. We will not have to start our case until tomorrow, and the delay works to our advantage.

Kevin brings a criminologist named Jeffrey Blalock to our evening meeting. He was formerly a detective in Bergen County, specializing in identity theft and computer crime. With the explosion of illegal activity in those areas, he left the force to set up a private consulting practice, and is now recognized as a leading expert in the field.

Blalock will be the witness through whom we'll make our claim that Stacy's background is fake, and he has spent the past couple of days going over the information Sam has gotten, as well as the documents Kevin brought back from Minnesota.

I usually like to spend far more time prepping witnesses as crucial as Blalock, but things are moving too fast to allow that. As I start to talk with him, I harbor a secret fear that he's going to say we're crazy, that Stacy Harriman is in reality Stacy Harriman.

He doesn't. "Stacy Harriman never existed. She was created out of whole cloth."

"How would this woman manage to do something like that?" I ask.

He smiles. "She wouldn't. This is WITSEC."

"They deny it."

"Under oath?" he asks.

"No, but to a court."

"Let me put it this way . . . ," he says, and then points to my desk. "What is that?"

"My desk," I say.

"If I tell you that's not your desk, are you going to believe me?"

"Of course not."

He nods. "Right, because you know better." He holds up the folder of documents relating to Stacy. "These are as clear to me as that desk is to you. This is WITSEC, no matter what they told that judge."

As much as I'm surprised that their attorney, Alice Massengale, would lie in court, what Blalock is saying instinctively feels right. Of course, there is always the possibility that Massengale herself was not told the truth and was representing to the court what she thought was accurate information.

I call Cindy Spodek at her Boston office. I don't want to involve her in the case any more than I have, because it seems to have caused her a problem with her FBI bosses. But this WITSEC confusion is bugging me, and I'm hoping Cindy's experience can help debug me.

I explain to her the situation and what transpired in court, and she listens without interrupting. When I finish, she says, "It sounds like WITSEC, Andy. I don't know how else these things could have been fabricated so completely."

"But their lawyer denied it in court, even though she didn't have to answer at all. She could have appealed the court's order to death."

"Who was the attorney?"

"Alice Massengale."

"It was Alice?" she asks, her surprise evident. "Then you've got a problem."

"Why? You know her?"

"I do. I worked with her a few times when I was based down there. There is no way she would knowingly lie in court. Absolutely no way."

For all Cindy's certainty, she is making an educated guess about Massengale's veracity. I'm inclined to go along with it because Cindy is a very good judge of people, and because it seems more likely that a good attorney would not intentionally and directly lie to a judge.

I head home and call Laurie before going to bed—or, more accurately, *from* bed. As always, she wants to be brought up to date on the case, and I do so. It actually helps me to verbalize it to her; it seems to clear my mind.

She also doesn't believe that Massengale would lie to the judge, both because it seems unlikely on its face and because she trusts Cindy's judgment. Nevertheless, for now I'm going to operate on the assumption that Stacy was in WITSEC; I just wish I could get it in front of the jury.

Laurie gives me a brief pep talk in honor of our starting the defense case tomorrow. She knows I'm not content with what we've got, and she wants to make sure that my concern doesn't impede my effectiveness. It won't, but I appreciate her effort.

Just before we're getting off the phone, I say, "How was your day?"

She laughs a short laugh and says, "It was fine, Andy. My day was fine."

"What was that laugh for? You don't think I care how your day was?"

"Andy, go to sleep. My day was fine, but you're in the middle of a trial. It's your days that are important right now."

After we hang up, I use up my yearly fifteen minutes of introspection to examine my feelings about Laurie's day. I love her deeply, and if something extraordinary happened today, or if she needed me for something, I would be very interested and unquestionably there for her.

But the truth is, if she had an ordinary day as chief of police in Findlay, Wisconsin, then I pretty much don't give a shit about it.

I'm not sure what that says about me, but it can't be good. Next year at introspection time, I'll try and figure it out.

• • • • •

"WE'VE GOT TWO matches," are the first words Pete Stanton says when I answer my cell phone.

He's reached me less than five minutes before my going into court for the morning session, and he's talking about the results from running the fingerprints through the national registry.

I'm actually a little nervous at finally finding out Stacy Harriman's real identity. Based on my inability to correctly predict anything about this case, I'm afraid it's going to be Margaret Thatcher or Paris Hilton. "Who was she?" I ask.

"Her name was Diana Carmichael, thirty-four years old when she died."

"Why were her prints in the system?"

"She was in the Army," he says, providing me a bit of a jolt in the process. I don't yet know how that piece of information fits, but I'd bet anything that it does.

"Pete, I'm late to get into court, so . . ."

"Okay, but I said we've got two matches. There's also one from one of the other prints, and you'll like this one even more."

"Tell me."

"Anthony Banks."

Lieutenant Anthony Banks. Deceased husband of Donna Banks, wealthy volunteer worker living in Sunset Towers in Fort Lee, and the recipient of the mysterious twenty-two thousand a month from Yasir Hamadi.

Lieutenant Anthony Banks, who, long after his death, seems to have managed to rummage through Stacy Harriman's things in the cabin, leaving his fingerprints in the process. Just as Archie Durelle, the man he died with, showed up to shoot at me on the highway.

We've got ourselves a group of dead guys who really get around.

"I'm going to have Kevin call you and get the details, okay, Pete?"

He's fine with that and also tells me he's making progress on checking into whether the type and amount of cargo coming through Franklin's customs office has significantly changed since his death.

"We're going to be meeting at my house tonight. Why don't you stop by?" I say.

"You mean that? So I'm on the team now?" he asks, sarcasm starting to return.

"Well, not the first team. But a damned good backup."

"Is that right? Well, how about if you kiss my—"

"Thanks, Pete. Gotta go," I say, and hang up, temporarily depriving him of the last word. As soon as I'm off, I bring Kevin up to date. I want him to call Pete and then take the information and see what Captain Reid at Fort Monmouth can add to it.

I reach the defense table moments before the judge enters, and Richard seems a little agitated at my uncharacteristically late arrival.

"Something wrong?" he whispers.

"Do you know the name Diana Carmichael?"

He thinks for a moment. "No. Should I?"

"You were engaged to her."

It is an unfair thing to do to him, since I don't have time to explain it fully right now. During the morning break I'll do so.

It's a strange feeling to be opening the defense case in front of the jury while the real action is going on outside, between Kevin, Pete, and Captain Reid. But that's what I have to do, and I start by calling Dr. Ruff, Reggie's veterinarian.

Kevin has had a chance to prep her on her testimony, and she's more decisive than during the hearing. She presents a compelling case that the Reggie she recently examined is, in fact, the dog that Richard owned and took on his boat those years ago.

Hawpe makes little effort to challenge her, and he concludes by stipulating that she is correct, that Reggie survived.

Next up for our side is Dr. Harold Simmons, a blood spatter expert. The fact that there is so much blood getting spattered in this country that we need experts on it is a rather negative commentary on our society, but Dr. Simmons is very good at what he does.

Dr. Simmons's contention is that the blood spatter on the boat was of a type and in a location so as to render it very likely that it was deliberately placed there. I ask very general questions and let him run with them, and he does so quite well.

Hawpe has some success in his cross-examination, focusing on the fact that it was raining that night and everything was wet. It could have washed away some of the blood and altered the spatter of what remained. Dr. Simmons gives ground very grudgingly, but Hawpe makes some points.

During the lunch break, I return a message from Kevin, telling me what he's learned. Diana Carmichael was in fact in the Army, stationed in Afghanistan and working for what was called the Afghani/American Provisional Authority. It was the operation hastily set up immediately after the fall of the Taliban to provide much-needed money for reconstruction.

A theory is forming in my mind, but I don't have the time right now to analyze it in depth. Hawpe has responded to my announced plan to call Jeffrey Blalock to the stand by asking Judge Gordon to refuse to allow his testimony. The judge has decided to convene a hearing, outside the presence of the jury and media, to consider the matter.

"Exactly what is Mr. Blalock going to testify to?" the judge asks.

"He is going to describe documents that he has reviewed that demonstrate conclusively that Stacy Harriman's background has been faked in an effort to conceal her true identity."

Hawpe stands. "Your Honor, unless he is prepared to present a credible explanation for how the deception was accomplished, it is pure speculation and should not be admissible."

"That makes no sense, Your Honor," I say. "He is going to be stating facts that exist independent of anyone's knowledge or understanding of how they came about. It is similar to a witness testifying to a cell phone call without understanding the technology behind it. But I might add that Mr. Blalock will also be advancing his view that the fake background was created in the context of the witness protection program."

Hawpe shakes his head. "The court has already convened a hearing on that matter, and it was determined that Ms. Harriman was not in that program. The U.S. Marshals Service very clearly represented that to the court."

"We think they lied or were misinformed," I say.

Judge Gordon does not seem pleased to hear this. "If you're going to stand up in open court and in effect accuse the government of lying, you'd better have more than what you just 'think.' "

"We have an expert presenting his point of view," I say, but I can feel this slipping away.

Judge Gordon shakes his head. "Not good enough. I'll allow the testimony regarding the background, but in the absence of new factual information, there will be no referencc to the witness protection program. Anything else, gentlemen?"

"Yes, Your Honor," I say. "We are in the process of determining Ms. Harriman's real identity right now. My intention would be to have Mr. Blalock review this new information tonight and then present it to the court tomorrow."

Hawpe starts to object, but the judge cuts him off so that he can question me about how we learned her real identity. I describe the process of getting the fingerprints from the cabin and running them through the national registry. I leave out the actual identities for now; they are not important to the issue we're arguing, and I don't want to give Hawpe a heads-up.

Unfortunately, Hawpe doesn't seem to need one. He argues that none of the fingerprint information should be admissible. There is no chain of custody, no way to be sure that Stacy left the prints there at all. Anyone could have gotten into the cabin in that time, and therefore it is impossible to say how they were left there, or who left them.

I argue the point, but I have no bullets to fire. Hawpe is right; no one can say with certainty that the woman we know as Stacy Harriman left those prints.

Judge Gordon rules the identity inadmissible unless and until further information is brought forth that could demonstrate its reliability. It has not been a good hearing for us; all we got out of it is the right to argue that Stacy's background was faked. Any second-year law student could have won that point.

The amount of information we're gathering is starting to take off, and I can feel us getting closer to the truth. It would have been nice to convey that truth to the people deciding Richard's fate, but his lawyer couldn't quite pull that off.

At least my client will have a great story to tell his cell mates.

• • • • •

KEVIN HAS SPOKEN to Captain Reid about Diana Carmichael, the woman who became Stacy Harriman.

The army lists her as deceased, but they are not referring to her death in the water off New Jersey. Her death is recorded as having taken place just three weeks after the helicopter crash in Afghanistan that supposedly killed Durelle, Banks, and the others. I suspect that they created this fake death as a way to ease her into the witness protection system.

Unfortunately, that's all the records show. The rest of her file is listed as classified, and not even Captain Reid or his boss has access to it. Reid considers this very unusual but is powerless to do anything about it.

Kevin and I struggle to come up with a theory, but what we wind up with is vague and only loosely based on facts. Our thought is that Stacy, which is how I can't help referring to her even though her real name was Diana, was likely stationed in Afghanistan. She was probably a witness to wrongdoing, and witnesses very often need protection.

The wrongdoing could have been misconduct by American soldiers, perhaps mistreating the enemy, or it could have been financial. There have been a number of stories written over the past couple of years about the chaos that existed just after the Taliban was defeated, and the corruption that was part of the reconstruction efforts. Billions of dollars were alleged to have been lost.

Billions. People have killed for a lot less.

It's possible that the government itself didn't believe that lives were really lost in that helicopter crash, or perhaps it knew of other bad guys that got away and would pose a threat to Stacy. In any event, those in charge obviously felt it necessary to tuck her away where she wouldn't be harmed.

Pete comes over and joins the discussion, mainly to report once again that no progress has been made toward finding Reggie, and that he seems to have disappeared off the face of the earth. I'm going crazy about it and getting more and more pessimistic that we'll never get a ransom demand. If we were going to get one, it would have come already.

We bring Pete up to date on what we know and what we suspect about Stacy's real identity and why she was a protected witness. He has a slightly different take on this. "If it's money that was stolen, maybe they put her in the program not so much so that she could someday testify, but rather to insure that she never would."

I don't understand, and I tell him so. He continues, "That money is gone; they're never going to see it again. If they catch the crooks and have a trial, then they have to publicly confront the embarrassment that they screwed up and lost billions of dollars. If they don't, then nobody finds out the truth about it."

"Right. But if there was some other kind of misconduct, like if she witnessed torture or something, the army might also want to keep that quiet."

Either scenario makes sense in light of the way the government has acted, trying to keep the case from being reopened and, failing that, attempting to thwart us at every turn.

We kick this around a while longer until it's time for Kevin and me to start our trial preparation for tomorrow. It's extraordinarily frustrating to realize that nothing that we have learned today or talked about tonight is going to make it to the jury.

Before Pete leaves, he gives me three sheets of paper. It is the result of the investigation I suggested into Franklin's work at customs, a comparison of the cargo entering before and after his death. I want to look at it because I still have no idea where Franklin fits into all this, but I just don't have the time right now.

Kevin and I are at it until almost one in the morning, including a half-hour walk that he takes with Tara and me. I've been trying to get Kevin to get a dog, since he loves them, and he's weakening. He explains that right now he's trying to figure out what he would do with the dog if he had to spend an extended time in the hospital.

"Why? Are you sick?" I ask.

He smiles weakly. "You have no idea; I just don't like to talk about it."

Oh.

Our first witness in the morning session is Michelle Miller, a travel agent with an office in Englewood. She met with Richard the day before Stacy died, and she testifies that the meeting was to finalize their honeymoon plans.

"They were going on a cruise through the Panama Canal," she says.

"Did he give you a deposit?"

She nods. "He did. One thousand dollars."

"Was it refundable in the event that they had to cancel their trip?" I ask.

"It was not."

I turn her over to Hawpe. "Had you spent a great deal of time with Mr. Evans and Ms. Harriman when they were together?"

She shakes her head. "No, I actually never met Ms. Harriman."

"I see. So you did not know what you would describe as intimate details of their marriage?"

"I did not."

"If the deposit had been refundable and then Mr. Evans committed suicide, would he have been around to receive the refund?"

I object and Judge Gordon sustains, but Hawpe's point had been made. A murder-suicide is an irrational act, and simply making a honeymoon reservation is no proof at all that Richard could not have done it.

We then call a series of witnesses who spent time with Richard and Stacy and who talk about how much they seemed to love each other.

Hawpe is basically dismissive of these witnesses, getting each one to admit that they have no idea what goes on behind the closed doors of anyone's relationship other than their own.

It's been a day of making small gains and pretending they are big, but we're going to have to do much better. And our chance will come tomorrow, when we call Dr. King and Jeffrey Blalock.

I head home for a long night with Kevin preparing for our witnesses. Dr. King presents an interesting problem, and a role reversal of sorts. In most cases where there has been a preliminary hearing, the witnesses that testify are almost exclusively those of the prosecution, since the purpose is to establish probable cause. The defense thus has the advantage of having heard the testimony before it is given again at trial.

In this case, because the burden was on us at the hearing to bring this to a retrial, it is our witnesses, like Dr. King, who have already been on record. It's an advantage for Hawpe, but one we have to live with.

It's almost midnight when we're finishing our preparations. Kevin's getting ready to leave, and I'm reading the report Pete left with me, when I immediately see it. "Look at this," I say.

Kevin comes over, and I hand him the papers. "It's the list of companies bringing large amounts of goods into Franklin's area of customs, before and after his death."

Kevin looks at it, but nothing registers. "And?"

At the bottom of the second page is a list of companies that have had dramatically less come through customs since Franklin's death. "If I remember correctly, a few of those names were on the list that Sam tracked down. The companies that Hamadi was dealing with."

I check back through the files and confirm my suspicions; four of the companies are on both lists. The man whom a worried Donna Banks called after my visit seems to have been involved with Franklin in customs activity. I don't believe in coincidences, but even if I did, this wouldn't be one of them.

By the time Kevin and I finish thrashing this out, it's one thirty in the morning and we've got a plan. At least, I've got a plan; Kevin cautions me against it.

The first part of the plan involves calling Vince Sanders. I want to do it now rather than the morning, because I will be heading for court early, and I want him to get on it first thing. Also, psychologically I want to get the ball rolling.

Vince groggily answers the phone with "This better be good, asshole." Apparently he's not so sleepy that he can't see his caller ID.

"I'm sorry to bother you, Vince, but I need a big favor."

He doesn't say a word, which could mean he doesn't want to, or else that he fell back asleep. I decide to push on. "Vince, I need to speak to Dominic Petrone."

"Is that all?" he asks, and then speaks to an imaginary person in bed with him. "Dominic, honey, Andy Carpenter wants to talk to you. And when you're finished, could you run over to the asshole's house and put a bullet in his head?"

"Vince, it's urgent, and I can tell you with one hundred percent certainty that he'll be glad you set up the meeting."

"You want to tell me what it's about?"

"I wish I could, but I can't."

"Repeat after me. If a story of any kind comes out of this, Vince is the person I will give it to, along with an exclusive interview."

I repeat the vow, and Vince agrees to call Petrone in the morning.

Tomorrow is showing signs of being an important day.

• • • • •

DR. GERALD KING has brought his A game to court today.

In direct examination, he is even more effective than he was at the hearing. He's a consummate witness; all a defense attorney has to do is wind him up and let him go.

I let him go over his assessment of what happened that night on the boat, and his absolute certainty that Richard did not take any pills. It's basically the same story he told at the hearing, with more charts and even more assertiveness.

Hawpe certainly has been preparing for him for weeks, but if he makes a dent, it's not worth calling the insurance company to repair. The best Hawpe can get from him is an admission that the prosecution's version of events is "not impossible," but even that draws a sharp comeback from Dr. King.

"Not impossible?" he asks. "Is that the standard the prosecution has to meet to send a man to prison?"

It's an unprofessional comment, and Hawpe's objection gets it stricken from the record, but the point is made, and the jury certainly heard it. By the time Dr. King gets off the stand, I think that Hawpe is ready to throw him a good-bye party.

Mercifully, a juror comes down with a stomach virus, and the afternoon session is canceled. I don't wish any-one ill, and if I could outlaw viruses forever I would, but if someone in America had to come down with one, I'm glad it's a juror on this case. I need the time to focus on our efforts to learn the truth about Stacy and why she was killed.

I call Vince, who tells me that he just got off the phone with Petrone's people. Whatever they talked about, it hasn't improved his mood any. "They want you at Spu-moni's Restaurant on Market Street at five thirty."

"Five thirty? That's a little early for dinner."

"That's because you're not invited for dinner," he says.

I want to make sure I have all this straight. "Who should I ask for?"

"Who are you going to see?"

"Dominic Petrone."

"Then why don't you start by asking for him and see how that goes? Oh, and they said you should come alone and unarmed."

"What did you tell them?"

"That not only will you not bring a gun, you probably won't bring any balls."

"Thanks, Vince."

Before he gets off the phone he makes me repeat the

"I'll give the story to Vince" pledge, which I willingly do. Vince is a major pain in the ass, but the next time he doesn't come through for me will be the first.

I call Marcus and give him the evening off. Ever the responsible bodyguard, he presses me about why, and I'm forced to tell him. He reluctantly agrees, and I only hope he's telling me the truth.

I show up at the restaurant at the appointed time. It has been on this downtown street for more than fifty years and is said to have extraordinary Italian food.

I just hope Clemenza left me a gun in the bathroom.

I've worn fairly tight jeans and a thin pullover shirt. I'm not trying to make a fashion statement; I'm just not a big fan of getting frisked by burly men, and I'm hoping this will render that unnecessary.

It doesn't work. I'm not in the door for twenty seconds before I've been frisked and ushered into a back room, where Dominic Petrone sits having a drink with two other men. He moves his hand almost imperceptibly, and they get up and leave the table. Three of Petrone's people take positions around the room, with their backs to the walls.

"Sit down, Andy," says Petrone.

"Thanks, Dominic," I say as I do so. "Try the veal. It's the best in the city." He doesn't seem to get the *Godfather* reference, which is just as well. But Sam Willis would have gotten it.

"Vince says you're here to help me."

"I was hoping we could help each other. I have some information you can use, and hopefully you can get information that I need."

"Let's start with me," he says.

I'm not going to get rolled here. "Do we have a deal?"

"Let's start with me," he says again, with a little less patience.

"Dominic, the way I envisioned this is—"

"You don't trust me?" he asks.

I just got rolled. "Of course I do." Strangely enough, I do trust him, though I know that were it in his best interests, he would kill me without spoiling his appetite.

I pause a moment to try to control the tremor in my voice. What I'm about to say can have serious repercussions, most notably to me.

"In the course of my investigation of the Evans case, I've learned that you have been sending large amounts of money, in small- and medium-sized bills, out of the country."

Petrone doesn't flinch, nor does he blink. He simply waits, probably deciding in his own mind how I am to be killed.

I continue. "I have not told anyone about it, but I have also learned something else. There is about to be an intense investigation into unusual activity down there, and if you have any cargo there or ready to be shipped in the next few days, it might pay to pull it back immediately."

"And you are the reason this investigation is taking place?" he asks, his voice completely calm.

I shake my head. "I have told no one about this other than you," I say, and for the moment that is true.

"And the information you need?"

"Four companies—I've brought the list with me—have been bringing goods into this country through the Port of Newark. They came in through Keith Franklin's section. I need to know what was in those shipments."

"And how would I know that?" he asks.

"You wouldn't. But I'd bet that you have the people down there that could find out."

He thinks for the moment, then takes a pen out of his jacket and writes something on a piece of paper. Hopefully it's not my eulogy.

He hands me the paper, and I see that it has a phone number on it. "Call me tomorrow at five p.m.," he says.

"I will. Thank you."

I walk out into the main area of the restaurant. One of Petrone's men points with his hand toward the exit door, which I will be thrilled to use. Before I go, I point toward the bathroom door. "My brother better not come out of there with only his dick in his hand."

He apparently hasn't seen the movie, either.

• • • • •

BEFORE CALLING JEFFREY Blalock to
the stand, I ask for another closed hearing.

I start off by bringing Hawpe up to date on what we
have now learned about Stacy's identity and background,
and I again ask that Blalock be allowed to state his view
that she had to be under the protection of WITSEC.

Hawpe, of course, objects. "Your Honor, as you know
all too well, we have been over this ground. There was a
specific denial in your court from the lawyer representing
the U.S. Marshals Service."

"I now believe she was parsing her words, Your
Honor."

"What do you mean?"

"I checked the transcript. She phrased her denial quite
precisely." I look at my notes and read the words she used.
"The woman known in this trial as Stacy Harriman was

never under the control of the U.S. Marshals Service in the witness protection program."

"How is that parsing her words?" the judge asks.

"I believe this is a DIA or CIA operation, probably using WITSEC's physical structure and operational capability. So I think that the Marshals Service could conceivably deny that she was 'under their control.' "

I go on to admit that there could be another explanation, that Massengale herself might have been kept in the dark and was therefore telling the truth as she believed it.

Hawpe cuts in. "Your Honor, with all due respect, Mr. Carpenter is making this up on the fly, with no facts to support him."

I'm prepared to argue some more, but Judge Gordon surprises me with a quick decision. He still prohibits Blalock's mentioning the witness protection program or WITSEC, but will allow his opinion that an unnamed government entity may have participated in or created the deception.

It's a partial victory for us, which right now feels pretty good.

Back in court, I take Blalock through all the documentation we have that demonstrates conclusively that Stacy Harriman was not who she claimed to be. In his expert hands the story is spellbinding, and it's not just my imagination in thinking that the jury is the most attentive it has been throughout the trial.

After we have gone through everything, I say, "A fake credit report . . . birth records . . . high school transcript . . . all these things—how could she have accomplished all this?"

"She couldn't," Blalock says. "She had to have help."

"You mean like a friend who was good with a computer?"

Blalock smiles. "No, much more than that. Far, far more than that. It would have had to be a government agency that made these organizations do their bidding. No citizen could have pulled this off."

I let him off, and Hawpe starts his cross-examination. He takes an interesting tactic, essentially conceding that Stacy's identity was a fake, but instead focusing on why that might be.

"Mr. Blalock, have you come in contact with many people who have created new identities for themselves?"

"Yes, quite a few."

"And they do so for a variety of reasons?"

"Yes."

"Would one be to get a fresh start, perhaps after a bad marriage?" Hawpe asks.

"It could."

"How about escaping financial problems?" Hawpe asks.

Blalock nods his agreement. "Certainly."

"And there could be many others?"

"Absolutely."

"Of these people who you've worked with that have changed their identity, have any of them been murdered?"

"No."

Hawpe spends very little time on Blalock, perhaps in an effort to diminish his importance. His cross-examination has been well done, effectively telling the jury that just because someone is not who they seem to be, that doesn't necessarily have anything to do with their murder.

All in all, I think Blalock's testimony went well, and

I tell that to Richard when he leans over and asks me. "Where do we go next?" he whispers.

"To the jury," I say, and then I stand and address the judge. "Your Honor, the defense rests."

The phrase "the defense rests" is unfortunately not to be taken literally. We don't rest at all after saying it; instead we prepare for any rebuttal witnesses the prosecution might call, and for our closing argument.

Resting is for suckers.

This time I'm going to get even less rest than usual, since at five o'clock I've got to place a call to Dominic Petrone, which in turn might lead me in any one of many directions, none of them restful.

I make the call, and the person who answers the phone gives me a different number to call. That call yields a third number. I assume this must have to do with some security concerns, but I'm not sure how.

I finally get through to Petrone, and he says, "I have your information."

"Great."

"Those companies you listed did not receive any goods coming through customs."

This both troubles and confuses me. "I have the documentation that they did."

"That was intentional. The documents listed shipments that never actually were delivered—that did not even exist."

This doesn't make sense. I expected arms, or drugs— "nothing" was not on my list of possibilities.

"Do you know why?" I ask.

"I neither know nor care."

"But you're sure about this?" I ask, and immediately regret the question.

"I only say things I am sure of," he responds. "As an example of that, let me say that I do not want to hear from you again." With that, he hangs up the phone. Just to show he can't push me around, I hang up my dead phone as well.

So Stacy Harriman was killed because she knew that certain people were smuggling nothing into the country.

I'm glad we cleared that up.

● ● ● ● ●

I FEEL AS if we are operating in parallel universes.

There is the trial, which is nearing conclusion and can certainly go either way. If I were inclined to make predictions, which I am not, I would say we're in some trouble.

Then there is the investigation operating outside the trial. We are making progress there, but not nearly fast enough. I am gripped by the fear that we're going to win the eventual investigation battle but lose the immediate war. I don't want to have to tell Richard the truth about Stacy in a visiting room at the state prison.

There is also the terrifying possibility that we can uncover the whole truth but that it will have no effect on the trial or on a subsequent appeal of another guilty verdict. No matter what happens in the world of Stacy, Hamadi, Franklin, Durelle, Banks, et al., it could be ruled irrelevant to Richard's case. A jury or an appeals court could say that yes, she was not nearly who she claimed to be, but that doesn't mean Richard didn't kill her.

The other, even more frustrating situation is Reggie's uncertain fate. It is terribly painful to think about, and it is a pain that Richard, Karen, Kevin, and I have in common.

Kevin shares my assessment that we need to take fast action. We discuss whether to turn over what we know about Stacy, Hamadi, and the others to law enforcement. At some point we will do that, but for now it simply doesn't serve our purposes. It will take too long, and if the government's performance on this matter to date is any indication, the actions they would take in response to our information may be somewhat less than vigorous.

The only acceptable option Kevin and I can see is to be aggressive and shake matters up. We've got a client to defend.

I place a call to Hamadi's business phone number at Interpublic Trading and reach an answering service. It's seven o'clock, and it's logical that no one would still be there. When your company's sole function is to arrange the importation of absolutely nothing into the country, not much overtime is required.

I tell the woman that I am trying to reach Hamadi on absolutely urgent business. Her reaction is not exactly heartening; she sounds as if she's falling asleep as I give her the message. I ask her to tell Hamadi that "I know about Franklin and the empty crates, and the world will know about it tomorrow."

I hang up with no confidence that the message will be conveyed tonight. I try to get Hamadi's home number from information, but the operator says it's unlisted.

This is obviously a job for Sam Willis, who laughs in the face of unlisted phone numbers.

I call Sam, who, for the first time in my experience, doesn't answer his cell phone. This is so unusual that if I were a good friend I would start calling hospitals to see if he's in a coma somewhere. Instead I leave a message that it's urgent that he call me back.

Kevin and I start to go over the closing statement I will be giving. As with my openings, I like to plan the main notes that I am going to hit, but not write out a speech or memorize anything. I feel I connect better with the jury that way.

Less than ten minutes goes by before the phone rings. I pick it up quickly, expecting it to be Sam. It isn't.

"Mr. Carpenter, this is Yasir Hamadi."

"Mr. Hamadi, you're about to be in a lot of trouble."

"Or we can both walk away from this with our respective goals achieved." He sounds unruffled and unworried. I, on the other hand, am very worried and thoroughly ruffled.

"Please explain that," I say.

"As I'm sure you understand, this is coming at me quite suddenly. I will need some time to deal with it, and providing me with that time will very much be to your client's benefit."

"How will my client benefit?"

"I will give you information that will result in his acquittal."

"How much time do you need?" I ask, though I can't imagine an answer that I will be willing to go along with.

"Ninety-six hours." I am struck not only by the absurdity of the number but also by its specificity.

"You're wasting my time. You have ninety-six *minutes* to tell me what I need to know, and then, if it's as valuable as you say, I'll hold off on reporting what I already know." I'm okay with making this pledge, since all I really have on him are suspicions without proof.

He doesn't answer for so long that I think he may have quietly hung up. Finally, "I will meet you tonight."

"In a public place," I say, thinking of Franklin's arranged meeting with Karen.

"No, it can't be. Believe me, that is not possible."

"Why not?" I ask.

"You don't know the people you are dealing with. But you can choose our meeting place, and you can bring anyone you want with you, so long as it is not the authorities. I will be alone."

I'm not thrilled with this, but I don't think I can push him any further. I direct him to Eastside Park, where I will have home field advantage, and he says he can be there by eleven. That will give me plenty of time to make sure my buddy Marcus is there by my side.

As soon as I get off the phone I call Marcus. He's probably right outside the house but doesn't say so one way or the other when we talk. I tell him what is going on and that I want him here at 10:45. He grunts either yes or no; I'll know for sure at 10:45.

"What will you do if Marcus doesn't show up?" Kevin asks when I hang up.

"Call Pete Stanton and ask him to come."

"Didn't Hamadi say no police?"

"I'll tell Pete not to show his badge."

Marcus shows up right on time, and I explain the ground rules to him. "I just want to talk to the guy. If he wants to do anything other than talk, you should stop him. As hard as you want."

Marcus and I drive to the same area of the park where we had our encounter with Windshield Man. It is on the lower level near the baseball fields, and to get there we drive down a road that we referred to as Dead Man's Curve when we were kids. While it's a fairly steep hill as it wraps around, the nickname we gave it shows that a child's perspective can be a little warped.

Marcus and I are there at a minute before eleven, and we get out of the car together. There's plenty of moonlight, and I walk a few yards to where I can see the curve, since that is the way Hamadi will be entering. There is no sign of him, but it's not that easy to find this place, so I'm willing to give him a grace period.

"Let's give him a few minutes," I say to Marcus, but he doesn't answer, which is no great surprise. What is a surprise is that when I turn to look at Marcus, I discover that he is gone.

"Marcus?"

No answer. I'm going to take it on faith that Marcus is still here but has decided that protecting me is more easily accomplished by staying out of sight.

With nothing better to do, I look back toward the curve. At about ten after the hour I see a car up above, beginning to make its way down. It's traveling slowly, as if the driver is unsure where he is going. That's a good sign.

The car moves silently along until it is about halfway down the curve, wrapping around and descending toward me, though still at least two hundred yards away. Suddenly I hear a deafening noise and see a sight so amazing I have to do a double take to make sure it's real.

The car is now completely engulfed in a ball of flames, yet it continues to roll down the curve. In the darkness it looks surreal; it's momentarily hard to realize that some-one has undoubtedly just burned to death in it.

Before I even have time to react, I feel a smashing blow in my gut, and I find myself off my feet, up in the air. In an instant I am literally flying, and I've flown maybe twenty yards before I realize that I have been lifted off the ground by Marcus, and that I am draped over his shoulder.

He is carrying me away from my car, probably thinking that it might be the next target. We travel like this across the field and to the pavilion, which houses the snack bar and restrooms but which is, of course, closed at this hour. Once we're there he puts me down, and we watch the burn-ing car complete its descent and crash into a tree.

Actually, I'm the only one watching it. Marcus has his eyes focused on the top level, since that is where the shooter must have been. What he used to shoot, I can't even imagine.

With Hamadi dead, I also can't imagine how the hell I'm ever going to find out the truth.

• • • • •

"THIS, AS I told you in my opening statement, is a very easy case."

That is how Hawpe starts his talk to the jury, who are paying rapt attention. I only wish they had been in East-side Park with me until three in the morning; then they would be as groggy and unfocused as I am.

I spent the hours after the explosion playing a balancing act with Pete Stanton and his detectives. I gave them Hamadi's identity and told them that he was coming to give me information about a case, but I revealed little else. Not knowing whether there are any federal law enforcement agencies I can trust with this, I decide to hold back for now.

I did take the opportunity to tell Pete Stanton about the money smuggling at the port, and Chaney's involvement in it. He'll go to the feds, and they'll start an investigation. Hopefully Chaney will go down, but Petrone will emerge unscathed, having been alerted by me as part of our deal. I'm not thrilled by my role in this, but it's the best I could do.

"And that is exactly what it has proven to be," Hawpe continues. "Richard Evans went out on a boat one night with his fiancée, and he killed her and threw her body overboard. He then tried to kill himself, an effort that was thwarted only by the Coast Guard.

"Witnesses have placed them alone on the boat together, and there has been no evidence to the contrary. The defense has suggested everything from murderous stowaways to marauding pirates but has offered not the slightest facts to back up their theories.

"We don't know why this crime was committed. Ms. Harriman told her neighbor that she and Richard Evans were having problems in their relationship, and she feared his temper. So perhaps he just flipped out in a momentary rage, then tried to kill himself when he realized what he had done.

"Or maybe he was depressed, and planned an evening that would provide a bizarre form of escape. Or it's possible that she told him she was leaving the relationship, and he couldn't handle the rejection.

"I can't stand here and tell you the answer, but I can tell you that it doesn't matter. We do not allow cold-blooded murder, no matter what the motivation.

"Now, the defense has raised the possibility—I would even say the probability—that Stacy Harriman lied about her true identity. And I cannot tell you why she did that. But none of the possible reasons—and they are many—could possibly justify her murder."

Hawpe walks over to the jury and stands maybe three feet from them. "If one of you took a gun out right now and shot me, thinking my name was Daniel Hawpe, you would be arrested. If later you found out that my real name was Bill Smith, or Carl Jones, it wouldn't matter. You would be just as guilty.

"On behalf of the State of New Jersey, I want you to listen to the judge's instructions, follow your common sense, and vote your conscience. If you do that, Richard Evans will never be in a position to murder again."

As soon as Hawpe sits down, I am gripped by exactly the sense of fear and anxiety and dread that I face every single time I give a closing statement. This is my last chance; once I sit back down I will never have another opportunity to influence this jury.

It's like a baseball pitcher who throws a three-and-two pitch with the bases loaded and two outs in the bottom of the ninth inning of the seventh game of the World Series. The pitcher is in control until the moment the ball leaves his hand, and then he has no control over his fate whatsoever.

Once I finish this statement, I'm a bystander.

"Ladies and gentlemen, I have been involved in a lot of trials, more than I sometimes care to remember, and I have seen many different prosecutorial approaches. A good prosecutor adjusts his case and his style to the facts he has to present, to the strength of his case.

"Mr. Hawpe is a very good prosecutor, and it is obvious that he carefully assessed his evidence before coming up with the tactic that best fit this trial. What he wound up with is the 'well, maybe, but' approach.

"You heard it throughout. When we proved that Reggie was alive, his response was basically, 'Well, maybe he is alive, but . . .'

"When it was shown that Richard did not take Amenipam in pill form, Mr. Hawpe backed off with 'Well, maybe he didn't, but . . .'

"When it was demonstrated that Mr. Evans could not have sustained his injury in the way it was presented, Mr. Hawpe allowed that 'Well, maybe he didn't, but . . .'

"And when it was proven beyond doubt that the very identity of the murder victim was a lie and a mystery, he conceded, 'Well, maybe it was faked, but . . .'

"Before a prosecutor asks you to send someone to a life in prison, he has to be certain of his facts. He should not be constantly amending them when they prove wrong. He cannot be allowed to tap dance his way to a murder conviction. Richard Evans deserves better than that.

"Stacy Harriman's entire life was a lie, a complete fabrication, even to her own future husband. This is not something that she would have done casually. How many people do you know that have done it? She was a young, beautiful woman so afraid of where she had been that she couldn't get herself to reveal it to the man she loved.

"She lived alone with her fear, her secret, until it killed her.

"Richard Evans has never done anything criminal—not on the boat that night, not in his life. Before this nightmare he was a dedicated public servant, a caring friend, a loving brother.

"He can be all that again, if you will let him. Thank you."

I turn around and walk back to the defense table. I see Karen in the front row, sobbing, and Richard grabs my arm as I reach him.

"Thank you," he says. "No matter how this turns out, thank you."

• • • • •

IT SEEMS THAT you can never get a good coma going when you need one.

My strong preference would be to remain in an unconscious state while a jury is deliberating. In fact, I'd like to be wheeled into the courtroom that way and not woken up until the very moment that the clerk is starting to read the verdict.

That way I would be able to avoid the anxiety, the doubt, and the second-guessing that I inflict on myself. I wouldn't have to go through my ridiculous preverdict superstitions, and my friends wouldn't have to deal with me at my most obnoxious.

This is not a fun time.

Making matters worse is Karen Evans's understandable desire to hang out with me while we wait. She knows I'll hear things first, so this is where she wants to be. This gives me the unwanted burden of having to be reasonably pleasant at a time when I am always impossibly cranky.

Karen also assumes I know more about this process than she does, but she's wrong about that. I have no idea what is going on in that jury room, or what decision they might reach. The entire thing is impossible to predict and, more significantly, completely out of my control. That is what makes it so maddening.

Kevin and I have tried, with little success, to divert ourselves with our investigation of Stacy's background, though it is too late for anything that could come of it to help in this trial. The reason it hasn't been that diverting is because we no longer know what the hell to investigate. By now Stacy, Durelle, Franklin, and Hamadi are all dead, which leaves us with precious few suspects.

In fact, the only suspects left from the dwindling pool are Anthony Banks; Mike Carelli, the Special Services chopper pilot; and Captain Gary Winston, the surgeon who went down with the others. We have never been able to locate any of them, and we certainly don't seem to be ready to start now.

Banks and Carelli are the most likely candidates for bad guy, since Hamadi's car was shown to have been blown up by a grenade launcher. Since surgeons are not usually trained in grenade launching, Dr. Winston is probably off the hook.

Sam Willis had a brainstorm yesterday to go to Hamadi's funeral and surreptitiously take pictures of all in attendance. Since Kevin and I had seen photographs of Banks, Carelli, and Winston in their army files, he thinks maybe we'd see one of them at the funeral.

The suggestion made very little sense to me, since if these guys are actually alive and in hiding all these years, the idea they would come out to attend the funeral of a man they killed doesn't add up. But Sam wanted to do it, probably so he could get to use a tricky hidden camera gizmo he recently bought, so I let him.

Sam has gone through all the pictures and printed them out off his computer. Digital cameras are amazing; I just wish I didn't find them so bewildering. When I want to take pictures, I buy one of those disposable cameras, take the shots, and then leave them undeveloped in the camera for years.

I call Sam and tell him he should bring the pictures over now. Karen and Kevin are both here, and I figure it will be good for Karen to think we're doing something proactive, even though we're not.

Sam brings in his computer and shows the pictures to us in something called PowerPoint on the wall. It's as if he were making a presentation to a board meeting. But he's enjoying the literal spotlight, so I pretend to be paying attention.

There are more than seventy-five pictures, documenting in excruciating detail the perhaps hundred and fifty attendees at the funeral. Most of the photos have five or more people in them, so obviously, many people are seen much more than once.

By the thirtieth picture, I haven't seen anyone that looks remotely familiar, and I'm so bored I would rather be at the ballet. Kevin's face tells me he's as miserable as I am, but I don't speed Sam up, because Karen is so into this. She keeps saying things like "Wait . . . hold on . . . that person looks like . . . can we focus in on him . . . ?" but ultimately she doesn't recognize anyone, either.

Just as Sam is gathering up his material to leave, the phone rings. A ringing phone while waiting for a verdict is equivalent to a drumroll and ominous music at any other time. Everybody stares at it for a moment, but I'm the only one with the courage to answer it.

"Mr. Carpenter?"

"Yes?"

"This is Ms. Battaglia, the court clerk. The jury has informed us that they have a verdict. Judge Gordon has convened a court session to hear it at three o'clock."

I hang up the phone and turn to Kevin and Karen. "We have a verdict."

"Finally!" Karen says, with obvious relief.

That one word completely sums up the difference between me and that strange group of people called "optimists." Karen is glad that there's a verdict; she sees a positive result as now a few hours away. I have no idea what the result is, but the fact that there is one is enough to make me physically ill.

Kevin is in another class altogether; he's always physically ill.

We hit a lot of traffic and don't get to the court until a quarter of three. The media is out in force to see the result of what has become a very public legal battle.

The public is kept behind police barricades, and as nervous as I am, I still reflect on what could possibly bring someone here to stand in the street. It's not as if they'll get special insight into the case; they'd be able to hear the verdict just as quickly on television. And they're clearly not here out of an intellectual interest in the workings of the justice system; the most intelligent question I hear is, "Hey, Andy! You gonna win?"

We're in our seats at five to three, and Richard is brought in moments later. Daniel Hawpe looks over at me, smiles, and mouths, "Good luck." He has the calm manner of a lawyer who doesn't have a client with his life on the line.

Richard seems under control, though I can't imagine the stress he must be feeling. He just looks at me and offers a weak smile. "One way or the other," he says.

I nod. "One way or the other."

Karen gets out of her seat in the front row and hugs Richard from behind. She's not supposed to do that, but the guards who would ordinarily prevent her understand that these are extraordinary circumstances.

Kevin looks pained and miserable. I have seen him in stressful situations like this, and they tend to increase his hypochondria fivefold. Right now I'm afraid he's going to have urology issues under the defense table.

Judge Gordon takes his seat at the bench and asks that the jury be brought in. It takes either ten seconds or ten minutes for them to do so; time doesn't seem to have structure or meaning at moments like this.

For some reason it always bothers me to know that the jury's decision has already been made, even though we're first finding out about it now. It's like watching a football game on tape and not knowing the final score; it doesn't help to root, because the boat has already sailed.

This verdict has already sailed.

Judge Gordon asks the foreman if a verdict has in fact

been reached, and he confirms that it has. He hands the verdict slip to the clerk, who hands it to Gordon.

Gordon reads it, and his face remains as unrevealing as those of the jury members. He hands it back to the clerk and asks Richard to stand. Richard, Kevin, and I all do so, and out of the corner of my eye I see Karen rise in her seat, a gesture of total solidarity. If I'm ever in a foxhole, I want her with me.

I put my arm on Richard's right shoulder, as much to support myself as him. He grabs my arm and holds it, and we brace ourselves. Here it comes . . .

The clerk starts to read at the pace of what feels like one word every three hours. "In the matter of the *State of New Jersey versus Richard Evans,* we the jury find the defendant, Richard Evans . . . guilty of murder in the first degree."

Richard lowers his head for about fifteen seconds, then turns to Kevin and me and says, "We gave it our best shot." The courtroom is deathly quiet, and I can clearly hear Karen behind me, sobbing.

I put my arm on Richard's shoulder and lean down toward him. "It's not over," I whisper. "I swear to you, it's not over." He doesn't answer, probably because he doesn't believe me. And there's no reason he should.

I'm sure Richard feels worse than I do, but right now it seems impossible that anyone could. My client was innocent, and I couldn't get a jury to believe me. Hawpe got twelve people to vote on his side, even though his side was wrong.

Judge Gordon thanks the jury for their service and schedules sentencing for three weeks from now. The gavel pounds again, bringing the proceedings to a close. The jury files out, and the guards lead Richard away.

If there's a moment in my life that I've hated more than this one, I don't remember it. Maybe when my father died.

Maybe not.

• • • • •

BEFORE I LEAVE, I ask the court clerk to get me in to see Judge Gordon.

It is not necessary to include Hawpe in the meeting, because the trial is over. This is just between Judge Gordon and me.

The clerk gets me back into his chambers right away, and Judge Gordon starts the conversation with "Tough loss in there."

I nod my agreement. "Very tough. Your Honor, I am here to report that I am aware of a crime about to be committed."

He's obviously surprised to hear this. "By whom?"

"My client, Richard Evans. As you know, even though it was told to me in a privileged conversation, I am permitted to reveal it because it involves a future crime. I am actually *compelled* to reveal it."

"What is the crime?" he asks.

"Suicide. Mr. Evans had revealed to me his intention to kill himself in prison should he be convicted."

"What is it you want me to do?" he asks.

"My request is that you take affirmative action to stop the crime from occurring, by ordering that Mr. Evans be kept on a suicide watch in prison."

Judge Gordon thinks about this for a while, but he really has no choice in what to do. He nods and says, "Thirty days, at which point we will revisit this."

"Thank you, Your Honor."

Karen and Kevin are waiting for me back in the courtroom when I leave the judge's chambers. Karen comes toward me and we hug, one of the longest hugs I can remember, without either of us saying a word.

When we break it off, she says, "You're not going to give up, right?"

"Right. Whatever it takes."

I want to talk to Karen about what she can do to keep Richard's spirits up, but I don't want to do it here. We make plans to have dinner tonight, even though I know my preference will be to hide under the covers.

When I get home, the answering machine tells me that Laurie has already called me twice. She's going to tell me how I can't blame myself, how I did the best I could, and how the odds were stacked against me. It has absolutely no chance of helping.

I call her back, and she tries her best to make me feel better, but I'm certainly not having any of it. "I started the case with an innocent client and a dog. Now my client is in jail for the rest of his life, and the dog is gone. I pulled off the daily double."

"Andy, I'm not saying you shouldn't feel terrible; I'm just saying that you can't wallow in it. And you can't let it prevent you from capitalizing on your progress."

"Which progress might that be?" I ask.

"Come on, you know as well as I do that you've learned an amazing amount about the crime. All along you've been operating on two parallel tracks, the investigation and the trial. You've been wishing that they could coincide, but they didn't. The good news is, you only had to win one of them to win."

She's right, of course. I could have won by getting Richard acquitted, but I can just as certainly win by finding out the real killers and bringing them to justice. And we have taken some substantial steps toward doing that.

Laurie and I talk it out for a while. The truth is, we know who Stacy Harriman really was, and we can assume that she was killed to prevent her from someday testifying. We even have a rough idea of the conspirators involved in her murder. What we need to do is keep pushing until we and the rest of the world know everything. And I'm going to make that happen if I have to hire every investigator in America.

I take Tara for a walk and then drive to Karen's to take her to dinner. The devastating verdict has left her subdued, and it's obvious that she has done quite a bit of crying.

During dinner we talk mostly about Richard and the need to keep him hopeful. It may be false hope, something I usually try to avoid in dealing with clients, but this time it's necessary. The suicide watch will not last forever, and if Richard is determined to kill himself, he will manage to do so.

Karen promises to do what she can and asks a bunch of questions about the status of the investigation. I tell her everything, and I can feel her optimism starting to return the more she hears.

It's almost eleven o'clock when we leave the restaurant. As we near Karen's house, she says, "Do you think I can visit Richard tomorrow?"

I shake my head. "I doubt it; they'll be transferring him back to Rahway. I'll be able to see him because I'm his lawyer. I want to explain to him that it's my doing he's under a suicide watch."

"Andy, I wrote a letter to him this afternoon. I wanted so badly to talk to him, but I couldn't, so it helped me to write it. Could you give it to him tomorrow?"

"Sure."

We pull up in front of Karen's darkened house, and we both get out of the car. Karen starts to get her keys out as we go up the steps, but it's hard for her to see in the dark. "I hope we didn't have some kind of power failure," she says.

"Why?"

"Because I'm sure I left some lights on."

I look over at the attached garage and see that there is a small light coming from underneath the garage door, which is open a few inches. I'm about to say that she obviously has electricity, when suddenly I'm gripped by a clarity of thought and an instinct I didn't know I possessed.

"Karen!" I yell, and I pull her arm just as her key reaches the door. She screams in surprise, and we lose our balance and fall back down the two steps. At the very moment this is happening, the front door seems to explode at its center in front of us.

Another noise comes from inside the house, and I grab Karen and we start to run. I make a quick decision that the street is not the place for us; it is too well lit. Instead I lead her into the alley, back into a darkened area that serves as a corridor between the houses on this block and the block behind it.

There are sheds and Dumpsters back there as well, but it's hard to navigate in the darkness. I can hear someone pursuing us from behind, so I pull Karen down behind one of the Dumpsters. It is so dark that I can't see Karen, which means the intruder shouldn't be able to see us.

My heart is pounding so hard that it feels like somebody is using the Dumpster we're leaning on for a bongo drum. "Andy?" Karen whispers—I guess, to confirm that I'm still there, since we're not actually touching. I reach out and touch her arm, hoping it will stop her from talking.

I can clearly hear someone coming toward us, stalking us. I'm in a near panic, not knowing whether we should try to run some more or stay there and hope the night makes us invisible. The danger in running is that we are likely to bang into something and call attention to ourselves. Based on what happened to the door, the shooter has such a powerful weapon that he will not have to be terribly accurate to hit us in this enclosed area.

I can hear the shooter coming closer. I can't tell how close, but I would guess he's thirty feet away. It is impossible to avoid the realization that this person is going to kill us unless I do something to stop him. I have no idea how to do so, and even if I did, I probably wouldn't have the courage or ability to pull it off.

On the other hand, I do have Karen, and she pushes something into me which feels rock hard. I reach out and take it; it feels like a piece of firewood. It makes sense; if she or her neighbor has a fireplace, this would be a likely place to keep the wood.

So I have a log, and he has a large gun. Advantage, bad guy, although I wouldn't feel confident even if the weapons were reversed.

I whisper to Karen: "Move as slowly and quietly as you can away from the Dumpster and back toward that wall." I say it so softly that I'm not even sure if actual sounds are coming out of my mouth, but she must hear me, because I can feel her slowly move away.

I can hear the shooter's footsteps move toward me, and I force myself to come up with a plan. It's not a good one, but it's the best that I can do.

As he gets closer, I slowly stand, dreading the clicking sound that my knee usually makes when I get up after sitting for a while. This time it doesn't; I wonder if fear-induced adrenaline is a cure for knee clicking.

Taking a deep breath, I quickly raise the lid of the Dumpster a few inches and let it drop. It is a distinctive sound, and I want the shooter to think we have taken refuge inside.

It seems to work, because I can hear him move quickly to the Dumpster. He opens the lid, and the next sounds I hear are bullets being fired into it.

Using that deafening sound to camouflage the sounds I will make, I stand and start swinging the log at the spot where his head and body are most likely to be. I seem to strike him a glancing blow, probably on the shoulder, and I hear him yell in pain.

I know that he must be readying the gun to fire, and I make an adjustment and bring the log down as hard as I can at where I think his head must be. It makes a crunching sound, and he moans and seems to fall.

I'm not taking anything for granted, and I keep swinging the log at him, alternating between hitting cement, Dumpster, and something else that I hope is his head. I'm sure the sound of wood hitting skull is quite disgusting to most humans, but right now it sounds pretty good to me.

I start screaming to Karen to run into the house and call 911. I eventually stop swinging the log, because the shooter is completely silent and apparently unmoving. Lights go on in Karen's neighbor's house, probably because they are wondering what the racket is about.

My eyes adjust to the dim light, and I can see the shooter at my feet. His head is literally smashed in, and a pool of blood is forming next to him.

I can't see his face, and I gently move him with my foot so that I'll be able to. I'm guessing it's Banks, Carelli, or Winston, since they are the unaccounted-for people in that alleged helicopter crash.

I've seen pictures of them all, but the damaged face on the shooter does not seem to match any of them. It's disappointing; there seems to be enough people in this conspiracy to fill Yankee Stadium, all of whom want to kill Karen.

Within a few minutes the area is filled with seemingly

every cop in New Jersey, and the paramedics arrive moments later. But this particular conspirator is not going to kill anyone ever again.

He is dead, just the latest bad guy to learn that you don't mess with Andy Carpenter.

• • • • •

KAREN AND I don't get back to my house until four in the morning.

It would have been even later, but Pete Stanton arrived on the scene at Karen's house and ushered us out of there faster than another detective would have.

After what happened, Karen hadn't wanted to spend the night at her house, which was totally understandable. Right now we're both exhausted, and I show Karen the bedroom where she can sleep, and head to my own to go to bed. I call Laurie to tell her what happened, since I know she would want to hear about it as soon as possible.

I wake her, but she quickly becomes alert when I start to tell her what happened. This is the first time I have ever told a story about my own actions that is simultaneously heroic and truthful. I faced death without Marcus to protect me, and I prevailed. The mind boggles.

Laurie has many questions for me about tonight's events, the last of which is, "Andy, are you okay?"

I know that right now she is referring to my state of mind, my emotional health. I have killed a man, violently and at close range, and that is known to have an often terrible effect on one's psyche.

Not on mine.

Maybe it will set in later, but I feel absolutely no remorse or revulsion about what I've done. This is a guy who deserved to die, whose intent was to gun down Karen and me. "Better him than us" is an understatement.

I get off the phone and try to sleep, and my exhaustion enters into a pitched battle with my adrenaline, the result of which is, I don't sleep well at all. I get up at seven to take Tara for her walk; it will give me time to consider the impact that what happened last night will have on our investigation.

Karen was obviously the target, since the shooter could not have known that I would be there. But the reason for the attempt on her life is bewildering. How could she possibly be a threat to their conspiracy? It's the same question I've been asking myself since she got shot, and I'm no closer to the answer than before.

Pete Stanton makes the situation slightly clearer when he calls and says that the fingerprints of the guy I killed showed that he was, in fact, Mike Carelli, the Special Forces officer who supposedly piloted the chopper. I didn't recognize him from the picture, but as in the case of Archie Durelle, the picture I had seen was seven years old.

Either way, I'm getting a little tired of people trying to kill people that I care about, including myself. And I'm getting more than a little angry about my government standing by and not doing anything to prevent it.

I call Alice Massengale at her Newark office and tell her I want to see her about her representations at the hearing. She seems reluctant, so I use the same approach on her that I used on Hamadi: I tell her that if she doesn't meet with me today, she can learn what I have to say by turning on the television tomorrow. It works again, and an hour later I'm in her office.

"Good afternoon, Mr. Carpenter."

Cindy Spodek said that Massengale can be trusted completely, but at this point I'm not ready to give her the complete benefit of the doubt. I'm certainly not concerned about the social niceties. "You misled the court about Stacy Harriman."

If she's cowed by my direct approach, she hides it well. "That's a serious accusation."

I nod. "And an inaccurate one. I should have said, "You misled the court about Diana Carmichael."

"Diana Carmichael," she says, concealing whether the name has any meaning for her. "Suppose you tell me what you are talking about."

I continue. "Here's some of what I know." I then proceed to detail some, but not all, of the facts I have learned about Hamadi et al. I tell her that a group of people stole billions during the chaotic reconstruction period in Afghanistan and then faked their deaths and disappeared.

"But it is difficult to disappear with a huge amount of ill-gotten money and exist in society. So an elaborate scheme was set up, whereby fake companies would do fake business with each other, showing huge earnings in the process. But in reality they were earning nothing; the money that they received was the stolen money, effectively laundering it. Hamadi was the front man for the operation.

"I know a lot more than that," I say, "and what I don't know, I am going to discover through the Freedom of Information Act."

"Mr. Carpenter, you can believe me or not, but the story you are telling is one I am completely unfamiliar with."

"If that's true, then you were set up to mislead the court, and you should want to help me get the truth out. Because I am going to prove that the government you represent knowingly withheld information, stifled investigations, and then deliberately misled the court. It resulted in my client twice being convicted of a crime he didn't commit."

"All I can say is that I will look into your allegations."

"Good. You should start with Hamadi."

She nods and asks me if I can write out all the particulars of what I know about him.

I start to do so, and I'm almost finished when I realize something else I can give her. "I have pictures of the people at his funeral. They meant nothing to me, but maybe . . ."

I stop talking, and the pause becomes so long that she says, "Maybe what?"

All of a sudden I'm not inclined to explain it to her. All I want to do is get out of her office and go home, because I just realized who is not in those funeral pictures.

On the way home I call Sam Willis and ask him to come right over with the pictures. I want to go through them again, just to make sure I'm right.

Next I call Kevin and ask him to check whether a golden retriever was reported missing to the Essex County Animal Shelter during a specific one-week period back in March.

Sam is already at my house and set up when I arrive, and I look at each one slowly and carefully. I still don't recognize anyone, which is exactly what I was hoping.

I call Karen, Pete Stanton, and Marcus and ask them all to come over on a matter of urgent importance. I want Pete with us where we're going, because law enforcement should be present, and I want Marcus with us in case we run into a couple of hundred bad guys with machetes and bazookas.

Karen, Pete, Marcus, and I are in the car and heading off within forty-five minutes. Kevin calls me on my cell while we're on the road, and he confirms exactly what I suspected about the animal shelter records.

Next I ask Kevin to check the records of Gary Winston, the surgeon who was on that chopper. What I want to know is what kind of surgery he specialized in. Actually, I believe I already know, and I just want to confirm it.

Karen is surprised when I tell her that we are heading for the cabin, and shocked when I tell her why. I'm encouraged when Pete hears what I have to say and doesn't ridicule it, but even if he did, it wouldn't matter.

I think I'm right.

I'd better be right.

It takes almost an hour and a half to get up there, and

we park close but out of sight of anyone in the cabin. I'm not sure how to go about approaching it, since there is a very good chance that gunfire might be heading our way when we do.

Pete and Marcus come up with a plan; they will sneak up and enter the cabin, disarming anyone who might be inside, while Karen and I wait by the car for them to signal to us that it's safe to come up. As far as I'm concerned, it's the perfect plan.

Pete and Marcus head off, and for the next fifteen minutes Karen and I hear nothing. No voices, no gunfire, no noise of any kind. I'm trying to figure out whether that's good or bad news, when my cell phone rings.

"Come on in," Pete says.

"Is there anyone there?" I ask.

"Come on in," he repeats, and hangs up.

Karen and I drive the rest of the way to the cabin. No one is outside and everything is completely quiet, and I have a brief flash of fear that Pete was forced to call me and that we could be walking into a trap. Then I remember that Marcus is with him, and I get a new infusion of artificial courage.

Karen follows me as I enter the cabin. Pete is leaning against the counter that separates the kitchen area from the main room. Someone I assume to be Anthony Banks lies on the floor unconscious, with Marcus standing over him.

In the corner of the room, lying on an area rug and chewing on a toy, is Reggie, looking none the worse for wear from his adventure.

And sitting at the small dining table is a woman I recognize as Yasir Hamadi's live-in lover/employee, Jeannette Nelson.

Also known as Diana Carmichael.

Also known as Stacy Harriman.

Even though she was expecting this, Karen doesn't recognize her at first, but slowly it starts to sink in. She stares at her as if trying to process what she is seeing. Stacy just sits there, sullen and silent, as Karen slowly walks toward her.

"You," Karen says slowly, "are a piece of shit."

● ● ● ● ●

YOU WOULD THINK that discovering that a murder victim is actually alive would be enough to quickly spring from prison the man wrongly convicted of the killing.

Unfortunately, the system does not work nearly that efficiently. The state has to endlessly investigate the developments, a hearing has to be scheduled, and witnesses have to be heard. That would all be fine, except that Richard is sitting in jail.

His reaction when I told him that Stacy was alive and Reggie was safe was not what I expected. I expected shock and euphoria; what I got was an almost dulled acceptance. This man has been battered and beaten down by events, and I have to get him out of that cell as soon as possible.

To that end I once again call to arrange a meeting with

Alice Massengale. This time she doesn't resist at all, asking me to come in right away, which I'm happy to do.

It is clear from the moment I arrive that Massengale is angry, and it doesn't take much longer to discover that it's not me she's angry with. "Stacy Harriman—Diana Carmichael—was part of WITSEC," she says. "I shouldn't be confirming that for you, but I am."

"Thank you for that," I say.

"I had been told otherwise, which is why I made those representations to the court."

I believe her, and I tell her so. I also tell her that I am here to negotiate with the U.S. government, and I have chosen her as their representative.

"I have no standing to represent anyone," she says.

"I think you'll have all the standing you'll need," I say. "All I ask is that you convey my terms to the appropriate officials and tell them they have twenty-four hours to respond."

She smiles; she doesn't yet know what my terms are, but she thinks she's going to like them. "Fair enough," she says.

"Good. Here's what I want. Richard Evans must be released from jail immediately; I don't care how it's done. I want him out and the conviction wiped from his record. Then I want ten million dollars to help compensate him for the loss of five years of his life, to say nothing of the pain and suffering he has had to endure. I believe he can get more in the lawsuit I will otherwise file."

"What are you offering in return?" she asks.

"Partial confidentiality."

"What does that mean?"

"Mr. Evans is free to discuss everything with the press,

with the following exceptions. He will not reveal that the government was aware of his innocence, that it misrepresented to the court, or that it tried to wiretap and otherwise sabotage his legal team. He also will not reveal the terms of the settlement."

"Ten million dollars is something of a reach, don't you think?" she asks.

"Not compared to what the government will recover when they start digging into Hamadi and everyone else. Either way, it's not negotiable. If my offer isn't accepted by close of business tomorrow, we file suit the next morning and start booking talk show appearances immediately. And with what I know about Afghanistan and the government's behavior in this case, ten million dollars to shut me up is a bargain."

She agrees to convey my offer, and I get the feeling she's relishing doing so. I also wouldn't be surprised if she testified for our side, should this ever go to trial.

I head home for a planned meeting with Pete Stanton. Pete is feeling pretty good right now; the arrests of Stacy Harriman and Anthony Banks are by far the biggest of his career. He's been all over the media talking about it, including an interview on the *Today Show* this morning. He has had to say repeatedly that he can't reveal details of the investigation, so basically all he does is smile a lot.

If Pete is grateful to me for putting him in this position, he's hiding it well. I tell him that there are a few things I still can't figure out, and ask if he can fill me in on where the investigation stands.

"I should tell you, a private citizen, about confidential police work?" he asks. "Why would I do that?"

"Let me take a shot at a reason," I say. "How about so

you're not forced to buy your own beer from now on at Charlie's?"

"On the other hand, we need more openness between law enforcement and the private citizenry," he says.

"Since it obviously wasn't Stacy, whose body washed up on shore?" I ask.

"Still no ID on that. We're checking missing-persons records for that period. Whoever it was, they took her hair and put it on the hairbrush at Richard's house and then put some of her blood on the boat, so it would seem to match Stacy's DNA."

"They would have had to find someone with the same body type, hair color . . ."

He shakes his head sadly. "Good reason to get murdered, you know?"

"Any luck finding Gary Winston?" I ask.

"Not yet . . . Hopefully Stacy will give him up. But he'll be found—surgeons aren't the type to hide in the wilderness eating leaves and shit. They like to come out and have a good meal once in a while."

As far as I can tell, and Pete agrees, Winston is the last missing member of the conspiracy. Had I realized earlier that Winston was a plastic surgeon, stationed in Afghanistan to deal with serious battle wounds, I might have caught on to the scam earlier.

I hadn't recognized Durelle or Carelli from their pictures and just assumed that it was because they were taken years ago. In fact, Winston had altered their faces enough to be consistent with new identities, as he had done with Stacy.

Karen was targeted out of fear that because of her closeness to Stacy, she might see through it and recognize her.

The night before she was shot, Franklin heard me agreeing to let her accompany me to Short Hills to see Hamadi. Their fear was that she might see Stacy then or shortly thereafter.

Stacy had obviously only pretended to be a witness for the government, to deflect suspicion from her. She was actually a key conspirator but allowed herself to be put into WITSEC, knowing full well she would not remain there.

"When is your client getting out of jail?" Pete asks.

"I'm working on it."

"Let me see if I understand this," he says. "You lose a murder case in which there was no murder, and you can't spring your client even though the victim turned up?"

"These things are complicated."

Pete nods. "I know one thing for sure. Clarence Darrow, you ain't."

"CHECK YOUR E-MAIL."

That is the short and to-the-point message from Alice Massengale that is on my answering machine when I return from my morning walk with Tara and Reggie. Tara is clearly loving having Reggie back, so much so that I'm thinking maybe I should get another dog when he leaves. I'll have to discuss it with her.

I turn on my computer, and I see an e-mail from Massengale, which seems to contain a document to be downloaded. After ten minutes of trying, I am forced to admit that downloading is simply not something at which I have the required expertise.

I am about to call Sam Willis, when the doorbell rings. It is Karen, coming over to find out in person if we've made any progress in getting Richard out of jail. The situation is even more frustrating to her than to me.

"Do you know how to download something from an e-mail?" I ask.

"You *don't*?" is her incredulous response.

"Of course I do. It's just that you said you wanted to help out on Richard's case, and—"

"Where is it?"

I take her over to the computer, and she sits down. She makes a few clicks with the mouse, and within thirty seconds she is jumping up and down and screaming with pure joy.

My instincts tell me this is good news, but I sit down and look at the screen to find out just how good. The document Massengale sent is a letter, for me to sign, essentially agreeing on behalf of the government to the terms as I presented them to her.

Richard is going to be free, and Richard is going to be rich.

Karen prints out the agreement, and I sign it. She offers to hand-deliver it to Massengale's office so I can focus on the mechanics of getting Richard out of jail.

I place a call to Hawpe's office and am pleased to learn that the process has already begun. Massengale had assumed I would find the terms acceptable, since they were my terms, and had taken the initial necessary steps.

Once I've done all I can over the phone, I head down to the prison. It is my opinion, based on very substantial feedback over the years, that I can be even more obnoxious and annoying in person than on the phone.

Even under my relentless prodding, there is a limit to how fast the bureaucracy will move, and it's not until three o'clock that I get to enjoy the sight of Richard Evans walking through the prison doors to freedom.

He sees me immediately and comes over. We just stare at each other for a few moments.

"It took you long enough," I say.

He smiles. "Sorry—I was tied up."

With that we hug. I'm not a big fan of hugs, and man hugs are my least favorite, but this one is okay.

"Come on," I say. "There's somebody at my house who wants to see you."

When we pull up to my house, Karen, Reggie, and Tara are on the porch waiting for us. Richard has the door open even before I bring the car to a full stop, and he heads for the porch. He doesn't quite get there, because Reggie comes bounding down the steps and leaps on him.

Within moments Richard and Reggie are on the ground, with Richard on his knees, hugging and petting him. Reggie's tail is wagging a mile a minute, and he seems to be doing his best to lick the skin off Richard's face.

"You saved me, buddy. You saved me." Richard says it over and over, punctuated by laughs. Reggie doesn't comment, so I assume he agrees and is being modest. And Reggie did save Richard's life, as certainly as Lassie ever saved anyone.

"Is this great, or what?" says Karen, constantly dabbing at her eyes. She comes over to hug Richard, but Reggie doesn't seem to be in the mood to share.

Yes, it's definitely great.

Tara stands off to the side, watching the scene, clearly bewildered that she is not receiving any of this affection. She comes over to me, and I pick up the slack and pet her, but she knows she's getting the short end of the stick.

We go into the house, and I fill Richard in on what I have learned from Pete or figured out on my own.

"Do you have any idea where Reggie was all these years?" he asks.

I nod. "With Stacy. She drugged you on the boat, and when you were unconscious, she left on another boat with one of her partners. She took Reggie with her."

"Why?"

I shrug. "I think she genuinely loved him. It's why she had him taken from my house."

"So how did he get away from her?"

"There was a storm last March, and a tree fell and badly damaged the house she was living in. My guess is that Reggie was home alone and that he took off when that happened."

"Where did he go?" Richard asks.

"Looking for you. The guy who found him, Warren Shaheen, lived only about six blocks from your old house."

This causes Richard to hug Reggie once again and call him an "amazing dog." He's got that right.

"So Stacy was with me because of my job? So they could work their customs scam?"

"I can't say that for sure, Richard." My statement is true; I can't say it for sure, but I believe he is right. And I believe she found a more willing conspirator in Franklin, which set this whole thing in motion.

"What are you going to do now?" I ask.

"Well, I have to find a place to live, I have to earn a living, and I have to pay your fee. Because if anyone has earned his money, it's you."

I look over at Karen and smile. "You didn't tell him?" she asks.

I have not told Richard about the monetary settlement. "No, I thought I'd leave that pleasure to you."

"What are you two talking about?" Richard asks.

"Let's put it this way," says Karen as she points to Reggie and Tara. "These guys are going to be sleeping in Gucci dog beds."

About the Author

DAVID ROSENFELT was the marketing president for Tri-Star Pictures before becoming a writer of novels and screenplays. His debut novel, *Open and Shut,* won Edgar® and Shamus award nominations. *First Degree,* his second novel, was a *Publishers Weekly* selection for one of the top mysteries of the year, and *Bury the Lead* was chosen as a *Today Show* Book Club pick. He and his wife established the Tara Foundation, which has rescued over four thousand dogs, mostly golden retrievers. For more information about the author, you can visit his Web site at www.davidrosenfelt.com.

• • • • •

"ANDY CARPENTER, LAWYER to the Dogs."

That was the *USA Today* headline on a piece that ran about me a couple of months ago. It was a favorable story overall, but the headline was obviously designed to make a humorous comparison between me and those celebrity attorneys who are often referred to as "lawyers to the stars."

While you would naturally think it would have exposed me to ridicule from my colleagues in the legal profession and my friends, it really hasn't. This is because I don't hang out with colleagues in the legal profession, and my friends already have plenty of other reasons to ridicule me.

Actually, referring to me this way makes perfect sense. Last year I went to court to defend a golden retriever who had been scheduled to die at the hands of the animal control system here in Paterson, New Jersey. I saved his life, and the media ate it up with a spoon. Then I learned that the dog was a witness to a murder five years prior, and I successfully defended his owner, the man who had been wrongly convicted and imprisoned for that murder.

Three months ago I cemented my reputation as a dog lunatic by representing all the dogs in the Passaic County Animal Shelter in a class action suit. I correctly claimed that my clients were being treated inhumanely, a legally difficult posture since the opposition took the position that a key part of "humane" is "human," and my clients fell a little short in that area.

With the media covering it as if it were the trial of the century, we won, and living conditions in the shelters have been improved dramatically. I'm in a good position to confirm this, because my former client Willie Miller and I run a dog-rescue operation called the Tara Foundation, named after my own golden retriever. We are in the shelters frequently to rescue dogs to place in homes, and if we see any slippage back to the old policies, we're not exactly shy about pointing it out.

Since that stirring court victory, I've been on a three-month vacation from work. I find that my vacations are getting longer and longer, almost to the point that vacationing is my status quo, from which I take infrequent "work breaks." Two things enable me to do this: my mostly inherited wealth, and my laziness.

Unfortunately, my extended siesta is about to come to an unwelcome conclusion. I've been summoned to the courthouse by Judge Henry Henderson, nicknamed "Hatchet" by lawyers who have practiced in his court. It's not exactly a term of endearment.

Hatchet's not inviting me to make a social call, and it's

unlikely we'll be sipping tea. He doesn't like me and finds me rather annoying, which doesn't make him particularly unique. The problem is that he's in a position to do something about it.

Hatchet has been assigned to a murder case that has dominated the local media. Walter Timmerman, a man who could accurately be referred to as a semi-titan in the pharmaceutical industry, was murdered three weeks ago. It was not your everyday case of "semi-titan-murdering"; he wasn't killed on the golf course at the country club, or by an intruder breaking into his mansion. Timmerman was killed at night in the most run-down area of downtown Paterson, a neighborhood filled with hookers and drug dealers, not caddies or butlers.

Within twenty-four hours, police arrested a twenty-two-year-old Hispanic man for the crime. He was in possession of Timmerman's wallet the day after the murder. The police are operating on the safe assumption that Timmerman did not give the wallet to this young man for safekeeping, knowing he was soon to be murdered.

This is where I am unfortunately going to enter the picture. The accused cannot afford an attorney, so the court will appoint one for him. I have not handled pro bono work in years, but I'm on the list, and Hatchet is obviously going to stick me with this case.

I arrive at the courthouse at eight thirty, which is when Hatchet has instructed me to be in his chambers. The arraignment is at nine, and since I haven't even met my client-to-be, I'll have to ask for a postponement. I'll try to get it postponed for fifty years, but I'll probably have to settle for a few days.

I'm surprised when I arrive to see Billy "Bulldog"

Cameron, the attorney who runs the Public Defender's Office in Passaic County. I've never had a conversation of more than three sentences with Billy in which he hasn't mentioned that he's overworked and underfunded. Since both those things are true, and since I'm personally underworked and overfunded, I usually nod sympathetically.

This time I don't have time to nod, because I'm in danger of being late for my meeting with Hatchet. Lawyers who arrive late to Hatchet's chambers are often never heard of or seen again, except for occasional body parts that wash up on shore. I also don't get to ask Billy what he's doing here. If I'm going to get stuck with this client, then he's off the hook, because I'm on it.

I hate being on hooks.

• • • • •

"YOU'RE LATE," SAYS Hatchet, which is technically true by thirty-five seconds.

"I'm sorry, Your Honor. There was an accident on Market Street, and—"

He interrupts. "You are under the impression that I want to hear a story about your morning drive?"

"Probably not."

"For the purpose of this meeting, I will do the talking, and you will do the listening, with very few exceptions."

I start to say *Yes, sir,* but don't, because I don't know if that is one of the allowable exceptions. Instead I just listen.

"I have an assignment for you, one that you are uniquely qualified to handle."

I nod, because if I cringe it will piss him off.

"Are you at all familiar with the case before me, the Timmerman murder?"

"Only what I've read in the paper and seen on television." I wish I had more of a connection to the case, like if I were a cousin of the victim, or if I were one of the suspects in the case. It would disqualify me from being involved. Unfortunately, I checked my family tree, and there's not a Timmerman to be found.

"It would seem to be a straightforward murder case, if such a thing existed," he says and then chuckles, so I assume that what he said passes in Hatchet-land for a joke. "But the victim was a prominent man of great wealth."

I nod again. It's sort of nice being in a conversation in which I have no responsibilities.

"I'm told that you haven't taken on any pro bono work in over two years."

Another nod from me.

"I assume you're ready and willing to fulfill your civic responsibility now?" he asks. "You may speak."

I have to clear my throat from lack of use before responding. "Actually, Your Honor, my schedule is such that a murder case wouldn't really—"

He interrupts again. "Who said anything about you participating in a murder case?"

"Well, I thought—"

"A lawyer thinking. Now, that's a novel concept. You are not being assigned to represent the accused. The Public Defender's Office is handling that."

Relief and confusion are fighting for a dominant position in my mind, and I'm actually surprised that confusion is winning. "Then why am I here?"

"I've been asked to handle a related matter that is technically before Judge Parker in the probate court. He has taken ill, and I said I would do it because of my unfortunate familiarity with you. Are you aware that the victim was very much involved with show dogs?"

"No," I say. While I rescue dogs, I have little or no knowledge of dog shows or breeders.

"Well, he was, and he had a seven-month-old, apparently a descendant of a champion, that his widow and son are fighting over. The animal was not included in the will."

This may not be so bad. "So because of my experience with dogs, you want me to help adjudicate it?"

"In a manner of speaking."

"Glad to help, Your Honor. Civic responsibility is my middle name."

"I'll remember to include it on the Christmas card. I assume you have a satisfactory place to keep your client?"

"My client?"

He nods. "The dog. You will retain possession of him until the issue is resolved."

"I'm representing a dog in a custody fight? Is that what you're asking me to do?"

"I wouldn't categorize it as 'asking,'" he says.

"I already have a dog, Your Honor."

"And now you have two."

"Can you keep a secret? A really big one?"

DON'T TELL A SOUL

A Novel
by
DAVID ROSENFELT

Tim Wallace's wife died in a boating accident several months ago. On New Year's Eve, his two best friends finally convince him to go out for the first time since Maggie's death—and that's when Tim's life goes from bad to worse. A drunken man confesses to a months-old murder, says "Now it's your problem," and walks away.

When the man turns out to have been telling the truth, Tim's life is put under the microscope by the cops, and they're not giving up. But neither is Tim. He's determined to uncover the truth—even if it kills him.

"This fast-paced and brightly written tale spins along.... *Don't Tell a Soul* is a humdinger."
—*St. Louis Post-Dispatch*

"Stellar...Rosenfelt keeps the plot hopping and popping as he reveals a complex frame-up of major proportions...terrifying and enlightening."
—*Publishers Weekly* (starred)